Paradise Falling

Fire Rose

ISBN: 978-1-9164743-8-3
Rapid River Publishing

The text type was set in Adobe Garamond Pro

For more information or to sign up to my newsletter, visit
www.authorfirerose.com

Content Warning:
This book contains strong language, sexual content, and other mature themes, including mentioning of past SA, and is intended for mature readers only. Please read at your own discretion.

"Paradise has never been about places. It exists in moments. In connection. In flashes across time".

Victoria Erickson

1

✺ ✸ ✺

CHELSEA

Hong Kong, People's Republic of China
February 2018
~~~~~

"Where's your fucking husband?" The brute raises his fist, exposing me to another whiff of his stinking body odor.

My stomach clenches and I gag, though the fear is an even greater motivator to puking up my breakfast than the stench. "I told you, I don't know." I choke on the words. Tears flood my eyes.

How did I get here?

How could my life change so drastically in the blink of an eye?

This morning, I was just getting ready for work as usual when I found the windshield of my car covered in blood. Sean was pulling my hand; I should've grabbed him and gone on the run. Instead, I froze.

Biggest mistake of my life.

That's when they plucked us right off the street.

The brute grins and delivers my punishment for non-compliance. When his fist connects with my cheekbone, my head snaps back. Tortuous pain explodes in my head. I cry out.

Through blurs of tears and swollen eyes, I can barely make out my surroundings.

"Bitch, do you like when I hurt you, or are you just dumb?" His breath reeks as foul as his body. "Give it up. The chump isn't worth it having your pretty face bashed in."

"I swear I would tell you if I knew." My whole body shakes like a leaf on a dying tree. Not that my fate will be any different; eventually, my body will be broken and gone.

What will happen to Sean?

He is my only concern.

"Tsk, you *are* fucking dumb." Jutting his chin, the brute signals to his buddy. He picks up a pair of pliers. So far, they've only broken one finger, so still nine to go. I close my eyes; the cracking of bone precedes the ear-splitting scream sucking the air from my lungs. Through the haze of black spots, I splutter, "Please, stop."

The words are no louder than a whisper and strained by deadly fear.

The brute's lips are right on my ear. "Then start talkin', bitch."

My brain scrambles in escape mode. Maybe I can bullshit my way out of this. "He said he'd have meetings all day. At his office."

The brute snorts out a laugh. "Don't you think we checked there already?"

I whimper.

"We checked fucking everywhere." The foul stench from his mouth has me gagging. "All his usual spots, everywhere the little rat could hide. Nothing. We aren't amateurs, lady."

"Then why do you think I'd know where he is?"

"Because you are his money tree. He would never leave you behind."

"But he did."

"Problem is, I don't believe you. Anyone who marries a Crimson Disciple and then convinces him to quit the organization knows the risk. They have a backup plan in case things go south. The past has a way of catching up, and Marcel Pierce surely knows that. He'd make sure that his money and his family can get out of Hong Kong before his fabricated life comes crashing down."

"Well, you give him too much credit." Marcel is probably on a plane to the States right now, not giving a damn about his family.

The brute's response is an elbow to my face, flooding my mouth with blood. Spitting it out, I shower his shoes with red rain.

He grabs me by the hair and yanks my head. "I didn't want to do this because I don't like hurting little kids, but you give me no choice." He nods at his buddy. "Bring him in."

"Mommy!"

The cry echoing off the walls has my heart come to a standstill. My breath stalls in my throat and every limb in my body goes numb.

No, not Sean.

"Please, I'll do anything you want," I plead through my tears. "You can have our money, the house, everything. Just don't hurt him."

The brute takes a deep breath. "Lady, when will you get it into your thick skull that we aren't interested in your money, or your house, or anything else, other than knowing where your fucking husband is?" As he spits out the words, his growl grows louder with every syllable.

"I swear on my son's life, I don't know where Marcel is."

As the brute crosses the room, his heels click on the cement floor like the seconds-hand on a clock winding down. Racking the slide of his gun, he moves a bullet into the chamber and presses the barrel against the back of Sean's head. My little boy sobs silently; the crotch of his pants is soiled from pee.

"Thirty seconds. That's all you have to stop the bullshit, or your son is dead."

2

✸ ✳ ✸

CHELSEA

Drogheda, Ireland
February 2024
~~~~~

"Chelsea, dear, this scone is wonderful." Adele McKenna, our next-door neighbor for as long as I can remember, offers me a toothy smile around a mouthful of buttered pastry. "Is that your mam's recipe?"

"Yes, ma'am."

For the thousandth time.

I'm glad for her patronage; she is one of my regulars, visiting the small tea shop three times a week like clockwork, but her memory is failing her more and more these days.

"And how is your mam?"

"Much better, thanks."

"Oh, was she sick?"

I internally groan. We had this conversation at least once every week for the last month. "She had to go to the hospital for a few days, but the doctors put her on a new blood thinner and she is doing fine."

"Oh, dear. I hope that will help her."

"Yes, me too." I brush a strand of my fringe out of my eyes and smile.

Respect your elders.

Mam's words follow me whenever I leave the house.

Mrs. McKenna focuses back on her scone and slurps her tea. The rain hits hard against the window and provides a backdrop to the silence. As usual, I have the heater going at its highest level; in miserable weather, patrons tend to buy more when it's toasty in the shop. Mrs. McKenna finishes her tea and slips into her arctic raincoat. Bidding me good-bye, she leaves the money for the tea and scone in stacked coin piles on the table. I count out the cash; she is seventy-five cents short. Still hasn't caught on that I had to raise my prices in the New Year to fight inflation.

With a sigh, I load the dirty cup and plate into the dishwasher. About to pour myself a mint tea to quiet the unrest that still haunts me every day even after six years, I look up when the old-fashioned bell over the door chimes. The new customer is some guy in his late twenties who is too well dressed to be a local. Stone gray cashmere suit under a short black wool coat, a crisp white shirt with a blue silk tie that displays a perfect knot, and fancy, shiny leather loafers. The whole outfit costs more than what I make in a month; not to mention it's totally unsuitable for Irish weather in the middle of February.

"What a miserable day." He shakes the wetness out of his thick brown curls and holds up a busted umbrella. "Do you have a bin where I can toss this?"

"Sure, just pass it to me."

Handing me the umbrella, he brushes over the bump of my crooked finger. His skin is warm and sends a tingle up my arm. As he stares at the menu above the counter, I study him from under my eyelashes. In another lifetime, I would've considered him attractive. The naturally darker skin and five o'clock shadow give him this renegade vibe that matches the energetic spark in his dark brown eyes. If I had to guess, I'd say he has Italian ancestry, or maybe Greek.

He purses his full lips. "I'd like a rooibos tea, with a dash of honey and coconut milk, if you have it."

Unusual choice.

"No problem. For here or to go?"

"For here. And one of the blueberry muffins, too." Looking around, his gaze lands on the framed photo of Sean on the wall by the cash register with the black ribbon and the rosary around one of the corners. "Cute boy. Was he your son?"

"He was." A hitch in my throat warns of impending tears, but I manage to keep it together. If I ever get my hands on Marcel, I'll make him pay.

"I'm sorry for your loss." Curious eyes drill into me. "How long ago did he die?"

Nosy much?

"Six years. He was only three."

"I'm truly very sorry."

I set the glass with the tea onto a tray so hard that a little bit spills on the saucer and grab the tongs for the muffin.

He has zero tact, asking me about Sean.

"Sorry, but I think I'll get this to go after all."

"Of course." Trying to steer the conversation as far away from my son as possible, I go on the offensive. "First time in Ireland?"

"What makes you think I don't live here?"

"You have an American accent." Plus no dude in Drogheda will waste their money on that suit.

"Well, you are right, I am from the States. New York, actually. Have you ever been?"

The Big Apple is the city where I met Marcel. Desperate to avoid more questions, I go with a lie. "No, I've never been to America."

"That's a shame. I think you'd like it there."

And why is that?

An assumption because I sell international tea brands?

You don't know me at all, asshole, so stop prying into my business.

Placing the bag with the muffin and the paper cup on the counter, I twist the golden band on my finger. "That would be seven euros and fifty cents, please."

With a startle, he raises his gaze from my hand and pulls a wad of money from his pocket. "Keep the change."

Before I have a chance to ask whether he'd like a receipt, he picks up his purchases and ambles out of the shop right back into the pouring sheets of rain.

What an odd character.

I unroll the euro bills and a piece of paper drops to the floor. Bending down, I pick it up. The carefully crafted note has me gasping.

> If you are curious where your husband
> is hiding, meet me tonight at 8
> at Clarkes Bar.

3

✹ ✹ ✹

BASTIAN

Drogheda, Ireland
~~~~~

With the muffin bag tucked under my chin and the teacup in my hand, I slide into the passenger side of the rented Ford Focus.

Anton squints sleepily at me from behind the wheel. "And? Did she take the bait?"

"I'm sure she did. She'll show up tonight."

"I hope so." He stares gloomily into the rain. "I hate this fucking weather."

"The wind is the worst. My umbrella snapped just walking the short distance to the café, and I stepped into a puddle on my way back, so my shoes are drenched."

He grumbles "better you than me" under his breath and I roll my eyes.

Fucking moron.

Setting the teacup into the holder, I toss him the bag with the muffin. "Here, I got you something."

"What's that?"

"Blueberry muffin."

He wrinkles his nose. "You know I'm not a fan of blueberries."

"Don't be a brat and eat what I feed you."

"And why should you get the coffee? I'm fucking jet lagged and have to drive." He leans over in an attempt to snatch the cup right from under my nose, but I beat him to it.

"It's rooibos tea, but you are more than welcome to have some if you ask nicely."

"Fuck no, and you're taking this health craze too far. No caffeine, no booze, no cigarettes. What's the fun in living if you can't have any of that?" With a sigh, he drops his head against the seat.

Silence falls over the car as I help myself to the spurned muffin, washing it down with the tea. The quality of the stuff is actually quite good and can measure up with my favorite breakfast joints in New York. The rain is relentless, pelting onto the roof of the car in a steady rhythm that doesn't ease up.

"So what was your first impression of her?"

"Okay, I guess, though she has a photo of her dead kid hanging right there on the wall, which made it a little awkward."

"Seriously?"

"With a black ribbon and a rosary. It's almost like a shrine."

He quirks a brow. "I didn't know she's that religious."

"All Irish people are religious. It's part of their DNA."

"And if faith is what gets her through the day, good for her. It's tragic what happened to the kid. And to witness it, too." Anton turns his head. "Do you feel bad about it?"

Fuck, yeah. If someone hurt my son, I'd feed him to a pack of wolves. Literally. "Nico went against orders. He shouldn't have messed with the boy."

"You can't blame him for wanting to make sure. He thought the bitch was lying through her teeth to protect her husband."

"I know, but Nico didn't have to shoot the kid. Threatening her that he'd harm him is one thing, but then actually pulling the trigger. That's sick. He went too far."

"Under normal circumstances, I'd agree, but you weren't there."

"And neither were you." I take the last swig of the tea and toss the empty cup onto the backseat. "Besides, what's done is done. Nothing will bring the boy back, so it's pointless to talk about it."

Anton straightens in his seat. "There she is. She must have closed the café early. Should—"

His last words bounce off me as my attention is drawn to a text message on my phone. Nico sent a thumbs down.

Fuck.

Murphy must be playing hardball and I don't feel like driving to Dublin in this shitty weather to straighten him out. For once, I wanted to put up my feet and watch some TV, maybe even get a massage before meeting Chelsea at the pub.

Anton squeezes my arm. "Bastian, you listening? I asked if you want me to follow the girl."

I raise my finger to shush him and write a hasty text message back.

Can U handle?

Nico's reply is almost instantaneous. Another thumbs down.

I glance at Chelsea's car turning left at the stop light. "Nah, she's driving home. Probably shook up about the note."

"Okay, are we going back to the hotel then?"

"We can't. Nico is having some issue with Murphy, so we need to get down to Dublin asap."

Anton groans. "I'm fucking tired."

"C'mon, let's go. The faster we take care of Murphy, the faster your whiny pussy-ass can take a nap."

"Fine," he grumbles. Turning on the blinker, he merges into traffic, just to whip the car to the left when he almost hits oncoming traffic. "This driving on the wrong side of the road is fucking nuts. Who came up with that?"

I smirk. "Aren't you full of complaints today?"

"Ha, I want to see you driving in this shit."

Not happening. Being a chauffeur is below my pay grade.

For a breath, he takes his eyes off the road and glances at me. "What if the girl blows you off tonight?"

"Don't worry, she won't."

"And the mother? She is old and frail. What if Chelsea doesn't want to leave her? I mean, she's the only close family she has left."

"Don't." I pinch the bridge of my nose to fight a sudden stab in my head. "This is the best lead we had on Marcel Pierce in six years, and I'm not going to let him slip through my fingers again. Chelsea will help us, and if the mom truly becomes an issue"—I stare out the window into the pouring rain—"then we'll just have to take her out."

4

✴ ✴ ✴

BASTIAN

Dublin, Ireland
~~~~~

Murphy is holed up in a run-down pub not too far from the Guinness Storehouse; I expect the streets to be crawling with tourists, but the area is surprisingly desolate. Entering the bar, I find an equally forlorn picture. Two patrons, one of them Nico, and an older man who could only be Murphy nursing their respective beers, a sole bodyguard loitering nearby. If I ever saw a criminal organization on its last leg, it's Murphy's shop. Icarus wasn't kidding when he told me that collecting the debt would most likely be a fruitless endeavor.

I drop into the chair across from Murphy without waiting for an invitation and measure him up. Dude is way past his prime without a suitable heir in sight to take over, desperate to hold on to a legacy that has lost its spark. Absorbing him within our group will be an ultimate relief, even if he doesn't realize it yet.

His smug smile carries the arrogance of a delusional man who feels too comfortable on his own turf. "Are you the lad in charge?"

Before I can reply, Anton snags the basket of chicken wings sitting on the table. He keeps going and folds into a chair closest to the bar. Gaze on the barkeeper, he demolishes one of the chicken wings in under five seconds.

Murphy's furrowed brows smoothen; he apparently doesn't see the need to school Anton for his lack of manners.

My smile is cold. "Where is our money?"

"Like I told your man, I need a little bit more time."

"Icarus already granted you a rather generous extension, so I'm afraid that you'll have to settle the debt without any further delays."

"I had some issues—"

"I don't fucking care." I lean closer. "We supply weapons, no questions asked, and in return, we expect payment. It's a simple transaction."

"The IRA—"

"Dude"—I draw in an exasperated breath—"what part of "I don't care" don't you understand? I don't give a flying fuck about politics in your country."

It guarantees that I sleep better. If I had to worry about every cause those weapons were used for, I'd be a wreck.

He takes a swig of his beer and has the nerve to give me a wide smile as if this is all a joke to him. "Look, lad, Icarus and I go way back. I've been doing business with him when you were still shitting into diapers. He knows I'm good for the money, so why don't you and those two eejits get the hell out of my pub?"

I chuckle. The fucker has no idea whom he's dealing with.

Standing up as if I'm about to leave, I bend forward and grab a handful of his graying hair. Without much resistance, I slam his face into the table, ensuring that the sharp corner smashes his nose. He howls like a little bitch. Enough of the spilling blood pools on his lips to shut him up.

Out of the corners of my eyes, I confirm that Nico has his gun trained on the bodyguard. Anton, once again, has my back by shielding me from the bartender. Time to get down to business.

"You got twenty-four hours, and then you either pay up or supply us with a list of your associates with an appropriate reference that will let them know that you went out of business." His well-established contacts will make lucrative trading partners with future revenues well above what he owes us. "If not, I'll kill you, your wife, kids, grandkids, even your fucking dog, if you have one, and then I'll burn everything you own to the ground. Don't make me come back here."

He groans. "Oh, feck off. Threatening me will get you jack shit."

I chuckle. "You still don't get it, do you? I have diplomatic immunity, so I could blow out your brains and piss on your skull right in the middle of the fucking St. Patrick's Parade, and all your government will do is ask me nicely to leave and not to come back. I'm untouchable, motherfucker."

He gulps but is smart enough not to give me lip again.

I jut my chin at Anton. "Let's go."

Slowly, we back out of the pub. Nico stays at the door with his gun drawn in case Murphy loses his mind and sends his bodyguard after us.

I pull out the phone from my suit pocket and dial the top number on speed dial. The receptionist picks up after the first ring. "Georgiou Logistics."

"It's Bastian. I need this line secured, and then put me through to Icarus."

A few clicks later, and the familiar snarl hits my eardrum. "All good?"

"Murphy is petulant. I think I got through to him, but if not, I need a crew and a cleaner on standby."

"Consider it done. How far are you with the girl?"

"Meeting her tonight, but she should be in the net."

"Good. This situation with Marcel Pierce has been dragging on for far too long. I want his head, Bastian. No more excuses."

"I promise I'll handle it."

"And if the girl doesn't play ball, tie up loose ends. And no mess this time, like it was in Hong Kong."

I roll my eyes. The fuck up in Hong Kong was totally on him. "Don't worry, theíos. If I see the need to eliminate her, I'll make it squeaky clean."

5

✵ ✵ ✵

CHELSEA

Drogheda, Ireland
~~~~~

I've been to Clarkes at least a dozen times, and as a local who grew up just a few miles outside of Drogheda, I recognize half of the patrons. As I try to catch the barkeeper's attention to order my drink, my old classmate Áine ambushes me to fish for the latest gossip.

The typical Friday night at an Irish pub.

I keep an eye on the door to check for new arrivals while smiling and nodding at the right time to avoid being rude. No sign of the man in the suit.

Don't you dare skip out on me, mate!

When all of the sudden a creeper breathes down my neck, I jump and almost knock the glass out of Áine's hand. She stalls mid-sentence, giving Mr. Fancy Suit an appreciative once over. He has changed into black jeans and a maroon merino wool sweater that add to the renegade vibe.

"Get lost." Despite the pleasant smile, the coldness in his eyes doesn't leave room for discussions.

Áine quirks a brow as her gaze travels from his face to mine, but Irish people seldom complain when someone is offensive, so she only squeezes my arm. "*Slán go fóill.*"

I glare at Fancy Suit. "You could—"

"Why don't you tell me what you'd like to drink"—he points at an empty table—"and then be a good girl and sit right over there."

I would like to give him a good tongue-lashing with some creative Irish slang that would wipe the smug smile off his face, but the information he has on Marcel's whereabouts is important enough to let his ill-manners slide. "A pint of Bulmers."

Omitting the please is a small victory in itself.

Somehow, he manages to catch the barkeeper's attention on the first try; a couple of minutes later, he sets the frosted glass with the amber liquid on the table and takes a seat across from me.

I eye the empty space in front of him. "You're not having a drink?"

"This isn't a social meet-and-greet."

I fold my arms. "Well, you have an advantage over me. You know my name, but I don't know yours."

"It's Bastian."

"So Bastian, why don't you start by telling me where my husband is?"

"I have no clue, but I know a guy who most definitely has that information."

How cryptic. "Okay, I bite. Who is it?"

"Jackson Pierce."

"Marcel's brother?" I laugh. "Your intel is bad. Jackson hates Marcel for joining the Crimson Disciples and would've killed him if their paths had ever crossed again."

"In times of dire need, blood tends to be very thick."

I lean closer. "What evidence do you have that Jackson knows where his brother is?"

"Trust me, my lead is solid."

"Then why don't you go and ask him yourself?"

"Because we both know that you don't just walk up to Jackson Pierce unless you are in his circle of trust or have a death wish."

"And why would it be any different for me?"

"You are still his sister-in-law, so he won't shoot you. Granted, he also won't talk to you, but that's not required. All we need is for you to be in his proximity for fifteen seconds to pair his phone and spook him enough to call Marcel."

"It only takes fifteen seconds to pair a phone?"

"With our tech, yes."

I lean back and run my fingers over the rim of the cold glass. Anything Jackson Pierce-related was an off-limits topic for my husband, so Bastian's plan is bound to fail. Even on the slim chance that Jackson knows where his brother is, those mercenaries who shield him will never let me get close enough to make this work.

"Sorry, not interested. What you are asking is insane."

About to stand, his hand covers mine. Hard eyes that send a cold shiver down my spine keep my butt in my seat. "You should think about this very carefully. It might be your only chance of ever finding Marcel."

"After he abandoned me in Hong Kong, what makes you think I even want to find him?"

"Oh, I could think of five million reasons. That's how much money he stole from you, didn't he?"

Give or take a few hundred thousand euros. "I'm sure that money is long gone."

"Maybe it is, but then there's also the issue of your son. Marcel just left Hong Kong, even though he knew it could only end badly for you guys. If I were you, I'd be itching to get even with him."

I gobble down a few mouthfuls of Bulmers to hide that he hit a nerve. "Why are you interested in him?"

"That's not important."

"Will you kill him?"

"Why would you care?"

Fuck, the man is evasive. "Look, I know nothing about you, so why should I trust you?"

His lips twitch. "Because I'm the only one who can help you find Marcel. That makes us allies, and I can guarantee you one thing: as long as you cooperate and don't try to double-cross us, my organization means you no harm. You can even keep any money we recover."

"Are you a Crimson Disciple?"

He rolls his eyes. "Names are just labels. Marcel pissed off so many people that half the world is looking for him. I'm one of them, and that should be enough."

Fucking easy for him to say. As far as I can tell, he has no stakes in this alliance other than realizing he got scammed with a bad lead. Jackson Pierce won't blow *his* brains out. "I need to sleep on it."

"No, you don't." He sighs. "Please, don't make this difficult. I already have enough problems as it is."

"Maybe it would help if I had something to relax."

Thoughtful eyes drill into me. "I got plenty of that in my hotel room."

Smuggling drugs into the country—even if only for personal use—means that he can't be working for any of the government agencies that are after Marcel, which makes him nothing but a fancy crook. Now I just need to figure out who his boss is. "How much?"

"I don't want money." He offers a smug grin. "No, if you want those little magic pills, you'll have to give me something more ... intimate."

C'mon, mate, don't make it that easy.

I figured I'd have to break into his hotel room to dig up any dirt on him, but now he's literally giving me access to the information hotline. I dip my hand into my coat pocket and fist the small baggie of ground up sleeping pills I brought just in case. They will send him to la-la-land well before I have to take off my clothes.

"Where are you staying? Is it far?"

"It's the D-Hotel in Scotch Hall right down by the Boyne. We can walk from here."

Also a short distance from where I parked my car, which would allow for a quick getaway. "Okay, you got yourself a deal."

6

✳ ✳ ✳

CHELSEA

Drogheda, Ireland
~~~~~

Bastian's hotel room is a nice size with a king bed in the center and enough space to walk to the other side without bumping my knee on any of the other furniture. Quite different from the hotels Dad used to run when he was still alive. Many of his rooms hadn't been larger than prison cells, but they were cozy and had turn-of-the-century character. They also were stuffed with antiques that were superior to the sleek modern furniture filling Bastian's temporary home. My gaze falls on the minibar, the only requirement for my plan.

Slipping out of his sweater, Bastian stretches until his t-shirt threatens to tear; a move undoubtedly meant to impress. And it's working. Having lacked a man between my legs for six years, I can't help for my imagination to run wild. His arms are made of sculptured muscles with well-defined biceps hinting that his chest is chiseled, and he has the type of abs that could give me the feels. A masterpiece of nature, just like Marcel, that turns off the rational function of the brain and unleashes wild, uninhibited urges designed to keep the human species alive. It has always been easier to blame my attraction for my husband on biology rather than my bad taste in men.

Bastian clears his throat. "I'll be right back."

As he disappears in the bathroom, I leap for the minibar to put my plan into action. Whiskey, gin, vodka—it would help if I knew his preference. In the end, I go for the whiskey since I've never met a man who'd refuse this Irish staple. With trembling hands, I fill up two glasses, almost spilling one of the small bottles on the desk. Pulling out the baggie with the sleeping pill powder, I dump the contents in the tumbler to the left. Slightly rotating the glass, I mix the substances as best as I can.

Just don't confuse them, dummy.

At this very moment, Bastian makes a reappearance and my breath catches in my throat. Somehow, he managed to rinse off in just a few minutes and is now gazing at me with hooded eyes in nothing but a towel wrapped around his waist. Water droplets glisten on his skin. His hair is damp and unruly, practically begging me to smooth it down with my fingers.

Fuck, he is ripped.

I lick my lips and hold up the glass. "Here, I fixed you a drink."

"Oh, thank you, but I don't drink alcohol."

"You don't?" I gape at him like an idiot, my mind close to a meltdown.

What now?

In my shock, I'm about to down the whiskey in my hand for courage but freeze with the glass already on my lips.

Crap, that's the spiked drink.

He smiles. "But you can go ahead and drink as much as you want." He opens the little fridge and helps himself to an apple juice. "I don't mind."

I set the glass down. "Are you a recovering alcoholic? If so . . ."

"No, not at all. Alcohol is bad for my health, so I tend to avoid it."

Oh great, a health nut.

He twists open the bottle and gobbles down the juice. His Adam's apple bops in quite the sexy way. Lowering himself on the bed, he turns up the heat with a panty-dropping pout. I glance at the door.

Abort plan!

I ignore the rational command; my hormones snap into overdrive and release a gush of arousal. He has trouble written all over him, but I can't fight the temptation. He is simply too hot and after years of abstinence, I'm starving for his touch. Like a puppet pulled by a string, I saunter toward the bed in my best hip-swinging style. His pupils dilate with appreciation.

"Take off your clothes."

I slowly shed each piece of clothing until I'm left with only my panties. He gets off the bed and the towel slips. I cock my head to admire his hard erection. He is nice and large, but not so big that he will hurt me. Stepping closer, I run my fingers over the smooth skin of his rib cage just above his hip. That's where Marcel had his lion-head tattoo, the mark of the Crimson Disciples. Bastian couldn't belong to them or he'd have the same tat.

Instead, the ink on his body is a climbing vine with several branches that start on his right hip and arch over his pubic area to his other hip before continuing on his back. I squint at one of the leaves.

Are those initials?

"Does your tattoo have a meaning?"

"If you're already injecting your body with ink, it should symbolize something, don't you think?"

"Then what does yours mean?"

"We don't have to share secrets in order to have sex." He pulls me into his arms. "As a matter of fact, I'd prefer if we weren't talking at all."

This is my last chance to get away, but his hard shaft has settled right between my legs, teasing my clit. With my intimacy-starved body, all my defenses are immobilized.

I look up and find his eyes. They are burning with desire. "Do you have a condom?"

"Sorry, but I don't use condoms."

My brows furrow. "You don't drink alcohol because it's bad for your body, but then you have unprotected sex? What about STDs?"

"I'm getting tested frequently, so I'm clean." Slipping his hand inside my panties, he pushes a finger into my drenched canal. "And judging from the tightness of your pussy, you haven't had sex in a very long time, so that only leaves pregnancy. If you want, I can get you a morning-after pill."

Not needed. "I had my tubes tied after Sean."

His eyes narrow. "But you were only twenty when you had your son."

"Marcel didn't want any more kids." My voice is thick and I drop my gaze.

"That wasn't his decision to make." Bastian cups my chin and tilts my head back to reinforce eye contact. "You seem like a good woman who deserved better than a husband like Marcel."

That might be so, but I'm done talking about this. Pulling his head to mine, I seal his mouth with my lips.

No turning back now.

7

✷✹✷

CHELSEA

Drogheda, Ireland
~~~~~

Bastian drops me on the bed and slides off my panties. Pulling my nipple into his mouth, he draws out a moan. My needy body quivers under his gentle strokes. The heat is building so fast that his exploring fingers in my folds drive me close to the edge. When his cock pushes inside me, all those feelings I fought against for so long come rushing back.

Passion.

Fire.

Craving.

Pulsing energy to heal and forget. A temporary bandage to cover the scabs left by my husband's treachery. Giving myself to another man closes a door that can never be reopened.

Bastian's thrusts are hard and fast and my muscles squeeze around his hard shaft. He knows when to slow down and how to stop the building heat from exploding too early. I buck my hips to force him deeper inside me. My skin hums with so much pleasure that I won't be able to hold on for much longer. His sucking lips around my nipple seal the deal. Waves of lust rush through me with such force that the muscles in my lower region contract; his hot cum shooting inside me releases another burst of pleasure. He keeps me locked in a tight embrace with his cock still inside me; the warmth of his body radiates against me like a protective shield. When he finally pulls out, I'm exposed to the cold and my heart shatters all over again.

A good fuck, nothing more.

No emotional entanglement.

Not that I could use that right now.

It still hurts all the same. I'm the abandoned wife Marcel discarded. His love was never sincere or he wouldn't have left Sean and me in Hong Kong to die.

Bastian spoons me from behind and nuzzles his nose into my hair. No lame small talk about how amazing the sex was. It's fine by me; otherwise, my voice might reveal that a few tears escape and burn on my cheeks.

His breaths become even after a while and his arms loosen around me. It's easy to free myself without disturbing him. I slide off the bed and watch him sleep; his face is relaxed and he looks content. Chances are he won't wake up as long as I'm quiet.

Heading for the bathroom to attend to pressing matters, I gaze around as I relieve myself. His toiletry bag stands wide open on the ledge of the sink and allows for a quick peek while I wash my hands. No medication of any kind other than a couple of vitamin supplements and a bottle of Advil.

I tiptoe back into the bedroom and rummage through his bag. A Glock is at the top and an array of different drugs is hidden between the various layers of clothes. With my back to the wall the way Marcel taught me, I keep an eye on the bed. Bastian's chest is rising and falling at steady intervals and he hasn't moved an inch. Opening the side pockets of his duffel, I finally strike gold. Two passports are stuck in the compartment.

Let's see who you truly are.

I open the US passport first. His first name is in fact Bastian, last name Artino. The date of birth puts him at thirty-one. Birthplace New York—the whole document looks legit. The second passport is from the Republic of Cyprus with matching information, which makes him either a dual citizen or he has a top-notch forger. I return the passports to their proper place and open the zipper pocket. An envelope filled with photographs that are sorted by packs and held together by paper clips is my first find. One batch shows me in different settings: at the tea shop, leaving my house, taking Mam to Tesco.

How long have those fuckers spied on me?

A second set of photographs caught up with Jackson Pierce, although there are fewer pictures of him taken from a much greater distance. I glance at the bed; Bastian is still in the same position, breathing evenly. I stuff the photos back in the envelope and return it to the bag. About to pull out another envelope, a *click-clack* behind me has me freeze. I slowly turn around and find myself staring into the barrel of a gun.

Note to self: don't trust walls with connecting doors.

The man's imposing body takes up the entire doorway, as if the frame were made for him to complement his massive build. With his muscled arms that are the same size as my legs, he gives me bodyguard vibes. Modern crew-cut hairstyle, a little goatee, surprisingly fine features; all in all, he's not a bad-looking chap if it weren't for his dark blue eyes that are as cold as the deepest waters of Bantry Bay in the middle of winter. As his glare roams over me in scrutinizing assessment, I drop my hand to cover my nakedness and wrap my other arm around my chest.

He smirks. "No need to hide your assets, sweetheart. I'm not interested in women by any means." His gaze flicks to the bed. "Hey, Bastian, wake up. You got yourself a bed bug."

8

✳ ✳ ✳

BASTIAN

Drogheda, Ireland
~~~~~

"Hey, Bastian, wake up. You got yourself a bed bug."

The words take a moment to penetrate my sleep deprived, jet-lagged brain; I sit up and rub my eyes to bring a rather bizarre scene into focus. Anton, taking up the entire frame to the adjacent bedroom, has his gun pointed at Chelsea, who stands like a little lost girl next to my duffel. Her cheeks are flushed; Anton must have caught her red-handed peering through my stuff.

"What's going on?" I lift my brows at Chelsea to offer me an explanation before Anton loses his patience and shoots her.

"Uhm—uhm—" She shuffles her feet; her attempts to diffuse the situation are adorable.

In her defense, if I had Anton glare at me with this death-stare, I'd be worried, too.

"Uhm, you said you'd give me something to relax. I have to leave and didn't want to wake you, so I thought I'd get it myself."

Nice save.

"So you just searched through his bag?" Anton growls, though he lowers his gun and secures it.

I raise my hand to call him off. "It's fine. Do you want nose candy or are you more of a pill popper?"

"Some Molly, if you have it."

I cross the room with a few long strides and search my bag for the colorful ecstasy pills. Wrapping her hand around the baggie, I jut my chin at the desk. "Before you leave, make sure to write your phone number on the notepad."

"I haven't agreed—"

"No? Because I can have my associate shoot you simply for going through my stuff. Of course, if we were business partners, I'd refrain from giving him such an order." She drops her gaze and I smile. Smart move. "We'll be leaving for the States in the next two days, so be ready on short-notice."

Five minutes later, Chelsea is dressed and the door to my hotel room closes behind her. I drop the notepad with her number on top of the duffel, ready to go back to bed.

Anton folds his arms. "Are you just gonna let her walk out of here without repercussions? She searched your bag. What if she knows who you are?"

I shrug. "She would've found out eventually. Besides, what am I supposed to do? Kill her? At the moment, she is the only one who can help us find Marcel Pierce."

And if I were in her shoes, I'd be spying on me. Intel is power.

"Still"—he pouts, his tone turning whiny—"and why did you have to sleep with her?"

I smirk. "Aw, are you jealous?"

"You know I don't like it when you fuck girls."

"And you know that I don't discriminate." I fiddle with the top button of his shirt. "As long as they have a hole I can stick my dick into, I'm good."

"So you're not gonna make it up to me?"

"I didn't say that."

In the next breath, his mouth is upon me.

Hard. Demanding. Almost cruel.

He forces my lips apart, his tongue taking control. My body is still wired from Chelsea's touch and I gladly follow his lead. Arms and legs entangled, we drop on the bed. His strong frame holds me in place and his mouth takes what it deems to be his until he has to come up for air.

His fingers stroke through my curls. "I'm gonna fucking edge you until you beg to stick your cock in my ass."

I smile.

I'm down for that.

As he disposes of his clothes, his eyes are dark with lust. "Get on your stomach and don't fucking move until I give you permission."

I roll over with a low laugh while he grabs the vaseline off the nightstand. Two of his fingers push inside me at once; he knows my body well enough to hit the prostate on the first try. I grit my teeth to suppress a moan. My cock is as hard as a rock and jumps with anticipation.

With his fingers picking up the pace, Anton strokes the inside of my thigh with his other hand, almost coaching a moan out of me.

Fuck, this feels amazing.

My cock is ready for some action.

He chuckles. "Yeah, you like that, don't you? It's nothing like being with a girl. Those whores don't know what men truly like."

"Shut up and fuck me."

"Oh, was that a demand?" He hits me hard on the ass, sending sweet tingles up my spine. "Guys who fuck girls don't get to be in control."

His fingers slide in and out of me so fast that I can hear the popping friction. He hits the prostate every fucking time. The heat is building in my core; I moan into the pillow, ready to explode. Just as I'm about to succumb to my lust, he pulls out.

"I think you are ready for some cock."

I tug up my knee almost all the way to my chin and angle to the side to allow him easy access while he lubes up. The tip of his cock glistens with arousal and it takes all my effort not to beg to taste him.

He grins. "I know what you want, but you're not getting it. Not as long as your dick smells like her cum."

So at some point, he wants to continue the evening in the shower. Fine with me.

Not wasting any more time, he lies behind me and tests my opening with an inch of his length. "Feels good?"

"Mm-hmm."

Thrusting inside me, he fills me up, the side of his hard rod continuing where his fingers left off. The heat burns like fire in my core; three strokes of my own cock and I explode. The orgasm rips through me with such force that my body shakes. I pull him with me and we ride the last waves together.

Lust. Passion. Hunger.

A void to fill left by the persistent violence in our lives.

We are brothers in arms, something a woman could never understand.

My heart pounds in my chest.

Fuck, that was good.

A ping alerts me of an incoming message.

Jackson Pierce is on the move. Need you on the ground in Texas pronto.

9

✳ ✳ ✳

CHELSEA

Drogheda, Ireland
~~~~~

Leaving the hotel, I take a shaky breath.

This was so close.

The asshole bodyguard could've shot me and asked questions later. At least I got away. I hunker down and fight the oncoming tears.

Get a grip on yourself.

I got away unscathed, and that's all that matters.

Wrapping my arms around my chest, I rock back and forth to calm down. My mind strays to the warehouse in Hong Kong. The last time I faced death.

The stench of sweat and blood.

Of urine.

The fear in Sean's eyes.

I press my nails into my temples to kill the images. None of this is helping.

I press my nails into my temples to kill the images. None of this is helping.

Forcing my body back into the vertical, I walk swiftly through the dark. Bastian's hotel is at the far end of the shopping center and the storefronts stare at me like vicious black eyes ready to jump at me from the shadows. The river flowing toward the harbor on the other side of me is just as obscure, the surface rippled by little waves. My teeth chatter from a cold breeze, but at least it has stopped raining. Cuddling into my coat and pulling the hat down over my ears, I cross the pedestrian bridge that takes me into the middle of town. At a red traffic light, I dash across the road and only need to make one left turn to get to my car. Adrenaline shakes my body and it takes forever to settle down enough to sort through the jumble of thoughts.

What now?

I should check in with Conor.

Opening the glove compartment, I toss the servicing booklet into the footwell to get to the hidden burner phone. Conor picks up before it rings twice.

"Hey, it's Chelsea. No one is suspecting a damn thing, so the job is a go. Just as we thought, they don't actually know where Marcel is, but the lead they have on him seems solid and might pan out."

"And they need you to pursue it?"

"Yes."

I don't go into details about having to meet with Marcel's brother Jackson, and Conor doesn't ask. We've waited too long not to take a risk and pass on the one chance to find my husband.

"You be careful, okay?"

"Always. Plus I have a name for you. Bastian Artino. He doesn't have the tattoo, so I don't think he's a Crimson Disciple."

"How do you know he doesn't have the tattoo?"

"What do you think?" I roll my eyes and he probably does the same.

I did what I had to do.

"Okay, let me see if I can find him in the database." For a moment, only clacks from him working a keyboard drift through the line. He takes a sharp breath. "Fuck, Chelsea, not only is he a Disciple, but he's the one being groomed to eventually take over from Icarus."

Geez, I wasn't expecting that.

"What else do you have on him?"

"He has a US mam and a Cypriot dad, born and raised in Brooklyn, and he graduated with an international relations degree and a Juris Doctor from Columbia."

So our boy is smart with a fancy education to give him some clout on the international market. Good for him.

"His official job title is Cyprus's alternate representative to the UN, whatever that means, but it likely gives him diplomatic immunity. Married an Olivia Artino in 2013, and they have a son together, Vitaly, age twelve. Wife appears to be deceased."

"How did she die?"

More clacks fill the silence. "It looks like she died in the same car bomb explosion as Konstantin Pappas. That's when Bastian also became the heir to the Disciples' empire. He's Icarus's nephew, and his kid has been living in Nicosia with Icarus ever since the mam died."

I frown. "Why would Icarus take guardianship of a child?"

"Maybe he's already looking at the next generation after Bastian."

Sure, expose kids from a young age to violence and ruthlessness.

That will screw them up good and turn them into perfect criminals.

"Okay, anything else?"

Conor pauses and I can practically see him scratching his beard on the other end of the line. "Come to think of it, getting close to Bastian might get you to the end goal faster. If you were his new squeeze, he might take you home to meet his son and uncle. A rare opportunity, and if the Marcel lead works out, you could kill two birds with one stone."

Which would finally allow me to move on. "By the way, I haven't even asked how everyone is. Are you and the fam okay?"

"Everyone is grand. With school, video games, and all the other crazy stuff, life keeps us busy. The little ones can't wait for you to visit us again."

I smile. It has been six long years, but the ball is finally on the move. Now I have to wait to see if my patience paid off. About to wrap up the call, I jump when my regular cell buzzes in my purse on the passenger seat. "Conor, I have to go. Have another call, and it's probably Bastian."

"No worries. Keep me posted and stay safe."

I drop the burner phone into my lap and peel the buzzing cell out of my purse. Caller ID unknown, so my hunch was right. I pick up. "This is Chelsea Doherty."

Bastian's rich voice fills my ear. "Be ready in an hour. We are flying out to the States tonight."

10

✸ ✳ ✸

BASTIAN

Dublin Airport, Ireland
~~~~~

Anton pulls the Ford Focus right next to the front steps of the jet, killing the engine. I turn around and grin at Chelsea in the backseat. "That's us."

She gapes at the plane with her mouth open. "It's huge."

"It's a Gulfstream G650ER, the most modern private plane on the market. Accommodates up to thirteen passengers and has sleeping spaces for six."

Shit, I sound like a marketing brochure.

"There are bedrooms? Wow, you travel in style." She cocks her head. "Who are you working for? I'm sure a plane like this isn't cheap."

Woman, are you still trying to get information out of me?

I can't satisfy her curiosity, nor would I want to. Nagging people are annoying as fuck. "Let's just say you won't ever have to worry about breathing the same air as hundreds of other passengers or staying in a dump. First class travel and accommodations are a given."

"That doesn't answer my question."

"No, but it eliminates half the players on the board."

For now, that should be good enough.

As I get out of the car, Anton hauls Chelsea's suitcase from the trunk with a groan. "Why do women always pack so much luggage?"

"Stop whining and get the bags on the plane. I want to leave within the hour."

"What about the rental car?"

I glance at Chelsea; she hasn't moved and is still gathering her things on the backseat. "Park it next to the hangar and text Nico to come and get it once we are in the air. I don't want to see his face around here before then." Chances are that Chelsea would recognize him, and that could blow the whole thing.

"Got it."

"And Anton, be nice. She is our guest, and I don't want any snide remarks that could make her feel uncomfortable."

He rolls his eyes.

Huffing "moron" under my breath, I open the car door for her. "Let's go."

She walks up the stairs in front of me and swoons over the plane as soon as she steps inside. "Oh, wow, look at all this space." With a sigh, she plops onto the couch. "And this is so comfy."

I chuckle. She's like a freaking kid in a candy store.

Beth, our main flight attendant, pulls back the curtain separating the passenger section from the crew. "Good evening, Mr. Artino. Can I take your coat?"

Slipping out of my wool coat, I offer her a smile. "Sorry that you have to pull an all-nighter."

"It's fine. The other girls and I took a bus tour through Dublin and had a Guinness at the Temple Bar. That was a treat, and I'm sure we'll be back one day."

When Anton bursts through the entrance, she steps aside, but he still manages to bump her shoulder in a rather rough way. "Double whiskey for me, and take it easy on the ice or you can do it again."

"Straight away, Mr. Worcheck."

I mouth "I'm sorry" and she acknowledges the gesture with a timid smile. "Would you like something to drink, Mr. Artino?"

"A peppermint tea would be fantastic." I rub the space above my nose. "And if you could find any more of those prescription painkillers . . ."

"Are you having migraines again?"

"On and off." Not surprising considering the stress I'm under. I glance at our guest. "Chelsea, would you like something to eat or to drink?"

"Just water, please."

Compared to Anton, she seems low maintenance. I watch Beth sway away, appreciating her curves and firm ass that are emphasized by her tight uniform skirt. Icarus tends to hire women who are easy on the eye.

I drop into the cream leather chair across from Anton. "Do you always have to be so rude to the staff?"

"Oh, did the bitch complain?"

"No, but I'm complaining. When you are around me, I expect some professionalism."

He smirks. "Like the way you were with Murphy when you slammed his face into the table."

"C'mon, you know exactly what I mean."

"Those private flight attendants are just calculating whores. They take the job in the hopes of catching a rich man. When that doesn't work out, they file a HR complaint for sexual harassment and walk away with a fat settlement. It's always the same."

"Beth isn't like that. She has never made a pass at me."

"Because she knows we are in a relationship and probably thinks you are a lost cause."

"Anton, we aren't in a relationship."

"Oh, yeah? Keep telling yourself that when you moan into your pillow the next time I stick my cock into your ass."

My gaze flicks to Chelsea. "Keep your voice down."

"Why? Are you afraid she won't give you more of her pussy?" He snorts. "Don't worry, she's a woman. Their sole purpose is to spread their legs."

"You are a misogynistic dick."

"Yep, and proud of it." With the smuggest sneer, he takes the offered whiskey glass off the tray Beth is balancing on her palm. "Thank you, dear, and you look absolutely lovely tonight."

Beth tosses me a confused look as she sets the tea and the saucer with honey in front of me. "Can I get you anything else?"

Anton takes a mouthful of whiskey and smacks his lips. "This is perfect, dear."

"Why, thank you, Mr. Worcheck."

I kick him under the table. *Stop it*, my eyes warn.

He laughs under his breath.

I grimace at Beth. "Nothing else for now, but we will probably retire for the night as soon as we are in the air."

"No problem. I'll get the beds ready."

As she walks off, I shoot Anton a glare.

He shrugs. "What? I was nice, wasn't I?"

"You couldn't have been any more fake if you tried." I rub my forehead. The headache is getting worse.

About to sip from the tea, the buzzing phone in my pocket distracts me. I check the caller ID. It's Lydia, my son's nanny. My heart stalls for a couple of beats. Why is she calling me at this hour? It's after midnight in Nicosia.

Panic colors her voice. "Apologies for disturbing you so late, Mr. Artino, but it's about Vitaly. He's in the hospital."

I take a sharp breath. "Why?"

"It's his knee. He tore his meniscus, playing soccer, and the doctors believe he might need surgery."

Fuck. "When did this happen?"

"This morning."

"And why am I only hearing about this now?"

"I'm sorry, but Mr. Pappas didn't want me to call you at all. He said you are on an important assignment and didn't need the distraction."

Such a typical Icarus move. He has been trying to keep me out of my son's life as much as possible.

"Thanks for going against orders, Lydia. I owe you."

"And please don't tell him that I was the one who called you."

"Of course not." Otherwise, she'd be gone and I'd lose my last communication line to Vitaly. Tossing the phone on the table next to the teacup, I stare through the window into the night. My chest hurts. As a dad, I'm a total failure. "Anton, go and tell the pilot that there's a change in the itinerary. We are flying to Nicosia first."

His brows furrow. "Why?"

"Because Vitaly is in the hospital."

"And Icarus is okay with the delay?"

I massage my temples to fight the stabbing pain in my head. Why is he always so confrontational? "Do what you're told or get the fuck off my plane."

11

✳ ✳ ✳

BASTIAN

Nicosia, Cyprus
February 2024
~~~~~

We touch down in Nicosia just as the sun comes up and stop for breakfast at a small restaurant not too far from the airport. Chelsea took shelter in the smaller bedroom shortly after take-off and opted to stay on the plane, so it's just Anton and I being led to the table by a young waitress. Anton punishes me with silence while gazing around with his typical brooding expression.

He folds into a chair with his back to the wall and an eye on the window, slamming down his phone. "I think this is a bad idea. We are wasting precious time."

"Yes, you said that already." More than a dozen times. "And a few hours won't make a difference." I smile at the waitress offering me a menu. Flipping it around, I find nothing on the back. Smallest selection ever. "Sweet Tahini Pie and spearmint tea, please."

"Just coffee for me." Anton shoos the waitress away with a wave. "I'll eat on the plane. Hopefully, this hospital visit won't take long."

"It'll take as long as it takes."

"Trust me, you wanna make it quick. If Icarus finds out about the detour, he'll be less than pleased."

"He'll get over it. Vitaly is my son and I have a right to see him."

Anton rolls his eyes.

"What?"

"I just don't get why you want to assume this father role so badly. In the last four years, you couldn't have seen Vitaly more than six times. Why are you so eager to visit him now, when we are so close to finding Marcel Pierce, and risk pissing Icarus off by going against orders?"

"I don't like how things have been going with Vitaly lately. Icarus has too much control over him. I don't want my son exposed to the criminal activities of the Disciples at his age. He's only twelve and doesn't need that sort of violence in his life."

"Well, you and I have worked for the Disciples since we were teenagers and we turned out okay."

That's highly debatable. "I don't want to talk about this anymore."

"Fine, suit yourself, but don't complain when you get into hot water with your uncle. Once he finds out that you flew to Cyprus instead of the States, there'll be hell to pay."

I rub the space above my eyes to massage away the pain. I don't even want to think about what Icarus will do if I'm caught. "Hopefully, we will be back in the air and halfway to New York before he knows. Now let's eat a bite and visit my son." The rest will fall into place.

The Tahini pie tastes stale and the mint tea is too sweet; I leave without giving a tip and with close to an empty stomach.

By the time we pull up to the hospital, my headache is so bad that I'm sick; as I follow the nurse assigned to take me to Vitaly, the bright neon lights in the hallways hurt my eyes. Yet, the second I cross the threshold to my son's room, his lips split to the widest grin. This detour was so worth it.

"Babá!" He stretches out his arm for a side hug. Looking around me, he beams at Anton and changes to a throatier voice. "Yo, dude, what's up?"

"Not much." Anton drops into the visitor chair. "Your old man has been a pain in my ass"—he smirks at me and wiggles his brows—"but you know yourself how he is."

I shake my head at his inappropriate comment.

"What are you two doing here?" Vitaly's eyes shine like those of an innocent child.

I mock-punch him in the shoulder. "I heard you busted your knee, so, of course, I had to come and check on you."

"Grandpa said it's not that bad."

Icarus is not your grandfather.

I don't say the reminder out loud. It took Vitaly years to accept that Konstantin hadn't been his dad and I no longer force other family issues. "Well, I don't want to hear Icarus's opinion. How do you feel? Are you in a lot of pain?"

"Nah, just a little. I'm tough."

"That you are." I tousle his hair. "Although I don't think you'll be able to play soccer for a while."

"It's fine. That'll give me more time with grandpa. He showed me how to shoot a gun." Vitaly bites his lips. "He promised we'd go hunting soon."

The excitement in his eyes is sickening.

"Not sure if I like the sound of that."

His forehead wrinkles. "Why? What's wrong with hunting?"

"Guns aren't toys, Vitaly."

"I know. Grandpa said we have to respect them, that's why it's important that I learn how to shoot them properly."

Or not at all.

"Maybe you should ask Icarus to take you fishing. Leave the hunting and shooting bit for when you are older."

"I don't like fishing. My dad"—he clears his throat—"sorry, I mean Konstantin, he took me a few times when I was little. I always got sick on the boat."

"Then maybe you and Icarus can do something else that's fun."

Anything that doesn't involve shooting a gun.

"Don't listen to your babá, kiddo," Anton butts in at the most inopportune moment. "There's nothing wrong with guns."

I'm about to give him a snide reply when a knock draws my attention to the door. The intruder is Rostya, one of my uncle's personal goons he found years ago in an orphanage in Russia. The warmth drains from my face.

"Vitaly, *pes antío ston patéra sou.*" Rostya's Greek is as flawless as mine. He meets my gaze and doesn't even attempt to be amicable. "Mr. Pappas would like a word with you and Mr. Worcheck."

12

✳ ✳ ✳

BASTIAN

Nicosia, Cyprus
~~~~~

Icarus is out on the terrace, enjoying his breakfast next to an open laptop. I drop into the second chair at the table and cross my arms; Anton stands at a distance by the pool. It'll be up to Icarus how much of our conversation will be privy to Anton's ears.

Icarus takes a bite of the Halloumi cheese and chews. The silence between us raises goosebumps on my arms; his eyes are thoughtful without much emotion, which is worse than an open display of anger. Even though Konstantin took after his mom and had different features than his father, he had the same eyes as Icarus. The same golden-hazel color, the same fading shade toward the rim, the same flecks of green. Eyes that still haunt me in my nightmares. They are the monsters of my dreams.

Icarus sets down the fork. "Why are you not on your way to New York?"

"I had to see Vitaly." I raise my chin in challenge. "And the next time he's sick or in the hospital, I'd appreciate a phone call from you."

"So much entitlement." Scorn and mocking fill his voice.

"I'm his father."

"And I have been making sure he realizes that." Icarus dabs his lips with a napkin. "How did you find out he is in the hospital?"

A question I expected and an answer I rehearsed during the thirty-minute limo ride from the hospital to his home, with the main objective to protect Lydia as my source. "One of the nurses called me because I'm listed as his emergency contact in their system."

Those thoughtful eyes drill into me until I twitch.

"I have to admit, I'm very disappointed, Bastian. This is a major slip-up." Icarus's words carry a dangerous edge. "It's crucial to find Marcel Pierce and make him pay for what he did to our family. Konstantin is only dead because of him."

"I know, theíos."

"Then I'm asking you again: Why are you here?"

"Vitaly—" I choke on the rest of the sentence. This isn't working and it's time to stop beating around the bush. "It's not good for him to live with you anymore. After the summer, I want him to attend boarding school, preferably in the States, but I would consider settling for Switzerland or the UK."

Icarus's laugh is soft. "That's not going to happen. Vitaly is fine right here with me. You might be his biological father, but make no mistake, Konstantin was the one who raised him. I see a lot of Konstantin in him."

I clench my jaw to contain a curse.

My uncle leans closer. "I will teach him everything he needs to know, and then, when he is ready, I will turn him into a man the way you, Konstantin, and every other boy in our bloodline became a man."

The first kill.

A rite of passage for every Pappas heir.

Icarus pats my hand as if I were a fragile woman. "And if you try to stop him from becoming a Disciple, it won't work. Your own father was the best example. He tried everything, even changed his legal identity to that ridiculous last name because he was ashamed of his heritage, and what did you do? Got out of there when you were only fourteen and begged Konstantin and Liv to take you in. Back then, you proudly picked up a weapon and did what you had to do. What changed?"

Your son and his whore breaking my spirit and the organization sucking the life out of me. "I've always been committed to the Crimson Disciples, theíos."

"Alright, then prove your commitment by telling me who really called you about Vitaly."

I glance at Anton. His face is even and he stares out into the distance. He was right there when Lydia called. Could his betrayal run this deep?

The silence stretches into minutes. Icarus holds my gaze without blinking until I squirm in my chair.

What does he know?

He clears his throat. "Maybe this will refresh your memory."

A few clicks on the laptop and the replay of a recording brings my heart to a standstill.

"Apologies for disturbing you so late, Mr. Artino, but it's about Vitaly. He's in the hospital."

"Why?"

Lydia's voice is louder with my words fading in the background, so chances are that Icarus bugged her phone rather than mine. Not that it should come as a surprise. Ever since the car bombing that killed Konstantin and Liv, he is paranoid and is likely keeping tabs on anyone in Vitaly's close proximity.

I should've known.

As the recording winds down, the full implications of the situation hit me.

"Thanks for going against orders, Lydia. I owe you."

An unkeepable promise.

"And please don't tell him that I was the one who called you."

A death sentence. Icarus can't allow anyone on his payroll to disobey orders without repercussions or he'll lose face.

Icarus stops the recording. A disturbing calmness emits from him. He juts his chin at Rostya standing closest to the patio door. The bodyguard disappears into the house, just to reemerge, pulling a struggling Lydia with him. She is bound and gagged, her makeup smudged; a bruise on her cheek and blood on her lips and chin leave no doubt that Rostya roughed her up. Probably even raped her. When he forces her on her knees, her whole body shakes.

Icarus racks the slide of his gun and sets it on the table. "You need to prove to me that you are fully invested in this organization, Bastian."

My gaze flicks from him to her. My stomach is tight with seething nausea, the vein on the side of my head pulsing as if ready to burst. I swallow hard to kill the surreal buzzing in my ears.

Icarus nods in the direction of the pool. "Anton."

Cold metal from the barrel of a gun presses against my temple.

So much for having my back.

Icarus's stare is fixed on me in a way a snake locks on its prey. "You have a choice to make, Bastian. You either renew your commitment to the Disciples or today was the last day you got to see your son."

As I stand, the chair scrapes over the tiles with a screech. My hand closes around the grip of Icarus's gun. In a trance, I walk over to Lydia.

Silent tears run down her cheeks.

Her eyes plead for mercy.

Tremble after tremble bear witness to her deadly fear.

I raise the gun to her forehead and pull the trigger, the *bang* vibrating painfully in the core of my bones. Her body slams back from the force of the bullet. A glassy stare meets mine.

I turn away and set the gun on the table. Vomit and tears threaten to spill, but I manage to keep it together. I won't show a weakness, not here, in front of him.

Icarus's glare doesn't ease up. "You get one free pass for disobeying my orders because you are blood, but don't ever let there be a next time. Now get to New York without further delays."

13

✳✳✳

CHELSEA

Nicosia, Cyprus
~~~~~

I crane my neck to check for approaching vehicles, but the path toward the runway is deserted. The pilot parked the Gulfstream away from the busier side of the airport with the humming of roaring engines from commercial planes only audible when they takeoff or land.

Refocusing back on my conversation with Conor on the burner phone, I play with a loose thread of the blanket. He has been giving me an earful about missed opportunities because I stayed behind. "Look, Conor, I know what I'm doing. When Bastian asked me if I wanted to accompany him, I could see it in his eyes that he was hoping I'd say no. It would've been premature if I had imposed. Besides, he never even said where he was going. I only know about the son in the hospital because he and his bodyguard had a spat about it." Anton is a mega-arse who could become a real problem.

"Well, okay, I guess you are in a better position to judge the situation. What's the full name of the bodyguard? I want to run him through the system."

"It's Anton Wotcheck, or something similar, but don't ask me how to spell his last name."

"Nothing comes up, so let me do some digging."

I watch a limousine grow in size as it slowly makes its way toward the plane.

"Conor, I have to go. They're back." I end the call and stuff the burner phone into the little hidden side pocket of my bag. Getting off the bed, I leave the compartment to greet Bastian by the door. He storms into the plane with the bodyguard on his heels; I only catch the end of Anton's "talk about it."

Bastian ignores him, tossing his phone and a bunch of coins on the table as he addresses the flight attendant. "Beth, could you please let the pilot know that we need to leave for New York asap."

"Of course."

"And I need more painkillers."

"I'm sorry, Mr. Artino, but the two I gave you a few hours ago were the last ones. Would you like me to contact the pharmacy in advance and have them deliver a prescription to the plane once we arrive?"

Bastian groans. "That's fifteen hours from now."

Anton squeezes his shoulder; his mouth is already open to say something when Bastian recoils. The words die on Anton's lips.

Bastian's eyes are almost black and burn with resentment. "Don't you fucking touch me, not after what just happened."

"Bastian—"

Bastian stabs him in the chest with a warning finger. "Give me some fucking space."

Anton raises his hands and takes a step back. He blinks a few times, but I don't know him well enough to determine whether he is angry or upset.

What did he do to piss Bastian off like this?

Bastian rubs his forehead. "I'm gonna lie down." The smile he offers me is nothing short of fake. "Are you comfortable in the smaller bedroom, Chelsea?"

"Yes, I'm good."

"And if you need anything, just let Beth know."

I nod.

Bastian's face is strained and he looks defeated. "And Beth, could you please prepare one of the reclining chairs for Mr. Worcheck."

Anton huffs.

Confusion is edged on Beth's forehead as she acknowledges the request with a mumbled "sure." Bastian takes off without a further glance at anyone and heads for the back section of the plane. Awkward silence follows in the wake of his departure and I decide to get the hell out of there. Even though I'm dying to learn what happened between him and Anton to get him so wound up, Anton is not the one I'd ever ask about it.

Returning to my compartment, I smile to myself as an idea sparks in my head. I still have painkillers from when I fell off the stepladder at the tea shop in October, and Bastian is in dire need of some heavy drugs. This could be my chance to gain a favor and maybe even find out what transpired while he was visiting his son.

I get the prescription bottle from my toiletry bag and check for Bastian in the back of the plane. He is in the bathroom; when he comes out, he's dressed in nothing but his boxers with the rest of his clothes stuffed in a trash bag he left in the middle of the floor. Toothpaste clings to the corner of his mouth and his hands are red as if he scorched them under boiling water.

His brows knit together. "Do you need something?"

I lift the bottle with the pills. "I remembered that I still had painkillers from when I hurt my back a few months ago. You are welcome to have them."

"Are you sure?"

"Absolutely. You look like you need them."

"Thank you." He unscrews the bottle cap and swallows two of the pills dry.

I'm standing on the threshold to his bedroom and am about to move aside when he grabs my arm and pulls me closer. His mouth is upon me in the next breath; my lips part, more in surprise, and our tongues collide. His kiss is hard and demanding; there is no give, only take.

He slides his hands under my shirt and pinches my nipples so hard that it hurts. When he crowds me against the bed, my knees hit the edge and I fall backward. Covering me with his body, he trails little kisses down my neck, his lips hot against my skin.

"I can stop, if you want me to," he mutters in between heavy breaths.

I slip my hand into his boxers and stroke his shaft. His cock twitches and the tip is already moist with arousal. "Take them off."

Standing over me, he watches me with hooded eyes. He disposes of his underwear and slides down my panties. I move closer to the edge of the bed to give him access to my pussy. He plunges inside me without any foreplay; his thrusts are as raw and feral as his earlier kiss. This act is not about pleasure but a means to an end. Lust for the sake of lust.

Leaning closer, he curls his arms around me, his nails softly scraping the skin on my back. His lips seal my mouth; this time, his kiss is like a desperate cry for air. A drowning man reaching for a lifeline he didn't know he needed. Moving in and out of me at a fast rhythm, he shudders as he finds his release. Warmth fills my womb. Even though I didn't orgasm and the sex was only about him, I'm oddly satisfied. I scoot over to the wall to make space for him on the bed. This time it's me who spoons him from behind.

He lets out a bitter chuckle. "Sorry, that was selfish. I can—"

"Shh, it's fine. Just go to sleep."

"So, you understand?"

I scoff; is he for real? "I've been there, so yes, I understand."

14

✳ ✳ ✳

BASTIAN

Somewhere between Nicosia, Cyprus and New York City, USA

~~~~~

The door to the bedroom compartment slides open and I meet Anton's gaze. The coldness in his eyes sends a shudder down my spine.

He tosses my cell on the bed. "Here, you forgot your phone and a text just came in." Pulling the door shut with so much force that the latch bounces back, he disappears again.

I close my eyes and inhale to soothe the turmoil churning in my chest.

Fuck this shit.

Sliding off the bed quietly enough not to disturb Chelsea, I unlock the phone and look at the message.

Lost Jackson Pierce. Will send update when I know more.

I groan. This is bad. Running my hand through my hair, I fight fresh stabs in my head and the rising nausea.

With one more look at Chelsea, I get up and move to the open area of the plane. Anton is in his usual chair with one leg crossed over another, whiskey glass in hand. He stares out of the window into the black night. When I sit down, he doesn't acknowledge me. After he had a couple of mouthfuls of whiskey, I break the stifling silence.

"Look, about earlier—"

A swoop of his hand cuts me off. "I get it. You were mad, so you punished me by fucking a girl. No biggie."

Of course, it's always about him. "I was going to say that I don't appreciate you putting a gun to my head. You're my lover, so I expected your loyalty."

He snorts. "Are you fucking kidding me?" Chilling blue eyes cut into me. "You want me to bite the hand that feeds me for a man who told me just hours ago that we aren't in a relationship. Bro, you haven't done anything that would warrant me to choose you over the Disciples."

I stare down at my hands that committed so many atrocious crimes. After everything we've been through, it hurts that I can't trust him any longer.

He downs the drink and slams the tumbler on the table hard enough that a fine crack spindles up the side of the glass. "Besides, I think Icarus is right. You don't give a damn about the organization. Maybe you should consider stepping aside and let Icarus focus on Vitaly as his successor."

"Fuck no. Vitaly is my son, and I don't want that type of life for him."

A vicious glow sneaks into Anton's eyes, warning me that he's about to deliver a blow below the belt. "You were nothing but a sex toy in a fucked-up love triangle, who then turned into the lucky sperm donor." Ridicule colors his chuckle. "You are no father."

"Hey, I was the one who was married to Liv."

"Sure, because that was the only way she and Konstantin could keep you trapped and use you for sex, but in the end, they only allowed you to be a very small part of Vitaly's life. Konstantin was his real dad. He taught the boy everything he could, and it's a good thing, too, because you would've turned Vitaly into a wuss." Anton shakes his head. "Fuck, you were upset earlier about killing a woman you barely knew but who went against our number one rule, damn well knowing there'd be repercussions if she were caught."

"She was trying to do the right thing by calling me."

"That's bullshit, and you know it. Lydia had a thing for you and this was her ticket into your inner circle. She wanted you to be indebted to her."

"Still . . ." It's one thing to kill a man who's trying to cheat us out of money or causes trouble, but Lydia was not a callous business partner going rogue. "She helped me out and shouldn't have had to die for it."

Anton doesn't hide his eye roll. "Shows you're not cut out for leadership. If you take over the Disciples, people will run all over you. You are way too soft."

Anger boils in my chest; I need to keep my hands balled to tight fists to avoid decking him. "Really good talk."

"Just trying to be honest. And, of course, it doesn't change how I feel about you."

"Right. I'm the weak boy you saved from a bad situation and I should be thankful for eternity." My tone is bitter. "Would you like me to suck your dick now to show you my gratitude?"

"I didn't mean it like that." He clutches my fists and rubs my hands until my fingers uncurl. "What Liv and Konstantin did to you was really fucked up, and I understand that you needed to heal, but it's time for you to leave that fragile boy in the past and grow a set of balls. If you want to be a real father to

Vitaly, you need to teach him how to be a man. And for a Crimson Disciple, it means that you have to show him how to kill."

"And you see nothing wrong with that?"

"We are henchmen in a war, Bastian, and the only thing that sets us apart from other soldiers of this world is that we are getting paid better, and that our organization will not abandon us the way governments do when things go wrong. Yet, at the end of the day, people die all the same. It's that simple thanks to the fucked-up society we live in. There's nothing more to it."

I bury my face into my hands and massage my forehead with my palms. Of course he's right, even if I sometimes struggle to come to terms with this reality.

He squeezes my knee. "And if you want my loyalty, you need to be ready to commit. We have been fooling around for five years, but I'm the only one invested. I've been monogamous the entire time; fuck, I've never even flirted with another man, while you . . ." As the words trail off, the hurt in his voice makes me cringe.

"I'm sorry, Anton."

"And it's not that I expect some profound declaration of love, but it would be nice if you could stop sleeping around . . . especially with women."

"So guys are okay?"

He moves closer and his breath fans my ear. "I know you like threesomes, and if that's so important to you, I'm willing to give it a try, as long as there are three cocks in the bed."

"Are strap-ons okay?"

"Oh, fuck off."

I chuckle. "Hey, you deserved that."

"What did the text say?"

His question works like an ice bucket being poured over me. "Vic lost Jackson Pierce."

"Fuck. Icarus will want someone's head."

"Maybe I'll offer him yours."

"Shit, right now, I think your head will roll faster than mine."

"That's true."

He rubs his chin. "Maybe it's time to put Nico on this. He is our best man and it won't raise any eyebrows if he replaces Vic."

"Nico is still busy with Murphy in Dublin, and if Jackson Pierce has a mercenary job, he'll be off the grid for a few months."

"That's true, too."

"I think for now, it's best to stay put until Jackson resurfaces on his own again."

"And send Chelsea back to Ireland?"

I smirk. "Unless you want her to move in with us."

"Fuck, no."

"Then we are aligned. Who will take care of Vic?"

"You did your deed for the month, so I'll do the kill."

15

✳ ✳ ✳

CHELSEA

Drogheda, Ireland
June 2024
~~~~~

Closing up the tea shop right around the time when most offices in town allow their workers to escape, I decide on a walk along the Boyne. The last few days have been marked by temperatures in the low seventies, a sign that summer has arrived in Ireland. It has allowed me to break out my short-sleeved blouses and skimpy skirts. A soft breeze nips at the ends of my short hair and I inhale deeply. The tension in my neck and shoulders still doesn't ease. I check my phone for a text— an almost hourly habit, unless I'm asleep.

Crickets.

For close to four months, I've been waiting for a message from Bastian, but zilch. If he found another way to contact Jackson Pierce, I'm fucked. My mood drops to its daily low. Ending my stroll at Starbucks, I order a caramel latte as a special treat in an attempt to stay positive. The shop has a little terrace overlooking the river and I sit down at a round table. Slurping my coffee, I watch shoppers cross the pedestrian bridge; it's the same one I walked across the night I left Bastian at this hotel. Since then, my life has almost come to a standstill. It's stifling.

"Excuse me, is this seat taken?"

I turn my head at the sudden voice; it's a dude in his late thirties who has seized the backrest of the second chair. Shooting him a get-lost glare, I raise my hand with the wedding band as a line of defense. He frowns. I look around him to find a woman next to a baby buggy at the closest table. Warmth floods my cheeks.

Geez, he wasn't hitting on me.

I shouldn't jump to conclusions.

Smiling, I try to gloss over the awkward moment. "No, go ahead."

He pulls the chair to the other table and sits down. Fretting over the woman and the baby, he ensures they have everything they need from the little stirring aid and a stash of napkins to a cracker the infant sticks into a drooling mouth. A picture-perfect family, out and about for an evening stroll. Something Marcel, Sean, and I used to do. A pang of jealousy turns my focus back to the river.

In a screwed-up way, I miss those days. Marcel had been a charmer, overly caring and protective, until that fateful day in Hong Kong when he just upped and left, forgetting that he had a wife and a son.

We met in a bagel shop in New York that had similar vibes to a Starbucks. I had come fresh off the plane, clueless, and he made fun of me for not knowing what a schmear was.

"It's the spread they put on the bagel."

"Oh, really." Watching him from under my eyelashes, I admired his broad, muscular frame so much in contrast to his fine facial features. His mouth was what stuck out the most.

Full lips under a pronounced cupid's bow, crying out for me to taste them. He was light complected enough to sport freckles on his nose, which was mega cute. "What type of schmear would you recommend?"

"Chives, if you like it savory, or peanut butter and Nutella, if you like it sweet."

"No offense, but the combination of peanut butter and Nutella sounds a bit off."

His chuckle injected my knees with jelly. "Trust me, you haven't lived until you had peanut butter and Nutella. It's the best schmear there is on a warm bagel."

Before I could object, he had ordered for me; as he passed me the paper bag, the bump against my shoulder was ever so subtle. It made my wallet drop right out of my hand.

"Oops, I'm so sorry." Dipping down, he retrieved the leather pouch but held it in such a way for the contents to spill out. "Oh, no!"

He was fast at returning everything to its proper place. My driver's license was last. One look was enough to burn every detail into memory. A skill every Crimson Disciple has perfected.

"Why don't you let me take you for dinner?" The velvety hum of his voice melted the Nutella before it even hit my mouth. "I know the best sushi restaurant in town."

Back in those days, Drogheda featured a few Chinese take-outs, but sushi was something out of a *Hello Kitty* anime. I glanced at Siobhan, my BFF accompanying me on my US adventure.

He picked up on it immediately. "Of course, your friend is welcome to join."

We both knew she would never impose, that it would just be him and me because no one wants to be the extra wheel. His offer set off an avalanche of jittery emotions. The thought of going on a date with him was just as exhilarating as it was terrifying. Temptation and curiosity won in the end over caution and the guilt of ditching my friend.

"I'd love to go to dinner with you."

We agreed to meet at the restaurant; by the time I sat down at the small table, he likely knew everything about me. About my family's IRA ties that had peaked on Bloody Sunday when my granddad proudly took a bullet for the cause, about my father's recent surrender to cirrhosis as the many shots of whiskey over countless years had gotten the best of his liver, about the eight million Euros in my bank account that were my cut from the sale of his hotels.

After dinner, Marcel took me home to his place. I was untouched, unkissed, and naïve, unable to resist his charm and his skillful touch. A lover who made me crave for his cock and who taught me about naughty sex kinks that would make my mam faint. For two weeks, he was my tour guide; we explored anything famous New York City had on offer during the day and every inch of my body throughout the night. When it was time for me to go home, I was hooked enough to accept his invitation to stay. He was like a fatal addiction.

A gust of wind blows a napkin from the neighboring table into my face.

Fuck, how long was I tripping down memory lane?

I shudder in the breeze. A wall of thick clouds have swallowed the sunshine; they are dark enough to promise rain.

Four seasons in a day, a concept that only exists in Ireland.

Finishing the last mouthfuls of coffee, now cold and stale, I chuck the cup in the bin on my way to the car. I stop by a fast-food place for a take-out pizza and demolish it during the drive home. Mam isn't a fan of non-Irish food and complains whenever I bring it into the house. Fifteen minutes later, I walk up the driveway to our old farm on the water, soaking up the scent of brine drifting from the Irish Sea. The wind has picked up, causing waves to crash to shore. The first raindrops fall. Dorothy, my Irish terrier, barks from inside the house; I'm eager to curl up on the sofa with her and watch some TV.

About to unlock the door, wailing sirens distract me. A bunch of Garda cars fly by on the main road. They are an unusual sight for a rural area; crime here is almost non-existent and disputes among neighbors are handled without involving law enforcement. When their taillights disappear around the next bend, I turn back to the door. Cracking twigs and movement in my peripheral vision cause my muscles to freeze.

A man stumbles out of the bushes, staggering in a zigzag line. He is hunched over with a hoodie hiding his face, which only emphasizes the threat of the object he clutches in his hand. Even in the dim light of the approaching storm, its purpose is unmistakable.

A gun—lethal by design—and it's pointed right at the center of my chest.

16

✷ ✾ ✸

CHELSEA

Baltray, Ireland
~~~~~

The man with the gun raises his gaze and I breathe a sigh of relief.

"Bastian, what the actual fuck?"

He bends over, vomit spilling from his mouth all over Mam's *Fáilte* mat.

Welcome, indeed.

The gun swings uncoordinated from left to right as he pukes up more of his stomach contents. The rest of him smells as if he swallowed a whole whiskey distillery. I grab his wrist and point the barrel of the gun upward, releasing the lock of the magazine at the same time. As the magazine drops, I catch it with my other hand. Twisting his arm until he loosens his grip, I secure the weapon and ensure with a quick safety check that he wasn't stupid enough to load a bullet into the chamber.

Phew, danger averted.

I pocket the magazine and shove the gun, barrel down first, into one of Mam's flowerpots by the entrance.

Incomprehensible babble floats from Bastian's lips. The only words I can decipher are police and chase. At least that explains the Garda presence.

"Bastian, what are you doing here?" I narrow my eyes. An angry bruise under his right eye has colored his entire cheek in a deep red and blood has crusted on his cupid's bow. His nose is so crooked that it's likely broken. "What happened to your face?"

A hiccup shakes his frame and he sucks in a deep breath. "Anton."

"Anton did this?"

"Yep." He wipes drool off his mouth. "But I—I—I"—a smile curls his lips—"I hit him first." Pride seeps out of him. "I gave him a shiner."

"Wow, impressive."

He misses the sarcasm and nods eagerly. "Yep, I—I showed him. He can't push—push me around. I'm not"—he runs his tongue over the tip of his teeth as if checking that they were still firmly in place—"I'm not his little bitch."

Okay, so he took on a man who is at least six foot three and whose punch is backed up by around two hundred and fifty pounds of body weight.

Good for him.

'What did Anton do that made you punch him?"

"He—he bought us a sex"—he swallows—"a sex swing even though he knew it would trigger me."

I arch a brow. Now that's some interesting intel and puts Anton's hostility toward women into perspective, even though it doesn't explain why Bastian would take issue in a popular sex device.

Bastian takes in a raspy breath and clutches his hand over his mouth. "I'm gonna hurl. Too much talk—" The rest of the sentence collides with a fresh surge of vomit. Half of it lands on his Jordan's. "Fuck."

"Okay, let's get you cleaned up and into bed. You need to sleep it off." I wrap my arm around him and yank him toward the door. He sways and almost pulls us down. Avoiding the puke is a challenge, but I manage to get him over the threshold and into the hallway. Dorothy jumps up on him, her tail wagging like a whip.

"Mam, can you get the dog, please?"

My mother shuffles out of the kitchen, dressed already in her bathrobe with her hair under a net. Her gaze roams over me, then Bastian and his stained clothes, and her brows furrow. "*Ag magadh atá tú?*"

I wish I were joking. I grimace. "I'm sorry, but your Welcome mat is ruined."

"You bring home a drunk? What in God's name were you thinking?"

"He isn't my boyfriend."

Dorothy's massive body crashes into me in an attempt to land a slobber kiss on my chin. I stumble against the sideboard in the hallway. Mam's vase tilts dangerously toward the side but manages to swing back with a low *thud*. That gets Mam to finally restrain the dog and pull her into the sitting room. Before I can make a dash for the guest room, she is back.

"Is he foreign?" She gives Bastian another once over. "He looks foreign."

She'll have a fit if I admit he's an American. "He's from Cyprus. They are part of the European Union."

She huffs—her opinion about the EU is almost as bad as about the States. "Why can't you find a nice Irish lad—"

"Please, Mam, not now. There's nothing going on between Bastian and me. We are simply friends."

"How do you even know him?"

I scramble to come up with a fib that won't send me straight to hell. "He came to the tea shop and we talked, and then we grabbed a drink at Clarkes."

"Hm, he looks like he had more than one drink."

Can't argue with that.

Bastian appears to wake up from a daze and I struggle to keep him upright. His mouth opens and the most inopportune words spill out. "Anton is a dick. He—he shouldn't have gotten the sex swing."

Crap, swear words and sexual insinuations are a red flag for Mam.

Mam's forehead wrinkles. "What did he say?"

"Nothing. As you can see, he's totally out of it."

"He sounded American. Is he American?"

"Mam, I told you he's from Cyprus."

Bastian squints at her. "God save the King."

Oh, fuck no. That could start a war in this house. Mam already has one hand on her hip for a roasting when I give Bastian a good push that catapults him right by her. "I'll put him up in the guest room. See you in the morning."

"I have a shotgun, laddy, and I'm not afraid to use it, so you'd better keep your hands off my daughter," she yells after us.

Bastian's response is another heave of his stomach; luckily, this time, the puke stays in. I wrestle him into the guest room and slam the door shut.

Bloody hell.

He topples forward onto the bed, dragging me with him and burying me underneath his firm body in a way that his cock sits right on my crotch as if it belonged there. If he weren't so drunk, this might even arouse me.

He smacks his lips. "Don't think I'll be able to get it up."

"Don't worry, I'm not in the mood." Consent and his level of intoxication don't exactly go hand in hand, so he won't be seeing any action tonight.

With one hard shove, I roll him onto his back and slide off the bed.

Fuck, the man is heavy.

Gazing down on him, I look him over. Getting him out of the hoodie will be impossible, so that leaves his dirty shoes and his pants. Once he's fully asleep, I could ask Mam to set his nose. Six younger brothers who like to brawl have given her plenty of experience in that respect.

I slip Bastian's shoes off, but before I can pull down his jeans, he rolls onto his side and tugs his legs into a fetal position. Soft snores drift from his mouth and with the small smile on his lips, he looks utterly content.

His phone chimes; pulling it out of his pants pocket to set it on the nightstand, I catch a preview of the message before the screen goes black. The sender is Anton.

If U are with her, I'll f-en end U both.

17

✳✳✳

BASTIAN

Baltray, Ireland
~~~~~

I wake up in a strange bed in an unfamiliar room, still dressed in clothes that reek abhorrently. A nasty-sour taste in my mouth makes me fear the worst.

What the fuck happened?

Closing my eyes, I sift through my last memories.

Anton and I leaving the Burger King at the rest stop, him holding his phone under my nose with a picture of a recent purchase. "Look what I got us."

"Is that a fucking sex swing?" I squinted at the email confirmation and decked him before he had a chance to reply.

Slamming my fist into his eye felt fucking good.

Something that was long overdue.

He threw a couple of punches, likely more out of reflex, and was overly sorry when my nose bled by the truckload.

Fuck him.

I grin. While he was running back into the Burger King to get napkins, I left his pathetic ass.

It was as if a chip fell off my shoulder. A victory after a long, tiresome battle. I was fucking free of his constant whining.

The pressure on my bladder forces me out of bed; there's a small ensuite bathroom that takes care of business. After I leak enough piss to fill a well, I rummage through the cabinets. Whoever lives here is a pretty good host; I find a toothbrush still wrapped in its original packaging, toothpaste, a neutral deodorant, liquid cream soap that smells a little like peppermint, and body lotion for sensitive skin. Lots of towels, too, so everything I need. Discarding the disgustingly smelling clothes and rinsing off under a stream of hot water is like a salvation; after a few good belches and brushing my teeth, I re-arrive among the living. Now all I need is a gallon of water and my collision with alcohol will be a thing of the past.

Staring into the mirror above the sink, I frown. My face is fucked up with a huge bruise almost completely covering one cheek, though my nose is surprisingly straight as if someone already set it. Anton will face some major groveling to even stay on as my number two. I'm so sick of him and his know-what's-best-for-Bastian approach.

A soft knock on the door sets off a small panic. I still have no idea where I am and how I got here.

"Bastian, is everything okay?"

Fuck, that's Chelsea.

"I'll be right out."

A few torn pieces of memories connect in my mind. Stumbling up a few steps with her arms holding me upright, a massive dog jumping, some scary woman glaring at me. Something about a shotgun was in there, too, though that bit is really fuzzy.

Wrapped in only a towel, I unlock the door and soak in her appearance. She's wearing cute pajama shorts and a crop top offering plenty of creamy skin. Her short, black hair is tousled in a straight-out-of-bed sexy way—a look some women would pay a fortune for at a salon—and her sea-green eyes that always take me back to my summers in Cyprus shine with concern.

She cocks her head. "How are you feeling?"

"Never been better."

"No hangover."

"Nope. Just a little dehydrated." Awkward silence stands between us. "Can you tell me how I got here?"

"Not a clue. Do you have any memories at all?"

I plop onto the bed and run my hand through my hair. "Honestly, not many."

"What's the last thing you remember?"

"Leaving Anton at the rest stop—"

"You ditched Anton in the middle of nowhere?" She covers her mouth, her shoulders shaking with laughter. "I'm sure he was mad as fuck."

Judging by the dozens of pings from text messages I ignored, I'd say so. "I'm sure he found a way back to the plane. Anyhow, after I left him, I headed straight to Drogheda to pick you up, but your tea shop was already closed." That's when I went off the rails and bought a bottle of booze to kill the choking memories triggered by Anton's purchase. "At some point, I was driving toward your house and I vaguely recall taking off the mirrors on a row of parked cars in a narrow street." I grimace. "Maybe I caused even more damage. I'm honestly not sure, though I don't think I hit a pedestrian."

"You didn't. I have been monitoring the news and they only spoke of property damage caused by an accident last night."

I lift a brow. "I made the news for hitting a couple of cars?"

"Hey, this is County Louth and the accident happened right in front of the Garda station. Some bystander alerted them, and apparently, you were involved in a real Gardaí chase. Newspapers will talk about this for months."

"Fuck." I bury my face into my hands. "I don't even know what happened to the rental."

More shreds of memory pull together like pieces of a puzzle. Sirens behind me became louder and then were gone again. The Google Maps woman telling me to take a turn into a driveway that I then missed. The steering wheel not responding and the car flying into a ditch. Stumbling through a field.

All in all, it's a miracle I made it to Chelsea's doorsteps.

"Whose name was on the rental?"

I raise my gaze at Chelsea's question. "Mine."

"They might arrest you."

"They can't." My smile is smug. "I have diplomatic immunity, and if they found and towed the car, the worst the Irish government will do is bitch to my embassy." And the suits in charge don't take drunk driving and property damage too seriously, especially not if the culprit is a top Disciple. It will blow over with a phone call to Icarus and a request to reel in his man.

"Why do you have diplomatic immunity?"

Always so curious.

I entangle her fingers and pull her hand to my lips. Enough of an information exchange. "Come here so I can properly say good morning."

"What did you have in mind?"

"You can't tease me with this type of pjs and hope to get away with it."

As she takes a step forward, I pull her on my lap. Her ass wiggles on my cock and gets me hard. Trailing kisses along her bare shoulder, I slide my hand under her shirt and pinch the few extra pounds around her waist.

God, everything about her is soft.

Big tits, with one side larger than the other and a bit lopsided. Liv had been the exact opposite. Following a strict diet and exercise regimen, she had a body made of steeled muscles with model-type proportions. The perfect standard of beauty that made her cold and aloof. She could've never measured up to Chelsea, whose little imperfections make her real and so much more attractive.

I lift Chelsea to set her on the bed and dispose of her shirt. When I slide down those cute little shorts, my cock jumps with excitement. She is lying on the bed, biting her lip. Waiting for my next move. Patience without demands. Her areolas are a deep red, her nipples taut. Arousal glistens on the inside of her thigh.

"Touch yourself."

She hesitates for a brief moment but then runs her fingers through her folds. Her body reacts with a shudder and a moan escapes through parted lips. As she fastens her strokes, her hips buck into her hand.

Fuck, I want to taste her saltiness.

I get onto my knees and remove her hand from her crotch. Spreading her legs, I blow onto her wet pussy. More moans fill the air around us. With two fingers pushed deep inside her drenched canal, I let my tongue explore her clit. Her skin is heated and the muscles in her pussy squeeze around my fingers. She is close. I fingerfuck her harder, my tongue hitting her clit in an even rhythm. When the moans turn to little yelps, I decide I edged her enough. My cock is so hard that it's aching for a release.

I plunge inside soaked wetness. My thrusts are slow and my gaze locks on her face. Head slightly tilted backward, she has her eyes closed and breathes heavily through pursed lips. Her pleasure stokes the fire in my core. I relish her lust, her desire for me, her passion. The friction in her tight canal is amazing; a few more thrusts set off a chain reaction. As the orgasm rips through her, my cock explodes, her greedy muscles squeezing even the last drop of cum out of the tip. Panting, I fall onto the bed and pull her into my arms.

She shivers with aftershocks and snuggles against me. A satisfied sigh leaves her lips. Her heated skin emits warmth and I focus on her racing heart against my chest.

This was some fucking good sex.

Wrapping my leg around hers, I tug her close, my thumb caressing her hand. Two bones have hard knots; I could kill Nico for taking it too far and breaking them. I trace the cold metal hoop on her ring finger.

"Why are you still wearing your wedding band?" I expect an off-putting answer, an excuse to end this perfect moment.

"It's actually my dad's wedding ring, not mine. Mam gave it to me after he died, and I used to wear it on a chain around my neck, but after Hong Kong"—she nuzzles her face against my shoulder—"I had it resized. It stops men from asking me out."

I hug her tighter. "I'm really sorry about all the shit that happened in Hong Kong."

"I know." A few hot tears burn on my skin.

"You asked me once whether I'm going to kill Marcel. The answer is yes."

"Why are you after him?"

"He stole from us."

That's the official version—the reason why Icarus put a bounty on his head—and I'll make damn sure that Marcel Pierce will never get the chance to open up his big, fat mouth and contradict any parts of that version.

The truth will die with him.

End of story.

He's gonna take the fall for what I did.

18

✸ ✸ ✸

BASTIAN

Dublin Airport, Ireland
~~~~~

Scrolling through my messages once again, I scoff at Anton's last text.

If U are with her, I'll f-en end U both.

Is he truly that delusional to think that this would intimidate me? Or make me come back to him?

Motherfucking moron.

Approaching the plane, the driver slows down the cab just as Chelsea folds the soft cloth she used to wipe the earth from the flowerpot off my gun. "Here, all done."

"Aw, thank you. You did so much." Patching me up, washing my clothes, now cleaning my Glock. I slide the weapon into my holster and accept the offered magazine. "I still can't believe you had us sneak out of your house. What will your mother think of me?"

"Trust me, after that piss-ass introduction, she is the last person you ever want to meet face to face."

"You should've at least let me apologize for hurling all over her front yard."

She smirks. "The "God save the King" comment blew your chances with her. You were lucky you made it out of the house alive."

"Ugh." Such a dumb shit moment.

The cabbie stops the car and turns around. "That would be two hundred and thirty euros."

Say what?

The drive was less than an hour. Taxi rides in this country are extortion. I count out 5 fifties and pass the money across the seat. "Here's an extra twenty if you carry the luggage on the plane."

He raises a brow.

Buddy, seriously?

With a huff, I dig out another twenty euros. "Is that enough?"

He clicks his tongue as if offended but pockets the cash and gets out of the cab. Popping the trunk, he heaves Chelsea's suitcase out and carries it up the steps. I don't envy him. That thing weighs a ton.

He returns not even a minute later; I wait until he is in his taxi and on his way. Behind Chelsea's back, I slide the ammo into my gun and rack it before replacing it into the holster. Following her up the stairs, I step onto the plane. Beth's cheerful good afternoon can't hide her distress. Her eyes are inflamed and her cheeks are puffy and red. She has been crying her heart out.

"What happened?"

She can't hold my gaze.

Her despair fuels the anger burning in my chest. "Did Mr. Worcheck upset you?"

She glances at Anton and drops her voice to a whisper. "He was in one of his moods, but honestly, it's not a big deal."

Oh, it's a very big deal. He can be mad at me all he wants, but I won't tolerate this utter cruelty toward the staff.

Approaching him, I pull the gun and lodge the barrel under his chin before he can open his stupid mouth. "You and I need to talk."

Getting to his feet, he raises his hands; I grab hold of his dress shirt to keep the weapon in place. Slowly, he backs up until we arrive inside the office space. I close the door. The compartment is soundproof, which will guarantee that this conversation stays private.

"Threatening to kill me and Chelsea? Did you seriously think that would work?"

He blinks at me but stays quiet. The black eye I gave him is in full bloom and cuts down on his attractiveness. This will make the next part so much easier.

I huff. "I think it's time to set some ground rules. You are hired muscle, working for *me*. Case closed. That means you don't complain, you don't question me, and you keep your damn opinions to yourself. If you can't accept that, you're off my crew."

"Look—"

"I wasn't finished. I expect anyone who works for me to treat other members of the team with respect. That includes the crew of this plane. Is that clear?" I press the barrel of the Glock harder against his jaw to prove my point.

"Crystal clear."

"Then apologize to Beth." I lower the gun and snort out a bitter laugh. "You wanted me to grow a set of balls? Consider them grown. Now get out."

He doesn't move. "Look, Bastian, about the swing."

Fuck, does he have a death wish? I'm about ready to blow his brains out. "I have nothing else to say to you."

"You are coping the wrong way. After all this time, you need to face your inner demons—"

"I was raped, Anton. Several times a week. For eleven fucking years. And they used a sex swing to make me submit, so in which fucking universe did you ever think it'd be a good idea to put me through that again?" My voice trembles so hard that the words slur together. I was their helpless toy, bound and dangling in a restraint without any control over my own body. Fuck, they even made me believe I liked it because I got hard and ejaculated.

"You need to move on from the past—"

"I said get out!" Tears choke my words. I point to the door. "NOW, before I fucking kill you."

He finally gives me my space and slams the door behind him.

I drop on the couch, burying my face into my hands. Silent sobs shake my body; the tears spill out of me as if my eyes suffered from a permanent leak.

Fuck, I'm crying like a little girl.

Get a grip, Artino.

Stifling pain rolls through me, leaving me raw and vulnerable.

A soft knock has me dry my face on my hoodie. The door opens a tiny crack. "I'm so sorry to disturb you, Mr. Artino, but Mr. Pappas is calling on a secure line and insists on talking to you before take-off."

I swallow three times to get my voice back under control. "Thanks, Beth. Could you please put the phone on the floor and close the door."

She obliges without a breath of hesitation. I stare at the cell on the ground, lying upside down.

Please, not a FaceTime call.

No such luck.

Icarus squints at me from the other side of the screen. "You okay?"

"Yep, fine."

"What happened to your face? Did you get hurt in the accident?"

So he knows about the trashed cars. The wheels of the Irish government work swiftly. "No, not the accident. I had to put Anton in his place and he didn't like it."

Icarus's brows arch. "You want him replaced?"

"Not sure yet."

His eyes turn thoughtful. "To be honest, when you two were in Nicosia, I was glad that he was still a mindless soldier who followed my orders without hesitation, but if Rostya had pulled a gun on me, he would've been lying dead on the ground next to Lydia. Not trying to tell you how to run your crew, but if you put your life in the hands of your lieutenant, trust is of the utmost importance."

"I agree, theíos, but right now, the only one I'd trust is Nico, and as long as I'm working with Chelsea Doherty, he isn't a feasible option. Once I tidy up loose ends with Marcel Pierce, I'll consider making the switch."

"Okay, I will already keep an eye out for a new home for Anton. He earned his stripes, so something nice and easy without stress might be good for him."

I chuckle. A bodyguard to an older member of the organization who plays golf all day. Anton will hate it. "That might be in the best interest for everyone."

"About the accident. What happened?"

"I got plastered and took down a row of cars."

His lips twitch. "About time you blew off some steam."

I roll my eyes. "It was poor judgment on my part." And my recklessness could've cost me days of delay.

"You are too uptight for your own good. Men need to drink and whore. It's in our nature."

And knock women around in case they criticize us.

Not for me.

"Can you have someone in the office take care of the paperwork with the car rental company?"

"Don't worry, I'll get one of the girls to do it."

The plane vibrates under my feet as the pilot starts the engines. "I need to go, theíos. We are about to take-off."

"You have been very focused lately, and I'm happy we could put this unfortunate incident with Lydia behind us."

"Yes, me, too. Talk soon."

I end the call and grin. The act of playing the obedient nephew who has given up on his son is working like a charm. Now, I just have to clean up the Marcel Pierce mess before I can fully focus on my next task.

A silent strike.

My final kill.

And Icarus will never know what hit him.

19

✳ ✴ ✳

CHELSEA

Houston, Texas
June 2024
~~~~~

"Ouch." I flinch and rub over the sore spot, shooting the platinum blond dude a hard stare.

He shrugs. "A little bit of pain is the downside of this new tech."

"On the other hand, even if Jackson's men sweep you for bugs, this device will not be detected." Bastian cranes his neck to take another peek at the restaurant across the street.

The sidewalk glimmers; it's almost seven pm but the sun is still beating down on the streets of Houston without mercy. I rub my eyes. According to my biological clock, it's already the middle of the night, and the flight from Dublin to Texas with only a quick stop in New York was exhausting. I'm thirsty, hungry, and tired, and the sweltering heat that's trapped in the cramped space in the back of the van has me sweating like a hog. The atmosphere is equally pressing; Anton is brooding in a corner as he flips through a magazine. He and Bastian have not exchanged a single word since their blow up on the plane and

Anton looks as if he's about to snap and kill everyone within reach while Bastian has kept a pleasant smile on his lips.

The platinum blond dude, who introduced himself as Falk, taps away on a laptop attached to several monitors. He is the epitome of a nerd minus the glasses: zero build-up muscle tissue, fine-boned long fingers, and smart as a whip with lots of techie talk and a total lack of slang. "Remember, I need fifteen seconds to pair the phone and the signal only works within twelve feet of the target. That's about three and a half meters, in case you struggle with US measurements."

Irish people haven't used the metric system for very long and Mam refuses to stray from her old way of thinking, leaving us with old imperial dimensions. "I hope I'll get close enough to Jackson."

"Just be assertive and you'll make it." Bastian's eyes narrow as a few patrons leave the restaurant. "And like I said, chances are he won't shoot you, but in case he does, the closest hospital is only three blocks away."

"Oh, lucky me." Other than Falk who snorts, I get no reaction to my sarcasm. "How much longer is this meeting going to last?"

"Could be minutes or another hour. Jackson is paranoid, so cell phones are disabled at the start of a meeting and he sweeps for bugs religiously. At this point, I can't even confirm he is in there."

Fantastic. The whole plan rests on the whim of a client who owed the Disciples a favor and lured Jackson to the restaurant under the pretense that he had a job for him. What if the customer flipped and told Jackson the truth? I could be walking right into a trap.

Bastian's phone pings. "Here we go. Meeting just ended and Jackson is on his way out."

Anton opens the back door and stale, hot air drifts into the van. The expectant gazes of the three men signals me that it's showtime. Jumping out of the car, I almost buckle under a bout of fear.

This is insane.

I've never even met Jackson Pierce before. What if he doesn't believe I'm his sister-in-law? And does he even care? If he decides to shoot me in the head, even a hospital next door couldn't save me.

As I dart across the street, the muscles in my shoulders tighten. Three men in khaki pants and black shirts spill out of the alley next to the restaurant; they openly carry their guns in holsters and steer toward a Hummer SUV. Wide shades and brimmed caps hide most of their features, but since they are white, none of them could be Jackson. When one of the guys looks right at me, my steps slow; even through the darkness of his glasses, his gaze sends a shudder down my spine. These men are trained killers.

A larger group is right behind them; six walking rooks in a diamond formation shielding two people. I catch a glimpse of Jackson's stocky frame and immediately recognize his face from the picture Marcel kept in his nightstand.

"Jackson!"

My shout triggers one of the men from the earlier group to take a couple of steps in my direction to position himself between me and his boss. "Continue moving, ma'am."

Crap, this is definitely not twelve feet. With a quick side-step, I rush around him, ignoring his sharp intake of breath.

"I'm Chelsea Doherty, Marcel's wife. Please, I need to talk to you."

Jackson has stopped; eight guns are drawn, their barrels pointing right at me. An ever so slight wave of his hand freezes the bizarre scene.

The man who tried to stop me grabs my arm. "Move, bitch."

Turning a blind eye to the danger he represents is the only way not to bolt. "Did Marcel tell you that he got our son killed in Hong Kong? *Your* nephew. His name was Sean."

Deafening silence surrounds me. Even though Jackson has his head turned, I can't tell through the mirrored sunglasses hiding his eyes whether he's looking at me or at his man behind me. His face is void of emotion.

Swallowing hard to fight the building lump in my throat, I rip myself loose and edge closer. "Marcel just abandoned us. That's the type of man you're protecting."

A small shake of Jackson's head is all that it takes to get his goon to breathe down my neck again. The man presses the muzzle of his gun against my spine. "You got three seconds to walk away." With an outstretched arm, he forces me backward and I almost stumble over my own feet.

Tears blur my vision. What will it take to make Jackson listen? "I hope Marcel paid you your cut. He stole close to six million dollars from me."

A good shove throws me onto a metal gutter by the curb; I land hard on my hands and knees. The pain is crippling. By the time I grit my teeth and get to my feet, Jackson has gotten into the Hummer. The SUV takes off with its engine roaring. The rest of his entourage settles into two cars across the street. I wait until they have disappeared before limping over to the van. Only my clenched jaw prevents me from bawling. My pants are torn on one of my knees, revealing scrapes, and blood oozes from a few cuts on my hands.

Staring through the open door into the back, I meet Bastian's gaze. He shakes his head.

Falk grimaces. "Sorry, but you only got close enough for about five seconds."

Fuck, all this was for nothing. "And now?"

Anton's glare is filled with scorn; it's obvious he blames me for the botched attempt. "She's of no more use to us but knows too much, so we should tie up loose ends and kill her."

20

✳ ✳ ✳

CHELSEA

Houston, Texas
~~~~~

I play with a piece of asparagus on my plate, not really having an appetite despite my body's famished state. The restaurant Bastian chose is magnificent; an outside terrace nestled in between a bayou and a lavish park. A low breeze raises goosebumps on my arms—a nice change to the heat—and the candle on our table flickers as if fueled by magic. A romantic setting for an unromantic date overshadowed by fear and guilt. I owed Sean to find his father and set the record straight, an encounter that now seems more unlikely than ever, with the added burden that if it were up to Anton, I'd be dead already.

Bastian sets down the fork. "Is something wrong with the food?"

"No, everything is delicious."

"Then why aren't you eating?"

I shrug.

Bastian's warm hand squeezes mine. "Don't pay attention to Anton. He can be a gigantic jerk."

An understatement. "What are we gonna do about Jackson Pierce?"

"What can we do?"

"I want to try again."

Bastian clicks his tongue. "He gave my men the slip, so for now, I don't know where he is."

"How hard can it be to find him?"

"Jackson Pierce is one of the most sought-after mercenaries for a reason. If he doesn't want to be found, he won't."

"But don't you share a lot of the same contacts?"

"Many of the people who hire him also buy weapons from us, but that doesn't mean they would ever risk betraying him. There are other arms dealers, but there's only one Jackson Pierce. He knows his stuff and is considered *the* expert when it comes to eliminating high-value targets. Why do you think he surrounds himself with so much security? Plenty of people would love to see him dead, but he has even more international connections who want to stay in his good graces."

"So he's pretty much untouchable."

"Let's just say he's outside the reach of my organization."

I decide to put the cards on the table. "Which is hard to do, considering you are a Disciple."

Bastian's eyes narrow. "What makes you think I'm a Disciple?" His question carries a dangerous edge.

"Nicosia. That's where we went the last time and Marcel told me that Icarus Pappas lives in Cyprus. Since he is the head of the Disciples, it would be a pretty big coincidence if you went there without being affiliated with him."

"Well deduced. I think I gave you too little credit." Bastian picks up the fork and takes a bite of his duck. Chewing, he smiles, though his eyes can't hide a certain wariness.

I will have to tread carefully but went too far out to back down. "What did Marcel steal from you?"

"What difference does it make?"

"Let's call it an incentive. I risked my life for you today and once you find Jackson, which you undoubtedly will, I'd be willing to try again, but I want to know if it's worth it for me. You said you want to kill Marcel, but right now, that could be a lie to secure my cooperation."

"Why would I lie?" He sips from his water, his gaze locked on mine.

"Maybe you want to get your hands on his money, then rough him up a little and call it a day. What guarantees do I have that you'd follow through? Knowing the stakes could put my mind at ease."

This time, the smile reaches his eyes. "Very nice. I like women who fight for what they want, even when knowing that it could bite them in the ass in the long run."

"Then what did Marcel steal?"

"Do you know what a NOC list is?"

"Sure. It's a database with info on all the covert agents of the US government."

"The Crimson Disciples have something similar. Not sure if Marcel told you, but we operate in crews. They are isolated groups that work mostly independently of each other."

I nod. "He said that this would guarantee that no one in the organization knows too much in case one of you is caught or decides to snitch." Damage control to ensure that the Disciples couldn't be taken down from the inside.

"Our NOC list contains the exact make-up of these crews. Who is in charge, what markets they operate in, their customer contacts, and so on. It also includes the locations of our safe houses and our dead drops. Needless to say, in the wrong hands, this information could prove deadly, and for both governments and our competitors, such intel is invaluable."

"Are you telling me that Marcel got his hands on your NOC list?" Now it all makes sense. Marcel's smug smile, the triumphant glow in his eyes, his boastful claim that the Disciples couldn't mess with him.

"It was his insurance policy to start a new life and it almost worked. Icarus ordered that Marcel was not to be touched as long as we didn't have a location on the stolen data, plus Marcel did a superb job of dropping from the face of the Earth without a trace. The identities he built for you guys were solid. If he had just stayed the course, chances are we would've never found you."

"Then what happened?"

"He got greedy. Started to sell the intel to the highest bidder, which triggered an international manhunt. Governments wanted him because he had the tools to take down the Disciples, competitors were eager to take over our networks, and we were scrambling for survival. Over night, Marcel turned into our enemy number one, and finding him was an absolute priority."

"Which brought you to Hong Kong."

"Unfortunately, yes, but the death of your son was not on us."

"So the man in the warehouse who shot Sean wasn't one of yours?"

"He wasn't a Disciple." Bastian's face is even and his eyes are clear of deceit; if I didn't know better, I would believe him. His lie hurts me more than it should and leaves a bitter taste in my mouth. What else was he untruthful about?

I slurp my cocktail, a tart concoction of tequila and juices. The icy liquid on my tongue manages to keep me calm. How should I proceed? Going home would be the prudent thing to do, a move that would set me back to square one. My other option is to keep up my game, swallow his story and pretend all is good between us even though the little trust we built just went down the drain.

Once again, I'm fucked no matter what way I turn.

I stare into the dark bayou, the candle flickering in my peripheral vision. Mumbling voices and clattering silverware drift across the terrace from the neighboring tables. Some of these words are honest conversations, others bullshit to keep up a false narrative. It's always the same. Just like everything else in life, candlelight dinners are simply a means to an end. The magic they offer dissipates as soon as the candles are blown out.

I turn back to Bastian and smile. "I'm glad you told me the truth. I don't think I could've continued working with you if the Disciples had been responsible for my son's death." The lie flows easily off my lips and I manage to stroke the back of his hand, even if looking into his eyes now makes me sick. "If you'd excuse me. I have to use the bathroom."

Asking a server for directions, I find the restrooms in the back of the restaurant. After relieving myself, I stare into the mirror as I wash my hands. To give Bastian credit, he did fill in a lot of the gaps that had been missing from Conor's files. If he had just been truthful about Sean . . .

A woman steps up to the sink beside me and our gazes meet in the mirror. Despite the buzz cut, she is quite pretty with cloud-blue eyes that are calming. Turning off the water, I dry my hands. She moves behind me. Too close for comfort.

I'm about to ask her to give me some space when she leans even closer.

Her warm breath brushes my ear and for the second time today, the muzzle of a gun presses against my spine. "If you want to live, don't make a sound."

21

✷✻✷

CHELSEA

Houston, Texas
~~~~~

The woman increases the pressure on my spine. "When we walk out of here, we're gonna turn left. The backdoor is only a few steps away. If you scream for help or try to alert your friend, you're both dead. Now move."

The barrel of the gun against my back is convincing enough to comply with her orders. The hallway outside the bathroom is deserted and the emergency exit opens without setting off an alarm. We stumble into a dark dumpster area. She shoves me toward a waiting limo with tinted windows. The trunk opens by remote.

"Get in."

I stare at the small space, my stomach cramping with apprehension. The last trip I took in the trunk of a car ended in the warehouse in Hong Kong.

The pressure of the muzzle on my lower back turns painful. "NOW!"

Heart throbbing in my chest, I sit on the edge of the car. My mouth is as dry as if I swallowed a bag of cotton wool. When I lower myself into the trunk, she supports my head with one arm; the other hand still holds the gun with the barrel now pointed at the part of my rib cage that protects my liver. The way she positions herself, I have zero chance to kick her or otherwise disarm her. She slams the lid down, leaving me in darkness. I force myself to breathe and not let the shadows overpower my senses.

Fuck.

As soon as the car moves, I close my eyes and count down the seconds to determine the length of the ride. I only get to sixty before we stop. The trunk is opened and four hands lift me out. Finding my footing, I stare at three men plus the woman. We are in some sort of courtyard in the back of a bakery.

The woman takes charge. "She was with Bastian Artino, which means that we have Falk Herrera on the other side. Everything needs to be triple checked, and you got five minutes." She claps her hands. "Move it, folks."

One guy approaches me with a scanner. "Lift your arms." He runs the device along my body. "Now turn around."

I comply without hesitation; this is not any more intrusive than the checks at the airport.

"Alright, now strip and put all your belongings in this bag." He tosses me the type of grocery bag Mam uses to transport frozen food from the store. "Everything needs to go in there, including any jewelry and your phone."

My cell, wallet, and ID are in my purse with Bastian at the restaurant. "I don't have anything—"

"Your clothes, including underwear and shoes, and your wedding ring. C'mon, let's go."

Unwilling to part with my summer dress, panties, and bra, I glance at the woman. She sits on the hood of the car, the gun resting on her knee. "Three minutes."

Our eyes meet and she raises her brows in a *what's-the-problem* kind of way.

The guy with the scanner groans. "She doesn't want to strip."

The woman raises the gun and points it at my forehead.

A very persuasive tactic.

Biting my tongue, I pull off my dress. My hands tremble as I unhook the bra.

Fuck this.

After a beat of hesitation, I determine that defiance is futile and pull down my panties. Standing naked in the middle of the well-lit courtyard is awkward and drives heat to my cheeks.

The man with the scanner stuffs my clothes into the bag. "Pen, she's ready for you."

The woman jumps off the hood and strolls over. Slipping on a pair of surgical gloves, she gives me a good once over. "Lift your boobs." She is rough as she runs her fingers along the contours of my breasts. "Now bend over."

What is she planning to do?

With one eye on the gun that is now in the possession of the dude with the scanner, I swallow hard but lean forward. She checks my ears inside and out, then snaps her fingers at something. Freezing cold liquid is poured over my head that smells like a chemical and burns my scalp. I splutter and spit but recover from my shock with a "fuck."

The woman hands me a towel and smirks. "Hope that's your natural hair color, or you'll look a mess."

Muttering "screw you" under my breath, I dry myself off. One of the other dudes passes me a set of clothes. "Put these on."

They are scrubs, the kind medical personnel wear in a hospital, and a pair of disposable panties. With my mind running on overload as one doom scenario is replaced by another, I get dressed. It's hard not to laugh about the bizarre situation, even though the reality of things slowly settles in.

Who are these people?

Why have they kidnapped me?

And where are we going?

Given their military demeanor, my money is on Jackson Pierce, but I can't be sure. About to fire off a bunch of questions, the woman claps her hands again. "Where are we on a possible tail?"

The third man looks up from a laptop. "No boy scout in the vicinity, so we are clear."

"Okay, then let's bag her and get her out of here."

"Where are we—" The rest of my words are cut off when a burlap bag is pulled over my head.

22

✳ ✳ ✳

CHELSEA

Houston, Texas
~~~~~

Being shifted from one vehicle to another, I lose all sense of time and direction. Our latest stop appears to be underground; it's cooler without even the slightest draft but sticky at the same time by the way the trapped air clings as a layer of sweat to my skin. The ground under my bare feet is smooth and warm like the driveway at home. I'm pulled by my arm; a ping and sliding doors give me hope that we have reached our final destination.

Time to get some goddamn answers.

The ride in the elevator takes forever and grinds my already frayed nerves. My heart is pounding and I'm nauseous with fear, but I'm also fucking mad that these assholes snatched me right from under Bastian's nose. Where was fucking Anton who was meant to secure the perimeter or Falk with his tech gimmicks that could allegedly track me anywhere. I rub my thumb over the sore spot from this morning. At least they didn't find the little device and I can only hope the rough search didn't damage it. If I'm going to come face to face with Jackson Pierce and Falk is online, the pairing thing might still work.

The elevator dings and I'm pulled forward once again. This time, the flooring is cold. Tiles. A quick look down confirms that they are terracotta and well lit. Someone's residence. My body quivers with anticipation—the uncertainty of what I'll be facing is worse than staring into the barrel of a gun.

A door gives access to the outside; a slow breeze fills the air with freshness. The burlap bag is pulled off and I blink to adjust my eyes to my surroundings. Judging by the neighboring buildings, I'm standing high on a small balcony surrounded by glass. Jackson Pierce claimed a table perched in a corner with his back to the wall; a filled dinner plate and a flute of red wine are sitting in front of him. Soft jazz music melts with the humming of the city life many floors below.

Head cocked to the side, Jackson takes his time looking me over. His resemblance to Marcel is undeniable. He is a few tones darker, which could be attributed to him spending more time in the sun, but his nose spots the same freckles. He has the same pronounced lips and fine facial features, just his eyes are a different shade. Marcel's deep brown was barely distinguishable from the black of his pupils while Jackson's color reminds me of the leathery whiskey my dad used to drink.

"Tell me about Hong Kong." His voice is a deep rumble that gives me goosebumps. He cuts a piece of the red-pink steak and places it in his mouth. As he chews, one of his brows is arched, demanding that I don't waste his precious time.

Folding my arms, I raise my chin in defiance. "Marcel's past caught up with him. One morning, when I was on my way to work, I found the windshield of our car covered in blood, but before it could even register what that meant, a couple of thugs grabbed me."

"And how was that Marcel's fault?"

"He left the house not even five minutes before me and was supposed to take the car. Instead, he must've caught on that he had been made and disappeared. Without any warning to me or our son. We walked right into a trap, and Marcel fucking knew what those goons would do to us. They tortured me for hours and then"—tears burn in my eyes—"they killed Sean. Marcel just abandoned us, no shits given."

"Let me assure you, he regrets this deeply."

"How would you know?"

"I spoke to him after you approached me today." Jackson's icy glare pricks like needles on my skin. "Had to make sure you are who you claimed you are. The pictures he sent were flattering. You look much older and kind of plain."

Why, thank you.

If he had his head drenched in some sort of chemical solution and were forced to wear these crappy clothes that are two sizes too big, he'd look fucked-up, too. "So you know where Marcel is?"

"No." He takes another bite of his steak and washes it down with a mouthful of wine.

"But you know how to contact him?"

"Obviously." A crack of a smile tugs at Jackson's lips as he gazes at me from over the rim of the glass. "He asked me to give you a message. The money is gone, so stop looking for him."

I snort with bitterness. "It's not about the money."

"Let me guess. You want to tell him that he ruined your marriage. How shit your life has turned out. That he took everything from you."

The burning sensation in my eyes turns into resentment. "Something like that."

"Trust me, this type of conversation doesn't go anywhere. Your and Marcel's stance on the matter is so far apart that you'd never find a common ground. When it comes to survival, people act out of instinct, and Marcel did what he thought to be his only option. You and your son were unfortunate casualties, but tracking Marcel down now to tell him that everything was his fault will never change the past."

It could still bring me closure. "Okay, if you don't let me talk to him, how about I tell you that you aren't any better than him. You inadvertently caused Sean's death."

The little amiability is sucked from the space. Jackson's body tenses. "That's a pretty big accusation, one I do *not* appreciate."

The hostility in his posture warns that I overstepped the limits. The woman who kidnapped me and who has stood silently by the door takes a step forward, but just like this afternoon, one slight shake of Jackson's head reels her in.

I take a deep breath to keep the tremble from my voice. "When Marcel decided to leave the Disciples to start a new life in Hong Kong, we needed new identities. None of his usual contacts could be trusted, so he had to locate a forger out of his network. Someone he couldn't have found without your connections . . ." A muscle in Jackson's jaw jumps and I press on. "And then, when he sold the intel he stole from the Disciples, he needed even better contacts with sufficiently deep pockets. Without your help, Marcel couldn't have pulled that off, so from where I stand, you are at least partially to blame."

The tension left in the wake of my allegations weighs heavily in the air. Seconds tick down in excruciating silence. Jackson finishes the last of his steak, his full focus fixed on the task. When he turns his head and dabs his lips with a napkin, the few emotions have drained from his face. "Nico Dessler."

"Excuse me?"

"That's the man you should be looking for. He's the one who shot your son, and he happens to work for Bastian Artino, so Artino is the last person you should trust. The Crimson Disciples are a disgrace to the profession, they groom their recruits from when they are children to force their loyalty, and they manipulated and molded Marcel into the man who abandoned you, something he would've never done before they got their hooks into him. They are the true enemy and helping them to find Marcel brings dishonor to your son."

I drop my gaze. If he only knew . . .

Jackson gets up and walks over to me. Cupping my chin, he lifts my head. His eyes are vacant; he's a man who has seen so much death and violence in his lifetime that he has become immune. He will kill without a second thought. "The way this works is that I give you a little and you give me a little. For your part, I need to know how you and Artino found me this afternoon."

"And if I refuse?"

"Then I'm afraid you won't be going home."

23

✵ ✵ ✵

BASTIAN

Houston, Texas
~~~~~

I chase back and forth in the empty parking lot, about ready to blow up the entire city. The restaurant is closed, everyone is gone, and it's only us that's left. The wait is driving me nuts. "It has been hours."

"We already established that." Anton yawns openly without taking his gaze off the phone in his hand for even one second. "Shit, I lost again."

I frown. "What are you doing?"

"Playing Yahtzee."

"Chelsea is missing and you are playing on some stupid app."

Anton shrugs. "What else is there to do? Besides, not sure why you are having a meltdown. You ordered me to stay put when Penina Cohn grabbed her and"—his smile turns smug—"I have the text to prove it. It's on you if something happened to Chelsea."

"Fuck you." Angry at myself, I kick the tire of the van. I shouldn't have risked it. When Anton texted that he spotted Jackson's number two entering the restaurant through a backdoor, I should've let him intervene. Now we might've lost Chelsea for good.

"Plus we got what we needed." Falk stares at me from his seat in the van with utter boredom. "The chick came through for us. Four paired phones, one of them likely belonging to Jackson Pierce. What more do you want?"

"I want her back here safely."

"Personally, I think Pierce killed her, so waiting around is just a big waste of time."

I huff. "You wouldn't think that if she were a Disciple."

"But she isn't, so if she's dead, who cares?"

Anton smirks. "Amen to that."

"You are both fucking morons." I shoot them a dark look.

Falk clicks his tongue. "What's your issue?"

"Oh, fuck off."

"If you have the hots for her, that's a bad move. You shouldn't get involved with an asset."

Anton chuckles under his breath. "Amen to that, too."

I pinch the bridge of my nose; the pain that has been pounding in my head since Chelsea's abduction is getting worse. These two are a lethal, migraine-inducing combination.

A van with a bakery logo drives slowly by the parking lot. The side door is open and I pull my gun. A body is pushed out, hitting the cement hard, followed by another object that looks like a small sack. Before I can take a breath, the van speeds off.

"Fuck."

I run toward the squirming person on the ground and pull the bag off Chelsea's head. The bastards bound and gagged her. Helping her sit up, I free her from the cloth in her mouth. For once, Anton proves useful when he pulls out his knife and cuts the cable ties around her wrists and ankles. They stuck her in some sort of scrubs; one of her upper arms is bleeding from a cut and a few scrapes mar the side of her face. If I ever run into Jackson Pierce, I'd make sure to repay the favor.

Chelsea blinks at me through unfocused eyes.

"Don't worry, you're safe now." I stroke a few strands of hair out of her eyes.

"Did the pairing work?"

"It did."

A smile lights up her face; it's amazing that she's still so upbeat after this latest ordeal. "Good. Now all we have to do is wait."

"I have to wait. You're going back to Ireland."

"But—"

"Not buts. We agreed that you'd help us get to Jackson Pierce. You did that. Now let the pros handle the rest."

She shakes her head. "I need to see Marcel. Talk to him. Once that's done, you can do whatever you want with him."

"Sorry, that's simply not possible." I have my orders. After tonight, we'll go our separate ways, at least until Marcel Pierce is eliminated. After that, we can determine if there's a joint future for us. "Can you stand?"

Before she can reply, Anton heaves her up by her armpits. "Here we go."

With her hand on my shoulder, I guide her to the van. She limps pretty badly and would hunch over without my support. A few groans hint to her pain. I lower her onto the ledge of the van. Falk hands me the medical bag.

Anton slips on some sterile gloves. "Let me take a look at your arm."

She snorts. "Yeah, right."

"Hey, I'm a licensed paramedic, so don't fret." He cuts through the fabric above the wound with a pair of surgical scissors. "She needs stitches, so it's gonna take a while."

I turn away since I've never done well around needles and pull out my cell. The time in Cyprus is eight hours ahead of us, but knowing Icarus, he's already up and about since the crack of dawn. He rarely sleeps past five am.

The call connects almost instantly and his usual snarl fills my ear. "Status?"

"We got a lock on Jackson Pierce."

"Excellent. Are Murphy and the girl still alive?"

"Yep, they are both okay."

"Do you want to tidy up?"

"I don't think that's necessary. By arranging the meeting with Pierce, Murphy repaid his debt, and the girl just wants her husband gone. They don't constitute a threat and killing them will only risk drawing unwanted attention to ourselves by the authorities."

"Then send the girl back to Ireland and let's leave things the way they are for now."

"Okay."

"What about Anton? Do you want to make the switch?"

I glance at him; he's just applying the bandage to Chelsea's arm and actually smiles for a change. "I'll let you know by the end of the week."

"Sure, that's your call."

"Have to go now, but I'll keep you posted." I hang up to get him off the line; these check-in calls where I have to pretend that everything is hunky-dory between us are turning into a nuisance.

Walking over to Chelsea, I peek over her shoulder just as Falk pulls the little pairing device from under her fingernail with the tiniest tweezers. Usually, that hurts like hell, but she doesn't as much as flinch. Anton must have given her anesthetic before he stitched her up. A few deep breaths and it's all over.

I search through the sack that Jackson's guys dropped off with her. "Looks like these are your clothes."

"Do you have my purse? I left it at the table."

"It's with Falk in the front of the van." The longing to spend the night with her is overwhelming. I want to hold her tight and make sure there isn't another scratch on her. "Say, what did you have to give Jackson Pierce for him to let you go?"

For a breath, I close my eyes.

Please, don't let it be sex.

Her forehead wrinkles. "I didn't give him anything."

Her statement is like a stab to my chest. My insides recoil; I have tried so hard to ignore my instincts, even whitewashing them at times. Discounting them as paranoia. Now, the blatant deceit is no longer deniable.

"Never mind. Falk will take you to the hotel, so you can pack, and then he'll drive you to the airport. You can take the Gulfstream back to Ireland tonight, and I'll let you know as soon as Marcel is dead."

Utter confusion reflects on her face. "That's it? Aren't we going to the hotel together?"

Anton opens his mouth to add his two cents, but a kick against his ankle shuts him up.

Smiling at Chelsea takes some effort. "I ran out of painkillers and need to fill my prescription." Practically pushing her into the van, I signal Falk. "You got this?"

"Sure." His face mirrors her confusion, but he is too low down the food chain to question my orders.

"So hotel, airport, no detour." My glare drills into Falk to ensure my instructions are crystal clear.

He nods. "Got it."

"Safe travels." I slam the door to the van shut and turn my back on her.

This is it.

My fling with Chelsea Doherty is officially over.

24

✳ ✳ ✳

BASTIAN

Houston, Texas
~~~~~

"What the hell was that about?" Anton's glare slices into me with anger. "You just let them drive off? It's the middle of the night and we are fucking stranded here. I'm exhausted and want to go to the hotel."

I raise my hand to quiet him. "Just give me a minute, okay?"

I drop on one of the benches in front of the deserted restaurant. Burying my face into my hands, I massage my forehead.

How could I've let it go so far?

Anton sits down across from me and pulls my head into his lap. His strokes through my curls to soothe the turmoil ripping through my body. "Hey, what's wrong?"

"She has been fucking playing me." A few tears are caught by Anton's jeans.

"You sure?"

"I tried to ignore it, but some of her reactions were totally off. Like tonight at dinner. I told her that her son wasn't killed by a Disciple, but from the way she looked at me, it was obvious she knew the truth. There were other times when I was almost certain that she was lying, but I always made excuses. And then she fed me this bullshit that she didn't have to give Jackson Pierce anything for letting her go." I huff. "I mean, how fucking likely is that?"

"Yeah, there's no way that happened." He leans over and cradles me close. "Don't sweat it. We all get fooled sometimes."

I snort. "When did you ever get played?"

"Maybe I'm the exception."

"What do you think she gave Jackson?"

"There are only two things. She either snitched on Murphy, or she told him the name of the hotel we are staying at. Could even be both."

"You don't think it might've been sex?"

"Nah. I heard that Jackson only visits brothels when he has a job in some backwater country and be done with it. That bitch Maren Birch burned him too good for him to mess with another woman in his own bed. No, I'm sure Chelsea either leaked that Murphy betrayed him or she gave up your location. Nothing other than that has value to Jackson."

That Jackson Pierce might know how to expeditiously find me sends shivers of dread to the pit of my stomach. "We should get another room and only go back to the old hotel for our stuff." And take enough manpower, just to be on the safe side, in case of a shootout. I huddle closer into Anton's embrace, indulging in the warmth emitting from his skin. The familiar scent of his spicy aftershave gives me an odd sense of comfort. Even the pain in my head is silent.

He rubs my back. "There's a hotel right next door."

"I don't want to move."

He chuckles. "I could toss you over my shoulder and carry you."

"Yeah, and give me a good few hits on the ass. I'm sure you'd like that." I free myself from his arms and search his eyes for the familiar spark. The shiner has faded enough to be barely noticeable and our fight seems like eons ago. I stroke the blemished skin.

He leans into my touch. "We should stop if you don't intend to take this further."

"I hate when we argue."

"In this instance, you had every right to be angry. I overstepped, and I'm sorry."

I arch a brow. "Anton Worcheck apologizing?" That's a first.

"Hey, I can admit when I'm wrong."

"Since when?"

"Since you grew a set of balls." He traces my bottom lip with his thumb. "I like this new Bastian."

"If you put it like that, let's get a room."

~~~~

Fifteen minutes later, I turn on the faucet and step into the shower. The new hotel room is a dump but will have to do for a night. With a sigh, I let the hot water pelt down on me. Emptiness pounds inside me, although I have no idea why Chelsea's betrayal upsets me so much. Sure, the time we spent together was nice and the sex was even better, but she's still a woman I hardly know. I shouldn't feel so crappy.

The door to the stall opens and Anton squeezes inside. It's tight but gives us a chance for some wet skin-on-skin contact. I lean against the wall and allow his mouth to claim mine; he's demanding and in control, his hand stroking the inside of my thigh. Our tongues rediscover each other and I desperately try not to compare his hard mouth to Chelsea's tender lips. His powerful hips to her soft curves. His cock pressing against my stomach to the warmth of her welcoming folds.

With an exhale, I let go of the tension and focus on the here and now. On Anton. On the good times we've had together. It almost works, even if a small part of me aches for Chelsea's touch.

Fuck.

Somehow, Anton manages to get on his knees. He traces kisses along my shaft, his tongue circling the tip of my cock until I'm as hard as a rock. As he sucks in my length, I push further into his mouth. His lips fit snugly around my dick and send shivers through my body. Thrusting my hips, I lean my head back and let the warm water caress my face. Anton takes me deep; the heat is building fast. I entangle my fingers in his hair to dictate the rhythm, slowing down when the fire is about to consume me and speeding up again as lust fades away. It's a back-and-forth until the burning need for a release takes over. I explode in his mouth. Breathing heavily, I ride out the aftershocks, not letting go of his hair until I'm fully drained.

Anton squeezes my ass. "I'll be waiting for you in bed."

Pulling a hotel bathrobe off the hanger, he disappears, allowing me my space. I take my time drying off. Anticipation is something I savor, and he needs to learn to be patient. As I'm toweling my hair, my phone pings with a message. It's from Falk.

Just got an alert. Murphy is dead.

So Chelsea did sell him out.

Closing my eyes, I sort through my thoughts. My fingers tremble as I reply.

How?

Falk's reply is almost instantaneous. *Initial report says heart attack. Dropped dead at the hotel bar.*

Injecting untraceable poison or spiking a drink to make a death look like natural causes is Penina Cohn's specialty. Since Jackson Pierce no longer operates on US soil, he sent his pet to do his bidding.

Check surveillance footage for foul play.

Falk responds with an okay emoji.

"Bastian, are you coming to bed or what?" Anton's low growl vents his annoyance.

Stepping into the room, I thumb-type one final message to Falk. *Want 24/7 location on Chelsea Doherty and tap her phone.*

Another okay emoji.

I drop the cell on the nightstand and grin at Anton. Stretched out naked on the bed, he gazes at me with a pout. His pupils are dilated with raw lust.

"Alrighty. Where did we leave off...?"

25

✷ ✳ ✷

CHELSEA

Baltray, Ireland
June 2024
~~~~~

The sun sits bright on a cloudless blue sky, emitting warmth to celebrate the rich life of a blessed woman. Someone I'll miss dearly during my hours at the tea shop. Adele McKenna had been the mother of five, who had gifted her many grandchildren and who sat by her bedside at the very end. Something I've always wanted to do for my mother, but so far, I've given her more cause for grief than happiness.

Mam has placed her hand on my forearm as we slowly make our way to the graveside at the end of the procession. The service was nice, lots of tears but also a few smiles during the eulogy, and the obligatory funeral attendance will soon come to an end. I'm itching to get back home, hide in bed with a gallon of ice cream, and binge-watch *Virgin River* for the fourth time, though knowing Mam, she will insist on dragging me to the get-together at the pub for a Guinness and some finger food. Since she doesn't drive, I'll have to take her. We reach Mrs. McKenna's last resting place and I catch Mam wiping away a tear.

I squeeze her hand. "You okay? Do you want to leave?" Tons of people surround us, so I doubt we'd be missed.

She shakes her head. "You know what they say. Death comes in threes. What if I'm next?"

"Trust me, the devil isn't ready for you yet. You still have a good few years in you."

Her smile carries the silent question.

What if I'm next?

She would be all alone.

About to squeeze her hand again, a short buzz in my suit pocket distracts me. My regular phone is on airplane mode, so this can only be Conor on the burner. And he wouldn't text me unless it were an emergency.

"Mam, I'll be right back."

She wrinkles her forehead but refrains from scolding me. I slowly back away and rush down the narrow path until I find a bench under an oak tree. Fingers trembling, I dial Conor's number. "What's up?"

"They found him."

The spit dries up in my mouth. "Are you sure?"

"Anton texted this Falk dude to get ready. They'll be leaving for Cambridge, Massachusetts, as soon as Bastian is done with his UN meeting, and since Falk doesn't get involved in the business side of things, it has to be Marcel."

I nod in agreement, even though it's silly since he can't see me through the phone. So Cambridge, Massachusetts, is where Marcel has been hiding. It makes sense. Deep down, he has always wanted to attend college, and picking a life in an Ivy League town would give him a sense of belonging to a crowd he could otherwise never be a part of. "But you don't have specifics on his exact location?"

"Unfortunately not."

Oh, well, there are other ways to find him.

I check my watch. It's only ten am. "Conor, do you think you could still get me on a flight this afternoon? I think I have an idea how to track Marcel down, but it only works on a Thursday." If I miss today's window, I'd have to wait until next week, and by then, he likely bit one of Bastian's bullets already. Literally.

"There are four flights to Boston starting at 2:00, so I'm sure I can still book you a seat on one of them."

"Good. Just text me the confirmation number when you have it."

"Where are you?"

"At the funeral of our neighbor with my mam."

"Oh, man, I hate funerals. So depressing."

"Yeah, well."

"And be extra careful. They say death always comes in threes."

I smirk. "Since when are *you* superstitious?"

"Hey, there's some truth to those old wives' tales."

"If you say so."

"By the way, how are you on money?"

"Still got enough."

"I'll wire an extra hundred k, just in case."

Just in case is his code for all the things that could go wrong. Hospital bills, lawyer fees, bail money, a list that goes on and on and could even include my own funeral expenses.

Sudden apprehension cramps my stomach. "Don't worry, I won't take too many risks."

"You'd better not. The fam would be devastated if you couldn't come to visit. I pretty much promised them it would happen in the next few months."

I close my eyes. The path ahead is still so long with so much potential for a fuck up that he shouldn't make that type of promise. "Have to go. Text me as soon as you booked the flight and I'll let you know when I landed. After that, I won't contact you again until it's done."

"Okay and good luck."

I will need it. Walking back toward the graveside, I grin.

But thank you, Anton.

If he hadn't sent that text message to Bastian's phone when Bastian showed up trashed at my doorsteps, Conor could've never gotten Anton's number off the tower ping and tapped his cell. It turned into our lifeline after Bastian made his prick move and cut me off.

Hot tears flood my eyes.

The persistent pain of the past week takes another good whack at my heart. I lowered my shields and allowed him too far in. Now, I'm paying the price, although it's the type of pain that hurts like hell but fades just as quickly.

I'll be fine.

Reaching Mam, I wipe my face dry on my jacket sleeve.

Her brows crumble. "Is everything alright with you?"

I nod. "I have to go away again. Please don't ask questions."

"I stopped asking questions a long time ago." Wise, gray eyes drill into me. "Just keep in mind that two wrong things don't make it right. Nothing will ever bring Sean back, so ensure that when this is all over, you can still look at yourself in the mirror."

26

✷ ✷ ✷

CHELSEA

Cambridge, Massachusetts
June 2024
~~~~~

Thanks to the five-hour time difference between Ireland and the East Coast, I arrive in Cambridge in the late afternoon. Checking into a hotel not too far from the Harvard University campus, I hunt for clues on the internet before I even unpack. About thirty minutes in, I hit paydirt. Of all the Chinese restaurants in town, only one sells Yan Du Xian soup. A staple food in Asian countries, it's a rare find in the United States but one of Marcel's must-haves. He's obsessed with this soup and when we were together, he'd go out to get it for us from a local restaurant every single Thursday night for dinner like clockwork. Even vacations were no exception. Unless he changed his habits, he will show up at the Golden Dragon tonight. I'm banking on it.

Leaving the hotel just after six, I get into the black Toyota Corolla I rented at the airport. Traffic is quite heavy; it takes close to thirty minutes for the two-mile ride and parking is a bitch, but I manage to find an on-road space three stores down from the restaurant. Now the waiting game begins. Angled and with my laptop open as if I'm working, I have a front-row seat of the entrance and watch as patron after patron walks in and out. The adrenaline keeps a constant tremble in my body and my thigh muscles twitch with impatience.

Six years without a peep from Marcel.

Time to plot my revenge.

Now that he's within reach, I'm close to a mental meltdown.

Keep it together, Doherty.

Over the years, I'd laid out careful words and repeated them over and over in my mind for hours on end.

Scenarios of how I'd react when I first encounter him again.

Actions I'd take that would speak louder than words.

When I finally catch sight of him, my mind goes blank. I struggle to breathe and the pressure on my chest threatens to crack my sternum in half.

Fucking bastard.

Time has treated him well. He is ripped, tanned, and self-confident, with a wide smile that bears witness to how much he's enjoying life. No sadness, no guilt, no desperation; feelings that have been constant companions for me since that day in Hong Kong. He didn't care then and he doesn't care now. Probably has forgotten all about Sean and me.

A bucket of mixed emotions is poured over my head. The hate and rage are overpowering, although there's also a part of me that weeps for lost times. Those times where our life was perfect with only the occasional ups and downs.

The day when we both said "I do" and swore to be there for each other in good times and in bad.

That evening I presented him during dinner with the little baby onesie that had the words "I'm Dad's Little Pumpkin" printed on the chest to tell him I was pregnant. Come to think of it, it might've been a Thursday night and we were enjoying Yan Du Xian soup.

The night in bed when we celebrated the baby's sex reveal and he told me that he was going to leave the Crimson Disciples. He didn't want that type of life for his family. Not with a child. He wasn't going to turn his son into a killer.

And then he threw it all away.

Tears flood my eyes and I have to bite the side of my hand to avoid a crying fit. Enough shed tears. It's time to get even.

Marcel leaves the restaurant with several paper bags in hand. I start the car and slide on my mirrored aviator shades. If Jackson taught me anything, it's the power of hiding my eyes. Marcel won't know what's going on in my head. When I confront him, he won't see the distress, the devastation, the vulnerability. No, the only thing he'll see is the stone face of a woman who will slice off his balls and feed them to him for dinner together with that damn soup before ending his pathetic life.

He must feel pretty confident because he doesn't take any precautions to lose a potential tail. No sudden turns, no unexpected u-banger, no speeding up or slowing down without a reason. He obeys the speed limit, signals in advance, and avoids sudden stops. Following him is as easy as pie.

We end up in a residential area screaming affluence. Without exception, the houses are big and well maintained, surrounded by sizable yards with grass that is meticulously groomed, and with several cars in their driveways that match the price of Marcel's fancy, silver Lexus. Marcel pulls in beside a midnight blue BMW coupe and from the look of things, he spent at least twenty percent of the money he stole from me on the cars and his new home.

When I'm done with him, I want to set the whole lot on fire.

He gets out of the Lexus and I'm about to follow suit when the front door to the house opens. A woman with long, chestnut-brown hair and a model figure appears on the threshold. Her frayed white shorts display sculptured, tanned legs and her overly large but even breasts suggest that she might've had a boob job. All in all, she is gorgeous with a smile and energy that goes along with utter happiness.

A little boy of maybe three or four appears next to her and takes off down the driveway. "Daddyyyy."

What. The. Actual. Fuck!

Marcel sets the paper bags with the food onto the hood of the car and catches the little boy. With the boy's arms outstretched, he spins him around, making airplane noises the way he used to do with Sean. The memory is choking me. Paralyzed, I sit in my seat, unable to make a sound as the woman joins them and is rewarded with a long, throaty kiss.

Fucking hell.

When I finally manage to breathe again, they are walking up the driveway. Marcel tousles the little boy's hair and the woman laughs. Pure positive energy surrounds them; not even a crack is visible in their idyllic, perfect existence. Does she even know about his past? That he had a wife and kid he abandoned? That he is nothing but a despicable human being?

As the front door closes behind them, the crushing pain is stifling. My cheeks are soon wet from my tears and I lean my forehead against the steering wheel, allowing the sobs to take over.

He fucking replaced us.

I could handle, even expected, another woman, but a child!

My body shakes so hard with rejection and anger that it takes forever to regain control. What the fuck am I going to do? I can't hurt him in front of the kid, but my thirst for revenge is pounding just as hard in my chest as it did for the past six years.

Confront him.

Get it off your chest.

Tell him exactly how you feel and that you hate him with every fiber of your heart.

The rest will fall into place.

I eye my purse with the gun I bought at a pawn shop in Boston as soon as I landed. If I take it, I might not be able to stop myself and shoot him right then and there in the head. Better leave it in the car.

Sucking in a deep breath, I close my eyes.

I'm ready.

This is the moment I've been waiting for, and if I don't act quickly, Bastian might get to Marcel first. Escaping the car, I square my shoulders, just to freeze when the now so familiar jab of a gun muzzle pushes against my spine.

Crap, not again.

27

✳ ✳ ✳

CHELSEA

Cambridge, Massachusetts
~~~~~

The familiar voice close to my ear churns my stomach. "Get slowly back into the car and keep your hands where I can see them."

I laugh under my breath. "And if I don't? What are you gonna do, Marcel? Shoot me right here in front of your neighbors and your son?"

"Trust me, I can make it look like self-defense in a robbery gone wrong."

Knowing how he can spin a lie, I don't doubt it. I open the door of the Toyota and get behind the wheel. With a few looks to his left and to his right, he joins me in the passenger seat.

"Drive."

I put on my seatbelt. The barrel of the semi-automatic is pointed right at my stomach and his finger is on the trigger; for now, I will have to play along. "Where to?"

"Just fucking start the car and go."

"What about your seatbelt?"

He snorts.

"The alarm will go off," I insist. "The beeping drives me nuts."

"Fine."

I don't take my eyes off the gun as he wrestles with the seatbelt to feed it behind his back. Just one second of him losing his focus will be enough . . .

My plan doesn't work. The latch plate of the belt clicks into the buckle and he angles himself with his back resting against the door to have optimum control of the weapon. "There. Now drive or I *will* shoot you."

I start the engine and pull out into the road. In the rearview mirror, his house disappears behind a bend.

His glare drills into the side of my head. "Why are you here? I told Jackson that the money is gone."

After I saw the house, the cars, and his neighborhood, it's another thing I don't doubt. "It was never about the money."

He cranes his neck to glance out the back window. "Take a right at the light and then keep straight. In about one point five miles, follow the signs to the transit station."

Sure thing.

With a gun trained on me, I don't have much of a choice. I signal and make the turn; the street is four lanes but still fairly busy for this time of night. Marcel turns the rearview mirror toward him to keep an eye on the traffic behind us. The silence in the car is so charged that a spark could set off an explosion.

For a breath, I take my eyes off the road and stare at him. His face is tense, but his hand is steady. Years of training with the Disciples have ensured that not much can rattle him. He is a trained killer and with the stakes as high as they are, my chances to overpower him are nil. If I want to make it out of the car alive, I'll have to come up with another plan.

He chews his lip; one of the few telltale signs that he is nervous. "How did you find me?"

I smirk. Not gonna make it that easy for him. "What do you think?"

"Do the Disciples know where I am?"

"Probably."

I shoot him a sideways glance. His jaw is clenched; he's starting to panic.

"What are you gonna do, Marcel? Go on the run again? Sacrifice another family?"

"Shut up and turn left at the light. Then immediately right." He licks blood off his lip; he has chewed it raw.

Oh, I hit a nerve.

We pass a row of parking garages and signs with *Passenger Drop Off Only.* A little further up is another sign announcing that this is Alewife Station. When the road curves, I'm about to turn, but he jabs the barrel of the gun into my ribs.

"Keep going straight."

It's the end of a one-way. "It says no entry."

"The park closes at sunset. We won't encounter traffic."

The street narrows; trees, bushes, and two jogging paths mark the curb on either side. It appears to be some sort of access road. "What is this place?"

"A wildlife reserve."

Deserted at this time of night. The perfect place to shoot someone without a witness and dispose of their body. My mouth dries up. I'm running out of time.

"Why did you do it, Marcel? Why did you fucking leave us in Hong Kong to die?"

"I didn't think they'd go so far and kill Sean."

"They held a gun to his head right in front of me. Do you have any idea what that did to me?" My voice shakes hard enough for some of the words to slur together.

Don't fucking lose it.

He can't see me cry.

Marcel clears his throat. "I'm sorry, if that helps."

His apology couldn't be any less sincere if he tried.

"Nothing you say will ever make this okay." I hate the tears burning in my eyes. "Why didn't you at least try to warn us?"

"I couldn't risk it. You saw yourself, a wife and a child are replaceable. My life isn't."

What the actual fuck!

A surge of rage forces my foot down on the gas pedal. I'm blinded by all the hurt, the despair, the guilt of the last six years. If I have to die, it will be on my terms.

Pulling the steering wheel to the right, I head straight for the fence dividing the road from the jogging path. The screech of metal on metal hurts my ears. The Toyota comes to a sudden halt; the airbags blow. As the seatbelt locks, pain shoots through my body. My face slams into the airbag.

Oof.

I blink away the black spots obscuring my vision and take a careful breath. One side of my body screams with agony; I likely cracked a couple of ribs. Opening and closing my hands still works and I can wiggle my toes in my sandals. A slight ache buzzes in my head. So far, I can't detect any major damage.

With a groan, I unbuckle the seatbelt and push the door of the Toyota open. Getting out is painful; every inch of my body is sore, but I manage to stay upright. I look back at the passenger seat. It's empty. Marcel's body lies motionless in the grass a few feet away. Thanks to his refusal to wear a seatbelt, he went straight through the windshield. I lean back into the car to grab the purse with my own gun. When it comes to his skills, I can't be too careful. For all I know, he's simply pretending to be hurt to get the upper hand.

Walking over to him, I prod him with my foot. The accident fucked him up. Several deep cuts mar his face almost beyond recognition and a bone sticks out of his twisted leg. His breath is shallow. It's a miracle he's still alive.

Though not for long.

I pull the gun from my purse and slide a bullet into the chamber. He gazes up at me without a sound. Fucking jerk knows that pleading with me to spare his pathetic life is futile.

I point the barrel of the gun straight at his head. "This is for Sean."

He blinks at me unfocused, his pupils dilated with pain. "I'm sorry, Chelsea." The words are barely audible over his raspy breath. "I really am."

I close my eyes to stop the tears from rolling down my cheeks.

This is not supposed to happen.

I'm not meant to feel sorry for him.

My hand shakes so hard that I almost drop the gun.

Pull the fucking trigger.

But I can't.

I fucking can't.

28

✳ ✳ ✳

BASTIAN

Cambridge, Massachusetts
~~~~~

I glare at the screen of the GPS where the dot that's Chelsea's phone has stopped moving. Things are about to get tight. "I told you not to keep that far of a distance."

Anton huffs. "Marcel isn't an amateur. If I had kept on his ass, he'd notice we were following them."

Marcel is probably shooting Chelsea right now.

We are gaining on the dot; one more turn and my breath hitches.

The fuck!

I stare at the surreal scene. The hood of Chelsea's car kissing the metal divider, windshield busted, glass scattered everywhere.

What the hell happened?

I jump out of the van before Anton has a chance to fully brake. Legging it around the crashed Toyota, I freeze. Marcel lies in a pool of blood on the ground, Chelsea standing over him, the gun she has trained on him trembling. I approach slowly so as not to spook her. The situation is unstable as it is;

the last thing I need is for her to swing around and fire a bullet at me because she feels threatened.

Sobs shake her body; if Marcel weren't hurt, he would've long disarmed her. I step behind her and reach around to steady her hand. "It's okay. I'll take this."

When I twist the weapon out of her grip, she doesn't resist. Gazing at me with tearful eyes from under her lashes, she lets out a low wail. "Why can't I do it? Why can't I shoot him?"

"'Cause you're not a killer."

She leans her forehead against my shoulder, her body quivering. I rub her back, whispering *"shh, shh"* under my breath.

The racking of a gun behind me foils the little strides I made to calm her. Turning around, I ensure that I'm shielding Chelsea from Anton's Glock. "Wo-ho, hold up. Now it's not the time."

"Now is the perfect time. Cleaner doesn't care if he has to get rid of one body or two."

This is the moment to pull rank. "Stand down, Anton, I mean it."

"Why are you protecting her? She has been playing us. You said so yourself."

"We don't have time to get into this right now."

"A bullet takes a second."

"Anton, I said stand down." I lock his gaze and hold it without blinking. "In case you forgot, I run this crew and what *I* say goes. There are still too many questions she needs to answer and tonight, our sole focus should be on Marcel."

Anton's nostrils flare, but he lowers the gun. I bought Chelsea some time.

I clutch her shoulders and shake her gently to get through to her. "The transit station is less than half a mile from here. Can you make it there on foot?"

"I think so."

"Then walk away and don't look back. Go straight to the station and find a cab that can take you to a hospital. Get checked out and then return to Ireland. I promise I'll contact you in a few days."

She glances at Marcel. His breath is shallow, but the thirst for survival has taken hold. For now, he's hanging in there. Her gaze travels to the car.

I squeeze her shoulders harder. "I'll take care of Marcel and make sure the car will disappear without a trace. Now go or I won't be able to guarantee your safety."

She nods in a daze. When I let go of her, she sways but keeps her footing. I make sure her purse is secure on her shoulder. Can't have her walk off without money and her passport. She takes a deep breath and then leaves without giving me any further hassle. As her figure blends with the darkness of the night, I turn to Anton.

He pops a piece of gum into his mouth, a sign that he's on edge. "I still think you're making a mistake, letting her go."

"Well, it's my mistake to make. Now take the van and secure the road. It's a one-way, so the only threat could come from this side." I point in the opposite direction of Chelsea's path.

"You sure you can handle Marcel on your own?"

I gaze at the piece of shit lying in the grass and snort. "Yep, I'm sure."

Anton doesn't argue further and gets into the van. As the taillights disappear, I'm left alone with Marcel. A half-broken streetlamp that flickers on and off is the only light source.

I squat and find his eyes. "Don't think we ever formally met. I'm Bastian Artino."

Marcel's lips twitch. "I know who you are. You were Konstantin and Olivia's little bitch."

I slam my elbow into his mouth; he gags and turns his head to spit blood into the grass. His body quivers and when our gazes meet again, tears of pain found their way down his cheeks.

"Fucking shoot me already," he growls.

A mercy kill would be a wasted bullet. "Tsk, I'm not done with you yet. As a matter of fact, we are just getting started. First off, let me show you what's going on at your house." I pull my cell from my pocket; not even a minute later, I have access to the secure video feed streaming right from his kitchen. I turn the screen around to show him I'm not bluffing. "My associates have orders to kill your family unless you cooperate."

Marcel closes his eyes. "The intel I stole is worthless by now, so what do you want?"

"After we restructured and you realized there was no more money in the data, you took it a step further. You sold someone insider information on Konstantin that got him killed. I need to know who that was?"

Marcel frowns. "I have no idea what you're talking about."

"Konstantin would visit his mom every other week for Sunday dinner. Only a handful of people knew about it. You were one of them, plus you knew her address. Selling that info was the only way to lay out a trap for him because he was too careful otherwise."

"Konstantin was like a brother to me. I'd never sell him out." A cough shakes Marcel's body, leaving blood on his lips.

I need to hurry or risk him taking a turn for the worse. "Nico, put on the screws."

With the phone screen turned toward Marcel, I only hear the sounds of Nico's handiwork.

Cries of a woman.

Pleads.

Claims that she has no idea about Marcel's shady past.

Sad thing, I believe her.

For a moment, I let Nico do his thing before lowering the screen. "Who did you sell the information to?"

A muscle in Marcel's jaw jumps. "I swear I didn't. Call off your man. My family knows nothing."

I scoff. "Seriously? You pretend to care? In Hong Kong, you didn't give a rat's ass about Chelsea and Sean when you left them there to rot."

"I'm sorry Sean died."

"You are not a very convincing liar, Marcel." I grab his hair to force eye contact. "Who did you tell where Konstantin would be that day?"

"I never told anyone."

"I don't believe you, so you better start talking. For right now, your kid is oblivious to what is happening. He is just in his room, playing with his toys, but I can tell Nico to go and get him."

Marcel shakes his head. "Please, Bastian, don't do this." More tears run down his face; I find the same type of distress in his eyes that I see in Chelsea whenever she talks about Sean.

"Last chance, Marcel."

"Please, I have no idea who killed Konstantin."

I lean so close to his ear that my lips touch his skin. "That's how Chelsea felt when Nico put a gun to Sean's head. She was totally helpless. You fucking abandoned her and your son, so whatever happens here today is on you."

"I swear I don't know anything." Fear and despair tremble in his voice. When his breath catches, he coughs up more blood.

"Stand down, Nico. I got the information." I kill the video feed. Point made, and there's no need to put his family through more trauma.

Marcel's eyes narrow. "But I didn't tell you anything."

I chuckle.

He catches on remarkably fast. "It was you. You sold the information."

Instead of a response, I pull the silencer out of my suit pocket.

"But why?" Marcel's gaze is drilling. "When you ran away from home, Konstantin took you in. Olivia was your fucking wife."

Standing up, I finish attaching the silencer to the barrel of the gun. He'd never understand. I raise the Glock and take aim at his forehead.

Pulling the trigger is easy.

Liberating.

The last loose end to tidy up.

The bullet finds its mark, leaving Marcel lying lifeless in the grass. I hunker down and force his eyelids shut.

He was the perfect fall guy.

He still is.

And now my secret died with him.

29

✷ ✷ ✷

BASTIAN

Nicosia, Cyprus
June 2024
~~~~~

When we pull up to Icarus's home, the sun is about to plunge into the ocean. Hues of yellow, orange, and red set the sparkling water surface on fire and I bathe in the sight, inhaling the scent of salt brought upon by the waves crashing against the cliffs just below the property. An idyllic picture if it weren't for the heavy ass cooler in my hand and the prospect of meeting my uncle. I walk behind Anton along the path that takes us out to the back of the house and step onto the terrace. Icarus's chair is reclined, his face tilted toward the sun. When I set the cooler down on the table with a *thud*, he squints at me through the shimmering air.

"Congrats on a job well done." He straightens the backrest and lifts the lid of the cooler. His lips twitch. "When I told you I wanted Marcel's head, I didn't mean it literally."

Oops, my bad.

He points at the chair across from him. "Can I offer you something to drink?"

What civil change compared to our last encounter. I sit down. "No, thank you."

He waves at Anton. "Grab a chair and join us."

I arch a brow.

What's this all about?

Anton isn't high enough on the payroll to have earned a seat at the boss's table.

He pulls a pool lounger closer and plops down on the very edge. The coward can't even look me in the eyes. Sensing another betrayal in the making, I fold my arms.

Icarus squeezes the juice from a small piece of lemon into his sparkling water, drying off his hands on a napkin. "What did Marcel tell you before he died?"

"He sold the info about Konstantin to Gezim Bajri."

Icarus clicks his tongue. "Can't say I'm surprised that the Albanians were involved."

"We always suspected it because they were the ones who gained the most from Konstantin's death, though it's good to be able to pin it on a specific clan." Limiting it to the Bajri family will avoid an extensive turf war. "What are you going to do now?"

"Declare open season and put a contract out. Ten million for each of the Bajri brothers' heads."

"That's a lot of money."

"Konstantin was my son and I want quick action. After four years, that's long overdue."

"Should I return to the usual business side of things?"

"There's another matter. Where are we on the girl?"

"Chelsea Doherty?"

"The very same."

"She still has a few questions to answer. I will take care of it."

My uncle glances at Anton. "I'm not sure you are the right person for the job. Anton informed me that you are sweet on her and that your judgment might be compromised. He requested permission to eliminate her."

I glare at Anton who stares out onto the water as if none of this concerns him. Breaking the chain of command will cost him. "Anton doesn't know all the facts."

"Then what are the facts, Bastian?"

I tear my gaze off Anton and focus on my uncle. "The girl has been playing us big time. Falk tracked her phone and noticed that there was another ping at times that was overlapping with the original signal. A second phone, though he couldn't find any official records, so he suspects it's a burner. He was able to tap into it and determined that Chelsea is working with a man named Conor. Now that guy is good, Falk called him an IT god. Apparently, this Conor has ways to bounce his signal from tower to tower, all around the globe, sending Falk on a wild goose chase. Falk has not been able to pinpoint his location. From his speech pattern and dialect, we suspect he is Irish, but technically, he could be anywhere in the world. We also have no idea how they are connected. Worst case scenario, he could be working for any number of governments or a rival group."

"And why am I only hearing about this now?"

"Those are fairly new developments, theíos. We only found out about Conor's involvement this past week. As you know, our full attention was on Marcel Pierce, so I need more time for a proper risk assessment."

Anton huffs and dares to add his two cents. "I bet that Chelsea would sing like a bird if we put her in a room with Nico for an hour."

Of course he'd like that.

"I don't doubt Nico can break her within minutes, but that could cause all kinds of issues for us. She had six years to dig up dirt, and with this Conor guy being a tech expert, we have no idea what she has on the Disciples. If we go about this the wrong way, Conor could call it and use the information to damage us. With the upcoming manhunt for Konstantin's killer, we don't need any more eyes on us."

"I agree. What do you suggest?"

I smirk at Anton. "Like Anton pointed out, she and I did have a thing, something I could now use as leverage. Gain her trust, show her that we are no longer the bad guys, then learn what her ultimate goal is. This would allow us to put appropriate safeguards in place; however, until then, I find it too risky to harm or eliminate her."

"Okay, starting now, I want your full focus on the Chelsea Doherty situation. We will reconvene in a month to see where we are on this."

"Of course, theíos." Enough time to put my next plan in motion. Everyone will be so busy finding the Bajris that I will slip by undetected. "I want to take Vitaly to dinner and a movie, and plan to fly out tomorrow." I find Icarus's eyes. "With your approval, of course."

"You deserve a night out with your son. Anything else?"

I look at the man who has been my brother-in-arms for the past five years. With his unswerving loyalty to Icarus, he could become a real threat down the line. "Find a new assignment for Anton. He's off my crew."

30

✵ ✵ ✵

BASTIAN

Baltray, Ireland
June 2024
~~~~~

From the rocks that divide the beach and the narrow coastal road, I let my gaze drift across the sand. Chelsea tosses a ball for her dog by the waterline; despite the nice weather, the area is pretty deserted but for a few colorful dots in the distance that could be joggers or people taking a stroll by the sea. Unthinkable for Cyprus where tourists flock to the beaches all year round. In a way, this type of setting seems frozen in time, emitting a peace and calmness I envy. My whole life has been one big rat race with violence and death as a routine occurrence.

I slip off my shoes and carry them in my hand as I make my way toward the crashing waves. The sand is wet and cool under my feet and the wind rips through my hair. The sun is by no means as burning hot as it is in Cyprus; the warming rays are more like a pleasant caress on my skin. Salt from the ocean weighs heavy in the air and each breath is like a cleanse. About halfway to my destination, Chelsea turns and shields her eyes from the sun. She stands frozen in place until I join her. Questioning eyes meet mine.

I give her a small nod. "It's done."

The big caramel-colored dog rushes toward me; our introduction is cut short by Chelsea picking up the ball and tossing it far into the water. With a few leaps, the dog follows and disappears between the waves.

When she looks at me again, tears sparkle in her eyes. "I know it's stupid, but I'm a little sad."

"You did love him, at least at some point. It's only natural to feel sad."

"I suppose." She wrinkles her nose. "What now?"

"Not sure what you mean."

Her gaze is on the dog swimming back to shore. "You could've called or even texted. Why are you here, Bastian?"

"I promised you—"

"You said you'd contact me. That doesn't require a visit."

The dog shakes the water out of its fur, showering us with droplets. To stall, I pick up the ball and toss it back into the ocean. With a happy bark, the Terrier takes off.

"Are you here to kill me?" Her question is mumbled under her breath and almost drowned out by the howling wind.

"If I wanted you dead, I would've sent someone else."

She folds her arms and turns away from me. A shiver runs through her body; it could be the cold as well as fear. Stepping closer, I pull her against my shoulder and nuzzle my nose into her hair.

"We know about Conor."

She tenses.

"But don't worry, no one has any idea where he is. He covered his tracks well."

"How did you find out?"

"The burner phone. Falk noticed a second ping, the rest was easy."

"So it's all over?"

"No. This is just the beginning, at least if you want it to be."

"Go on."

I drop my arms. "Why don't we take a walk?" Getting my blood circulation flowing will help me to sort through my mingled thoughts.

How much to tell her?

How far should I go?

Should I trust her?

This could become a make it or break it situation, and if it goes wrong, I will have no choice but to kill her.

Hand in hand, we stroll along the water, the dog chasing back and forth between the waves and our moving legs. The silence between us is charged. I'm terrified to trust her and risk another betrayal, but my chances of success without her are slim to none. It's time to find an ally.

I clear my throat. "I might be wrong, but my gut tells me that you aren't happy to let this end with Marcel's death. You want to hold more people accountable."

"That's a fair assumption."

I halt and turn toward her to find her eyes. "How far up the ladder do you want to go?"

She clicks her tongue and sidesteps around me. Whistling for the dog, she avoids glancing in my direction.

"Chelsea, how far are you willing to go?"

She spins around. "Why don't *you* tell me?"

I close my eyes; here goes nothing. "I want to take down the Disciples. And I want Icarus Pappas dead."

Her gaze stays on me for the longest time.

Dissecting. Leery. Doubtful.

"Why?" Her voice has an edge. "As far as I know, he's your uncle and you are being groomed as his successor."

She and Conor did their homework. "Let's just say that there's a lot of things I did that I'm not proud of. It's not how I want to live my life. I made bad choices, but that doesn't mean I have to continue to make the same mistakes. I want out, but as you know, you can't simply quit the Disciples, so dismantling the organization is my only option."

She snorts. "And you just want me to believe you? You've been lying to me from the start."

"You haven't been exactly truthful either," rests on the tip of my tongue, but I swallow down the words. I'm not here to argue with her. "What can I do for you to trust me?"

"Tell me who killed my son."

I turn my head. Giving up Nico, who's the only Disciple I'd still trust with my life, is not an easy feat. "His name is Nico Dessler."

"And he works in your crew?"

"Yes." When I glance at her, I can't shake the feeling that the information isn't new to her.

A smile plays on her lips. "You give a little, I give a little, so it's my turn. Yes, I do want to hold Icarus accountable, and I wouldn't mind destroying the Disciples in the process. Now what's your plan?"

"There is one thing I need to do before this final part. My son lives with Icarus in Cyprus and I don't want him caught up in this." Especially if things go south. "I need to get him out."

She nods. Again, the news about Vitaly doesn't seem to come as a surprise, but then again, she could've overheard

Anton and me discussing him on the plane before our detour to Nicosia.

"Okay, and how do we do that?"

"Call the dog. I'm getting cold and this will take a while."

31

✳ ✳ ✳

BASTIAN

Baltray, Ireland
~~~~~

Hiding in the bushes in Chelsea's backyard like a thief, I roll back and forth on the balls of my feet.

C'mon, hurry up and open that damn window.

A chuckle escapes from under my breath.

Sneaking into a house to hide from a parent.

That's definitely a first.

And a new low.

I'm a grown man and this is juvenile behavior at its best.

A creak draws my attention to a window on the second floor. The stern face of an elderly woman peers at me, her brows furrowed. "What ye think you're doing down there, laddy?"

I pull my head between my shoulders.

If there's a god, please turn me invisible.

My smile is crooked. "Waiting for Chelsea to let me in."

She narrows her eyes. "Aren't you that fella from the other night who showed up drunk?"

Guilty as charged.

"Yes, ma'am, and I sincerely apologize if I caused any damage or offended you."

"Hm." The deep wrinkle on her forehead doesn't smooth; I'm surely not forgiven. "Are you really from Cyprus?"

"Yes, ma'am."

"And that's all?"

Better not lie or her wrath will follow me until the day I die. "I'm also American."

"I thought so."

Now would *really* be a good time to be swallowed up by the ground.

Her eyes narrow even more. "Are you getting serious with my daughter?"

Stick to the truth.

"Honestly, I'm not sure, ma'am. Right now, Chelsea is helping me with some issues I have with my son."

Her tight lips curve to a mild smile. "How old is the young lad?"

"He's twelve."

"Tough age."

"Yep, I can confirm that."

It's the year things really started to go downhill with my folks.

"Well, if you and Chelsea ever get serious, you are welcome to use the front door."

"Thank you, ma'am, that's good to know."

She closes the window and I let out a shaky breath. That was worse than a dentist visit.

The window right above my head pops opens and Chelsea sticks her head out. "Come on, I'll help you."

I eye the ledge. The front door would be easier, but I'm not ready for that. Hoisting myself up, I wince as the sharp metal of the window frame digs into my hands. Chelsea pulls my arms.

For a beat, I'm in limbo. The tips of my shoes scrape over the wall of the house in a desperate attempt to find a purchase for a quick boost; once found, I'm able to get my hips across the windowsill and gravity takes over. Toppling into the room, I take Chelsea with me. She ends up buried underneath my body.

Fuck.

"Did you get hurt?"

She shakes her head. Laughter bubbles out of her; it's catching. My chuckles come in spurts until I'm out of breath. Gazing down on her, I'm tempted by her heart-shaped mouth. My lips find hers; she allows access and I take her for a deep kiss. Her hair and breath still smell like the salt of the sea; the surge of electricity her gentle touch sends through my body is intoxicating and gets me hard. I squeeze her ass. As we come up for air, she fumbles with the buttons of my shirt. I don't want to wait and simply tear the damn thing open, sending the ivory studs flying.

She straddles my hips and I lift her up to set her on the bed. Her chest is rising and falling in a rapid rhythm. She arches her hips and I take her pants off with one pull. We dispose of her respective shirts at the same time. My jeans are next. In my haste to shake them off, I get my legs entangled in my boxers.

Fuck.

Struggling to keep my balance, I somehow manage to toss away my last piece of clothing. My cock is so hard that it sticks out at a right angle; the shaft points at Chelsea's pussy like the barrel of a gun. I'm ready to shoot, too. Just the sight of her, panting on the bed in nothing but her lace panties and bra, gets my tip moist.

I move my thigh between her legs and begin a slow assault. Kneading her nipples between my fingertips through the fabric of her bra solicits a moan. Her eyes are wide open and her pupils are dilated with lust. I slip my hand inside the cup and free her breast. The little bud is deep red and hard like a rock. When I gently pinch it, her hips buck. Warm juices seep through her panties. I rub her crotch with my thigh until she's soaking wet.

"Fuck, Bastian, get this underwear off me."

I raise a brow.

Demanding?

She'd better not forget who's in control.

Stripping her of her last pieces of clothing is oddly satisfying. I love how her body reacts to me, and her heated pussy and hard nipples are sexy as fuck.

"Get on your knees. I want to take you doggie-style." I don't have to ask twice. I stroke her ass, my cock twitching. Aligning my tip with her heat, I plunge inside her. Her muscles squeeze around me.

Fuck, she's tight.

My thrusts are slow and I slap her ass. She cries out, a shudder running through her. Her tightening canal almost pulls me over the edge.

"Too much?"

"Do it again."

With a grin, I let my hand smack her other butt cheek. Her moan is like a purr. I rub over the redness with my thumb.

Fuck, this is good.

I relish the control, the domination, her utter vulnerability as she submits to my lust. Pushing deeper inside her, I fill her, stretch her, take it as far as I can go. I speed up; with every thrust, the heat builds. As I start to spiral, I spank her one final time; it sets of a chain reaction. Her orgasm rips through her with such force that I explode, my own waves of pleasure so strong that my head spins with dizziness. My body shakes and my breath catches. I'm unable to stay on my feet. Pulling my cock out, I collapse next to her on the bed and spoon her in my arms. My heart hammers in my ribcage.

"Sheesh, I think that was the strongest orgasm I've ever had."

"Same." She snuggles against me. "Can we cuddle for a bit before we talk?"

Hell, as far as I'm concerned, we can have a few more rounds of sex. I hug her tighter.

A satisfied sigh leaves her lips. "My mam will be leaving in a little while, then we have the house to ourselves for a few hours."

I wouldn't mind spending the evening in bed. "At some point, we should probably worry about dinner. Is there any place around here that delivers?"

"The Chinese place in town."

Chinese it is. "And I should probably check into a local B&B."

"Nah, as long as you don't ruin Mam's new welcome mat, she won't mind you staying here."

Smiling against her skin, I allow my hand to wander south. "I'd better keep you happy then, so I don't find myself in the street."

When I push two fingers into her drenched pussy, she wiggles her ass against my cock. "Don't worry, as long as you keep doing that, we're good."

32

✳ ✳ ✳

CHELSEA

Baltray, Ireland
~~~~~

I wave the chopsticks holding the jumbo shrimp in front of Bastian's mouth. "Okay, open up."

"And you swear it's not too spicy."

"It's sweet chili." Emphasis on sweet.

"Exactly. Chili could mean mega hot."

I roll my eyes. "You said you'd trust me."

That does it.

He obediently opens his mouth and I place the shrimp on his tongue. Chewing, he skews his lips but otherwise keeps a straight face. The fact that he downs half a bottle of water as soon as he swallows hints that the chili might've gotten to him after all.

He takes a deep breath and ignores my efforts to sneak another shrimp into his mouth. "What's the deal with Conor?"

How much to tell him?

Considering how fresh our allegiance is, I opt for the basics. "He is actually my half-brother."

Bastian arches a brow. "Not sure how we missed that."

"A well-hidden family secret. Our dad was married before and had Conor with his first wife, though we both didn't know about each other until we met at our dad's funeral. We lost contact again until after I returned from Hong Kong." And then he came through for me in my darkest hour. My throat constricts and I swallow hard. Without Conor, I would've been fucked. Eager to change the subject, I shuffle saucy rice into my mouth. "Now tell me about your son."

"His name is Vitaly and he is twelve."

"And he lives with Icarus?"

Bastian nods. "His mom died four years ago in a car bombing. Before the dust even settled, Icarus had a man on a plane to the States to pick up my son and take him to Cyprus. He then bribed a judge to grant him full guardianship. All that happened before I even realized Vitaly was gone, and when I insisted that Icarus should return him to my care, he told me to go to hell. I tried to get the guardianship papers revoked through the courts in America, but they refused to take jurisdiction unless the Cypriot court would surrender the case. Since Vitaly is also a Cypriot citizen, there was nothing I could do."

"But why is Icarus even interested in him?"

"The mom, Olivia, was in a romantic relationship with Icarus's son Konstantin. Konstantin practically raised Vitaly as his own, so Icarus considers him his grandson. He has done everything to keep me out of Vitaly's life and limited my contact. Now I barely even know my own son."

I reach over and squeeze Bastian's hand. "That must be very difficult."

"You have no idea." Jaw clenched, he turns his head and stares out of the window. A minute goes by in silence; only the chirping of the birds in the tree right outside my window drift through the cracked window. A few times, he wipes through his face; I suspect he tries to hide tears, but since I only have the benefit of staring at the back of his head, I can't be sure. This must be so hard for him.

I squeeze his arm to regain his attention. "How was your relationship with Vitaly before Olivia's death? Did you and her get along? I mean, it must've been tough to see her with your cousin after you guys broke if off."

He tenses under my touch. "Olivia and my relationship was complicated. It would take too long to explain."

Ah, a touchy subject.

He turns his head; the blazing hurt in his moist eyes hits me without warning. Those memories are a fucking nightmare for him.

"What's the plan of getting Vitaly out of Cyprus?"

"Icarus recently learned the identity of Konstantin's killer, which has triggered a global manhunt. With a few exceptions, every Disciple is looking for the culprits and as soon as they are found, Icarus will leave Cyprus to personally witness their execution. When that happens, security around Vitaly will be minimal. Everyone will want to be close to the boss to grab a piece of the action. Under normal circumstances, Icarus never leaves the island, so this will be my one chance to grab my son. If I miss it, I'd probably lose him forever. Icarus has been preparing Vitaly to join the organization and it'll be one to two years max before that happens. Getting him out now is my only opportunity to save him."

I chew my lip. This is way riskier than expected. "How do you plan to grab him?"

"That's the tricky part. I recently lost Vitaly's nanny, who has been feeding me information about him. In the past, he had an active life outside of Icarus's villa, but he hurt himself playing soccer a few months back, which confined him mostly to the house. Icarus took advantage of that and changed his routine. Instead of team sports, Vitaly now does martial arts and boxing, and Icarus has added a shooting range in the basement to show Vitaly the basics. Aside from school, Vitaly does not appear to leave the villa anymore. I took him for dinner and a movie last night to learn as much as possible about his new schedule, but he was evasive and didn't give me much. However, I did learn that he'll be participating in an exclusive summer program in his school, which will be our only chance to grab him."

Wow, that takes risky to a new level. I pinch the bridge of my nose. *Think of the end goal, Chelsea.* Having him as an ally will be invaluable in my quest to kill Icarus.

"How long do you think it'll take the Disciples to locate Konstantin's killers?"

"I anticipate anytime between a week and a month. We'll need to be ready to enter Cyprus on short notice because Icarus will only be gone for a few days. When it comes to border control, he also has his eyes and ears everywhere, so we can't just fly there without our names being flagged."

"Then how do we enter the country?"

"Cruise line."

I arch a brow. "You want us to go on a cruise?"

"It's the most inconspicuous way. All cruise ships that dock in Limassol leave from Greece and return there, and with both countries being in the EU and having historically strong ties, border patrols at the cruise port are lax. As long as you are part of a cruise tour, they wave you through without even checking passports."

"Okay, and once you get your son out of Cyprus, where are you gonna take him? I'm sure Icarus will send the full force of the Disciples after you once he realizes Vitaly is gone." Bastian will be a hunted man like Marcel, and I can't have him pull me down with him.

"We will disguise our appearance, so it might take him a while to figure out that it wasn't a ransom kidnapping. I'm also expecting that the execution of Konstantin's killers will cause a turf war. The Disciples will be busy defending their territory and keeping their business relationships intact, which will buy us at least enough time to find a safe place for Vitaly. The rest, I still have to figure out."

My laugh is filled with incredulity. "You are asking me to risk everything for a *still-have-to-figure-out* plan?"

He wraps his hands around mine. "If it were Sean who were trapped with Icarus, would you hesitate?"

"Not in a million years."

"Then I'm asking you, as one parent to another, please help me save my son." Tears sparkle in his eyes. "I can't live with the thought of him becoming like me. I don't want that type of life for him."

I swallow down the lump in my throat. *Manipulating bastard. "No, sorry, I can't do it,"* would be the sensible response. The words refuse to cross my lips. *Do I really trust him?*

Without a doubt, he hides many more secrets, though as it stands, I'm keeping my cards closer to my chest than he is.

I take a deep breath. "Okay, I'll help you, and I might even know a place where we can hide Vitaly to keep him safe."

33

✳ ✳ ✳

BASTIAN

Athens, Greece
July 2024
~~~~~

I step out of the barbershop and let my gaze roam over the plaza. Chelsea is engaged in an animated conversation with one of the street vendors, probably haggling over the price. She is a great bargain hunter and has saved me a bundle; not that I need it, but it's still nice to see that she doesn't spend money faster than I earn it.

With my backpack hanging from one shoulder, I cross the plaza and join her at the booth. Wrapping my arms around her from behind, I rest my chin on her shoulder. "What are you getting?"

"This bracelet." She lifts up a simple silver hoop with a few green inlays. "I think my mam would really like it."

"Then let me get it for her."

"You've already spent enough money on me. I'm not used to all this first-class travel and those mega large hotel suites."

"And there I would've thought that you and Marcel always traveled in style." They had plenty of money. When her body tenses, I hug her tighter. "I'm sorry. Talking about him must be a difficult and I shouldn't have mentioned him."

"It's fine. Marcel was a part of my past and there'll be times when his name will pop up." She looks at me from under her eyelashes with a sweet smile, though her lips are a little crooked. "And Marcel spent his money on other things. He was into expensive jewelry and bought himself a lot of designer clothes. And then there were the houses and the cars. Even in Hong Kong, he insisted on buying this mega expensive condo and he thought we needed a fancy SUV, even though the public transportation was perfectly adequate. And he was big on eating out. We spent an insane amount on restaurants and babysitters for Sean."

"You must have gone through a lot of money."

"Over two and a half mil in the three years we lived in Hong Kong. Before that, it was mostly the money he earned from the Disciples."

As Konstantin's top lieutenant, he was in one of the higher salary brackets. Icarus tends to compensate the men on his payroll well.

Chelsea hands the street vendor a few euros and accepts the bag with the bracelet. Escaping from my embrace, she cocks her head. "Let me look at you." Her brows furrow. "Not gonna lie, I don't like a platinum blond Bastian with a fully grown beard."

"Well, it's only temporary. Plus, look at this." I pull the horned-rim glasses with the tinted lenses out of my shirt pocket. "Do you think they hide my eyes enough?"

"Yep, it's the perfect disguise." She gets on her tiptoes and kisses my lips. A whiff of vanilla tickles my nose and my mind strays to forbidden places.

Sheesh, we've been fucking so much that we must be setting a new world record.

I still can't help but to squeeze her ass. "And you totally rock in that long, red wig." When this is over, I wouldn't mind if she grew her hair out a little.

"I don't think long hair suits me."

"I love it but ultimately, that's up to you."

"Good to know. Marcel always made those decisions for me and I'm glad you're not trying to turn me into your ideal woman."

"Nope, I like you just the way you are." Draping my arm around her shoulder, I pull her along the booths. "Where to now?"

"Hotel?"

I grin. Spending the rest of the afternoon between the sheets is just what the doctor ordered. My phone buzzes in my pocket. Still smiling, I pull it out. The message turns my stomach.

Found the Bajris. Icarus is leaving for Tirana tonight.

"Is it time?"

Chelsea's question barely makes it through the humming in my ears. I nod and grip the strap of my backpack. "I'm heading to the travel agent to book our tickets. You go pack and I'll meet you at the hotel for checkout."

One more quick kiss and we part ways; I flag down a taxi to drive to the port. Thirty minutes later, I've paid for our cruise and completed the pre-check-in for our departure. The sailing from Athens to Limassol will take two nights with one day at sea. It should get us into Cyprus with plenty of time to grab Vitaly before Icarus returns.

On foot, I jog over to the harbor and slip undetected through a side entrance that I used before when I was supervising the loading of one of our arm's shipments. The docks are busy with forklifts coming and going and cargo containers being lifted in the air. Walking along a connecting passage to the cruise port, I find our ship without any hassle. The first passengers are boarding and porters loiter around the pier. I pick a gruff-looking black dude. Most African workers are paid even less than their white counterparts and he looks as if he's out to make an extra quick buck.

I pull out a wad of cash. "My wife and I are staying in suite twelve thirty-five, and I have this backpack that will guarantee us a good time but would get flagged if we put it through the x-ray machine. Do you think you could get it onboard for us for say ... a thousand euros?"

He hesitates ever so slightly. "It's not a bomb, is it?"

I laugh. "Heavens no. My wife is into kink, you know handcuffs, gun play, whips, that sort of thing. The backpack will stay in our cabin the whole time."

"Make it two thousand and you got yourself a sex toy party."

I can live with that. Pulling out the extra cash, I hand him the backpack and the money.

"You said twelve thirty-five."

"Yep."

"The backpack will be there upon your arrival."

"Stash it in the closet."

"You got it."

"And if you double cross me, I *will* find you, and trust me, that's not something you want."

I give him an Anton glare that makes him gulp. Hopefully, the little fucker realizes that he'd sign his death warrant if he scams me out of my money or alerts the cruise line.

I retrace my steps to the entrance of the harbor and catch a cab that takes me to the hotel. Chelsea is already in the lobby, pacing. She has chewed her lip raw and appears unsettled.

I squeeze her arm. "Ready."

"Yeah."

"Then let's go. The taxi is waiting."

The first couple of miles are spent in silence. Chelsea chews her lip with vigor to the point where it pains me to watch.

"What's wrong?"

"Dunno. My gut is in knots. I'm just worried, I guess."

"We planned every little detail."

"Still." More lip chewing. "And you are sure Vitaly is in this summer program?"

"As sure as I can be."

"And he'll be alone?"

I internally groan. We've been over this at least a dozen times. "Like I said before, the music program is exclusive and the extra class is only offered to a handful of conservatory members. All the other kids in the program are boarders, so he'll be alone when he exits the school. His bodyguard is the only one we'll need to worry about."

She lets out a shaky breath. "Okay, it's gonna be fine."

"It will be." I squeeze her arm, though I'm not sure if the gesture is meant to calm my nerves more than hers. Her worry is contagious.

The taxi pulls up to the side of the terminal and I help Chelsea gather her things. For a beat, I meet the gaze of the black porter and he gives me a small nod. So far so good.

I smile at Chelsea. "You got your passport?"

"Yep. You got yours?"

I pat my coat pocket. The passport is spanking new, just issued two week ago at the US embassy in Dublin. The clerk never even raised a brow when I presented her with my original birth certificate that was issued prior to the name change. Chelsea's renewal was even easier since she and Marcel never formally divorced.

As we approach the check-in desk, Chelsea loops arms with me.

The woman behind the computer screen smiles at us. "Your names, please?

I return the smile. No turning back now. "Bastian Pappas and Chelsea Pierce. We are booked in suite twelve thirty-five."

34

✹ ✹ ✹

CHELSEA

**Somewhere at sea, approaching the port of Limassol, Cyprus
July 2024**

~~~~~

I ride Bastian slowly, relishing how the lust glowing in his eyes grows with every move of my hips. He is close to his orgasm and I let my own heat consume me. The slick friction of his cock hits me in all the right spots. Sucking air through gritted teeth, I try to prolong the inevitable. He cups my ass and forces his shaft deeper inside me. I moan, unable to hold back. The heat rips through me, my muscles clenching with shivers, greedy to squeeze even the last drop of cum out of him. He pulls me to his chest as we ride out the aftershocks; in his tight embrace, his racing heart hammers against my ribcage.

Fuck, this was good.

I cuddle closer against him to get the most benefit from his heated skin. "We should be getting ready."

On cue, a shudder runs through the large ocean liner.

"Nah, we still have at least an hour. Once we dock, they do some checks before we can disembark." Bastian squeezes my butt. "Though we should probably get dressed if we still want to have breakfast."

"Who needs to eat when we can have this?" I nibble his ear, ready to go again.

"True, but today will be a taxing day. We both need to preserve our energy."

His words sober me up and I roll off him. The dangers we'll be facing are real; they might even become more threatening than what went down with Marcel. It's not a given that we'll both make it back to the cruise terminal tonight.

Bastian scrolls though his phone.

"Any news?"

He looks up. "Icarus is still in Tirana. From the looks of things, everything is working as planned. Every available Disciple is eager to get their hands on the bounty and is sticking close to Icarus. Security around Vitaly will be minimal, just as we expected."

"Who is feeding you the info?"

He turns his head and gets out of bed.

I throw a pillow after him. "Who? We said no more secrets."

"Nico."

Fuck, I knew it. "And you are sure you can trust him?"

"Positive. A few years back, Nico really fucked up and ended up with a gun to his head. I saved his life, so he owes me." Bastian rummages through a drawer and pulls out a fresh pair of boxers. "I'll quickly jump into the shower. Don't join me or we'll never get out of here."

I grin. "Don't worry, I wanted to call Conor anyhow to give him an update."

Bastian disappears and I scour my backpack for the brand-new burner phone. A few seconds later, I find it and dial

Conor's number. He picks up on the first ring, as if expecting my call.

"We just docked in Limassol and booked a bus tour up to Nicosia. God willing, we'll be able to intercept Bastian's son as he leaves school and then we'll be back here before the ship leaves tonight. Tomorrow, we'll be in Greece and disembark, and then fly back to Ireland."

He sucks in a deep breath. "I don't like this plan. Too much that can go wrong."

"I know, Conor, but I promised Bastian I'd help him." And as a mom, I totally get why this is important to him. No risk is too high when it comes to your kid.

"Okay, fine, and at least this whole cruise ship idea keeps your exposure to a minimum when entering the country."

It's the only solid element in our plan. "Is there any chatter you picked up?"

"I monitored all the frequencies and things around Bastian are quiet."

"What about Icarus and the Bajris?"

"Plenty of chatter there. Several intelligence services, including the CIA, sent out alerts that there might be a turf war. They are drooling to get their hands on both the Disciples and the Bajri clan to split up their operations."

With any luck, they'll kill each other. "Let's wait and see what goes down."

"There's one more thing. Jackson Pierce put out a contract on whomever killed his brother. So far, he has no solid evidence that it was Bastian but eventually, this will come to light. Bastian will be a wanted man, so make sure you wrap things up with him before that happens. Ending up in Jackson Pierce's crosshairs is the last thing you want."

"Got it." I close my eyes. This is a complication I didn't need. "Conor, I have to ask you for a favor. If things go sideways, I need you to take care of my mam."

Silence drifts from the phone speaker. At least half a minute goes by before he speaks again. "That's a big ask, Chelsea. The woman wrecked my parents' marriage."

"C'mon, Conor, you are old enough to know that relationships aren't black and white. I'm sure it wasn't only Dad's fault that they split up."

More deafening silence hangs in the line.

"Okay, I'll make sure your mam is alright, but you'd better get your ass back here in one piece or the fam will be heartbroken. You can't do that to us."

"I promise I'll be extra careful. And tell the fam I love them."

"Call me tonight the second you get back to the ship." He hangs up without a good-bye, a sign that he is mad.

Bastian appears in the doorway. He's still wet with water pellets glistening in the most inopportune spots, the towel only used to dry his hair.

He smiles. "All good?"

Groaning, I pinch the bridge of my nose. The morning started out so promising and only went downhill from there. "Jackson put out a contract on Marcel's killer."

"That was to be expected."

"Aren't you worried?"

"I am, at least until I get an opportunity to talk to him, but I can't let that distract me. Chances are he's still putting all the pieces together and it might take weeks before he has a solid lead on us."

Let's hope so. "I should get ready."

I slip into a pair of black jeans and choose a sleeveless blue t-shirt to battle the heat. Spreading the suntan lotion all over my exposed skin, I eye the wig on the stand. I loathe the damn thing. The hairpiece scratches and the long red curls do not suit my face. Unfortunately, it's also my main means of disguise. In hindsight, I should've insisted on shorter hair and a wig that doesn't weigh a ton.

Bastian tosses me a glance. "You need to take a jacket."

"Why? It's roasting in the sun." And with the artificial long hair, it'll be torture.

"To hide this." From his open suitcase, he takes a gun and sets it on the nightstand.

My forehead wrinkles. "How did you get a firearm onboard?"

"Oh, I have my ways."

"And you think I need it?"

Cautious eyes meet mine. "Anything could happen today and you want to be prepared."

35

✳ ✳ ✳

BASTIAN

Nicosia, Cyprus
July 2024
~~~~~

We spill out of the bus together with thirty other tourists in the center of Nicosia. So far, the plan is holding up. As anticipated, the immigration officer didn't check our passports when we disembarked at the Limassol cruise terminal, though it was still a relief that everything went so smoothly. Three weeks of preparation went into this trip and today will show if our efforts to evade the Disciples and snatch Vitaly from right under their noses were enough.

The tour guide raises an umbrella with the cruise logo. "We'll be exploring the Leventis Municipal Museum first, so follow me."

I slip him a hundred-dollar bill. "My wife and I would prefer to discover the city on our own."

"No problem, sir. The bus will leave from this exact same spot at five pm to take the group back to the cruise port. Don't be late because I'm unable to wait."

"Don't worry about us. My wife is pregnant and we might leave earlier already. We'll find our own way back to the ship."

I wrap his fingers around another hundred-dollar bill to avoid further questions.

He catches my drift. "Then have a good day, sir."

He herds the other passengers away and I motion to Chelsea to follow me across the road. We sit down in a coffee shop; it's the best place to kill the last hours. As we wait for the server to take our order, I drum my fingers on the table. My gaze roams over the faces of the other patrons and the passersby. This is almost too easy.

"Bastian."

Chelsea's hissed word rips through me like a bolt of lightning. I'm sweating and my hands are clammy.

Take a deep breath and calm the fuck down.

"Sorry, did you say something?"

"I asked you twice how far Vitaly's school is from here."

"Four blocks."

"So that's what? . . . About a ten-minute walk."

"More like fifteen."

"And he gets out at two?"

I nod. "It's summer school, so it might even be a few minutes earlier."

As time winds out, every second stretches like rubber. I pat my pocket with Vitaly's birth certificate that will allow me to get his US passport at the embassy in Greece. We'll still be on hostile territory and I'll have to watch my back. In this part of the world, Icarus has a fuckload of government officials in his pocket; this is his stomping ground and anyone here could turn out to be an enemy.

I let out a shaky breath.

Chelsea squints at a building across the street.

"What?" I turn around but find the sidewalk empty.

She shakes her head. "For a second, I thought I saw Jackson."

I snort. We are both spooked. "Let's try not to be afraid of our own shadows."

"Aren't you nervous at all?"

My stomach is in such turmoil that I'm in danger of losing my breakfast. "It's gonna be alright. We just need to keep our cool and stick to the plan."

"Yeah, the plan is solid."

"Very solid." Except for the trillion things that could go wrong.

I order another spearmint tea to distract myself. The next hour passes by in silence; Chelsea is reading a book on her phone, though I can't detect her turning the pages. Together with the heat that has reached boiling temperatures, I'm a bundle of nerves by the time one thirty rolls around.

I toss the crumpled-up napkin I tore to shreds onto the table. "Time to go."

She is on her feet in an instant. More silence ensues as we walk along the street. Due to the heat, the foot traffic is scant and we encounter mostly women and small children. School is out for the summer and the beaches are calling. Many people who live and work in Nicosia take July off to spend time by the sea.

One more turn and the old brick building stands tall across the street. Vitaly's school takes up an entire block, the esteemed halls funded by private tuition and donors like Icarus to guarantee the best education money can buy for their offspring. Two cars are parked in front; the limo my uncle uses to chauffeur Vitaly around and a white SUV of a parent whose kid must be another summer school attendee. This one was not anticipated.

I pull Chelsea into a waiting area at a bus stop to hide from view.

She bites her lip. "You said Vitaly would be the only one being picked up. What are we gonna do now?"

"We stick to the plan. If the other parent is still around when Vitaly's bodyguard drops, you just yell, "oh, my god, he fainted," and then use the commotion to disappear."

"And you think that will work?"

"There won't be another opportunity to grab him today and Icarus might be back as early as tomorrow. It has to be now or never."

She nods, though judging from her tight lips, she isn't convinced. Neither am I, but I'm running out of options.

I nudge her shoulder. "Okay, here we go."

The front doors to the school have opened and Vitaly walks down the steps, talking with a pretty girl about his age. He's putting on the moves, beaming and listening, without once breaking eye contact. They arrive at the bottom of the stairs and head for the white SUV just as Chelsea and I cross the road.

Vitaly opens the passenger door of the SUV. "I'll see you tomorrow, and maybe my grandpa is back and we'll be allowed to go for pizza."

"That would be nice." The girl lets out a flirtatious giggle.

I roll my eyes. Kids today start so young in the dating scene.

Chelsea passes through the gap between the cars while I round the trunk of the SUV. Right about now, the school's cameras will pick us up, but our disguises should be solid.

She approaches Vitaly's bodyguard. "Excuse me, but I'm totally lost." She holds up a map. "Could you show me the way—"

"Fuck off," the man grumbles.

He turns toward Vitaly. It's the moment Chelsea strikes; the needle of the syringe with the tranquilizer enters the guy's body just above his hip. He blinks a couple of times and falls over like a freshly cut tree.

Man, that's some potent shit I got on the dark web.

My son is frozen in place, staring at his bodyguard with an open mouth.

I stretch out my hand. "Vitaly."

He snaps his head around. "Babá?"

"Yes, it's me. C'mon, we need to go."

He shakes his head. "Grandpa said—"

"Fuck what Icarus said. You are my son, and you need to do what I tell you."

He stares at me with wide eyes.

In that very moment, the driver's door of the SUV opens and a dude gets out. What is it with people these days, not minding their own business?

Chelsea plays her part. "Oh, my god, he just fainted. Call an ambulance."

I grab Vitaly's arm. "Let's go."

He hardly fights me and we gain on the street corner.

"Hey, where are you taking him?" the SUV parent yells.

Chelsea pulls her gun. "If you value your life, get back into the car and drive away." Her face is a solid mask; her death glare is downright terrifying.

My son tears from my grip. "I want to go home."

"Vitaly—"

As he tries to get back to his bodyguard, Chelsea intercepts him. She cups her hands around his shoulders and shakes him gently. "I know you have no idea what's going on and this is fucking scary, but you need to listen to your dad. He's doing this because he loves you."

A few tears run down Vitaly's face and he allows her to pull him away. By the time they reach me, a spark of stubbornness remains in his eyes, but his bottom lip is quivering. He's close to a crying tantrum. I drape my arm around his shoulders in a desperate attempt to comfort him.

Rounding the street corner, I come to a screeching halt. Not even six feet away, a man blocks my way; he's tall, lean, and lethal. Even though the mirrored aviator shades hide a good amount of his features, I immediately recognize his face from the few photos Falk managed to snap of him and his entourage. With the next breath, a gun rests in his hand and he trains it right at the center of my forehead.

36

✳ ✳ ✳

CHELSEA

Nicosia, Cyprus
~~~~~

Jackson!

So it *was* him whom I spotted across the street from the coffee shop. He had been in my sight for only the blink of an eye before disappearing again, but I'd recognize those aviator shades anywhere. Too bad I didn't listen to my gut.

He pulls out a gun, pointing it straight at Bastian.

Fuck no.

I'm not gonna let Jackson shoot him right here in front of his son.

A hard shove transports Bastian out of the line of fire; he almost topples into the road and I ignore his surprised gasp.

"It's me you want."

Jackson turns his head.

"I killed Marcel, but it was self-defense. It was either him or me."

Even though the shades hide his eyes completely, his glare burns on my skin. Just as quickly as he drew the gun, it disappears. A motorcycle speeds up and Jackson gets on the back without losing a beat. Engine revving, the driver takes off. A helmet with a tinted window hides their face, but from their frame and slender fingers, my money is on the woman who abducted me.

Phew, that was close.

"Are you fucking insane?" Bastian's face twists with a mix of desperation and anger. "You just signed your death warrant."

"I think he believed me. Otherwise, why didn't he shoot me?"

"Because Vitaly was with us. Jackson is known never to leave an eyewitness, but he would equally never harm a child. Sooner or later, he'll catch up with you and trust me, he won't hesitate a second time."

Crap. "What should I do now?"

"I'll put the word out that it was me who shot Marcel, which will hopefully get you off his radar." Sirens blare in the distance and Bastian glances over his shoulder. "For now, we need to get out of here. The SUV dude or the school must have called the cops and they are on their way."

Bastian grabs Vitaly's arms and pulls the reluctant boy forward. We move quickly up the block and dart across the next street to disappear in a park. The trees offer shade, but the air is hot and stale. I struggle to breathe and sweat pours from every pore by the truckload.

Silent tears run down Vitaly's face. "Why can't I go home?"

"Because you can't." Bastian's voice hitches; he's close to losing his cool. "You're never going back, so stop nagging."

"But why?" Vitaly's question is no louder than a whisper and Bastian ignores him.

I squeeze his arm. "Once we are safe, your dad will explain everything."

Vitaly sobs. "He isn't even my dad."

Bastian closes his eyes and takes a deep breath. Wrapping Vitaly into his arms, he allows him to cry on his shoulder. "I know I haven't been around much, but that wasn't my choice. I wanted to spend way more time with you, but Icarus wouldn't allow it. I love you and want us to be together. You want that, too, right?"

Vitaly nods, his whole body shaking with sobs.

Bastian rubs his back. "And if I take you home now, I'll never be able to see you again. Do you understand?"

Vitaly gives him another nod.

"So do you want us to be together?"

"Yes, Bábá."

"Then I need you to pull yourself together." The hurt in Bastian's voice has me wince; he's just as lost in this new father role as his son. "And once things settle down, I promise that you and I will sit down and talk. Man to man. I'll tell you everything you want to know, about your mom and Konstantin, and about grandpa and my reasons why I don't want you to live with him anymore. I'll answer any question you have. Deal?"

"Okay." Vitaly dries his face on his shirt. He offers me a small smile. Quizzical eyes take me in for the very first time.

Bastian catches on. "This is my friend, Chelsea."

"Hi, Vitaly."

He acknowledges me with a small nod. "Is she my new mom?"

His father chuckles. "No, not yet anyways."

My heart lurches. It's the most inopportune moment to hope for a Bastian-Chelsea future, but I still can't suppress the huge grin spreading on my lips.

Sirens blast by our location mere feet away and Bastian cranes his neck. "We need to move and then I have to find us some transportation."

Vitaly points at the other end of the park. "I know there's a taxi stand at the entrance. Anton took me there the other day when the limo had a flat tire."

Bastian raises a brow. "Icarus assigned Anton to be your bodyguard."

"He was until grandpa had to go on his trip."

At least luck was on our side this once. Even with my wig, Anton would've likely recognized me and would've never allowed me to get close enough to knock him out with the syringe.

Bastian squeezes my arm. *Are you okay*, his eyes ask.

I nod.

"Aright." He straightens, resuming full control. "Let's find a cab and get the hell out of Nicosia."

~~~~

Ninety minutes later, we are approaching the port gate of Limassol. I turn around in the passenger seat; Bastian is staring out the window and Vitaly has fallen asleep. During the drive, a few hushed words were exchanged, mostly in Greek, and Vitaly's face was twisted with despair. If I had to bet, he was having second thoughts again and asked to go home. This must be all so confusing for him. Bastian will have his hands full to convince him that he's only doing this for his son's own good without giving too much away about the Disciples' atrocious practices.

The burner phone buzzes in my pocket and I close my eyes. Conor would only contact me in a worst-case scenario. With I sigh, I pull the device out and check the message.

They're on to you. Whatever you do, don't go back to the ship.

Bastian has been watching me and I hand him the phone. Leaning back in my seat, I rest my head against the cool window.

How the hell are we going to get out of Cyprus?

Bastian leans closer to the driver. 'Pull in over there. We prefer to walk the rest of the way."

The cabbie slows down and Bastian wakes Vitaly. The boy rubs his eyes, disoriented. On Bastian's motion, he gets out of the car without a complaint, and we are soon left standing on the sidewalk in the pressing afternoon heat. The taxi and its pleasant air conditioning drives away.

Looking around, I wrinkle my nose. "What now?"

"We need to check out what's going on at the port."

Getting to the cruise terminal is quite the hike and I'm drenched by the time we duck behind a cargo container to inspect the comings and goings of passengers.

"Shit, they are checking passports," Bastian hisses.

"Then what are we gonna do?" As far as I know, he hasn't gotten his son's passport yet, but even if we had all the proper documentation, I doubt they'd just let us walk onboard.

"Our exit route is blown and we'll need to find another way off the island."

37

✸ ✸ ✸

CHELSEA

Limassol, Cyprus
~~~~~

Find another way off the island.

Bastian's voice is as nonchalant as it can be, as if it weren't a big deal to be trapped on Icarus's turf. It's likely his attempt to keep Vitaly calm, but it's not fucking working for me.

I'm about to freak out.

"If you have another brilliant idea, now would be the time to speak up." The words come out harsher than intended and get me a raised brow from Vitaly.

Bastian squeezes my hand. "Don't panic, I got this."

His eyes beg me to take it down a notch and from Vitaly's *should-I-bolt* expression, I understand why. I take a deep breath and give him a brave smile.

Take the lead. I follow.

A few minutes pass in which we stare at the entrance to the cruise port where the border patrol officers still check the passports of every passenger entering and leaving the docking area. Unfortunately, they neither magically disappear nor give the impression that they are about to give up.

Bastian points at the taxi stand. "Let's grab a cab. A friend of mine lives close by and might be able to help."

I quirk a brow. "And you think we can trust him?" Marcel had no friends aside from the Disciples; it's one of their safeguards to keep people isolated within the organization.

"It's a she and yes, I explicitly trust her."

So an old girlfriend. Not ideal, but we also don't have an alternative.

The taxi ride only takes ten minutes and is spent in utter silence. Both Bastian and Vitaly brood in the backseat; with their lips pursed and their brows puckered, their resemblance is undeniable. Except for the bone-straight hair that is a lighter brown than Bastian's usual hair color, Vitaly is a younger version of his dad.

We get out of the cab in a residential area where villas line the waterfront. Boats of all sizes bob in the wind at private docks and the properties are meticulously maintained. This is an affluent neighborhood well within Icarus's reach. Another big risk.

Bastian steers straight toward a house at the end of the row that is a little bit more secluded. We arrive at the door and his gaze cuts into me. "I'll do the talking, so please just go with the flow."

I nod a *got-it*. Vitaly chews his lip. Without a doubt, it won't take much for him to blow our cover.

Bastian rings the doorbell.

Steps approach from the inside. A woman opens the door, the smile dying on her lips. "Bastian? What are you doing here?" She hurries outside and closes the door behind her but for a crack. With panic, she glances over her shoulder.

"I didn't know where else to go. Icarus has half the island looking for us."

"You kidnapped your son. What did you expect?" She tosses another glance inside the house. "And Christos is here. If he catches you, he'll kill you himself."

On cue, a man's voice drifts from inside the house. "Who is it, Solara?"

She opens the door a little more. "Just the neighbor. Their dog ran away again."

Bastian tries to peek over her shoulder. "What is he still doing here? He was supposed to go to New York on Monday."

"He caught a stomach bug, and surprise, surprise, no one could get a hold of you to stand in for him at the UN. He's loaded about that, too."

"Shit. When is he leaving?"

"Tomorrow morning."

"So we could still take the jet—"

"No, you can't take the jet. The pilots will notify Christos if I call in with a new itinerary."

"Fuck, Solara, you need to get us off the island." He clutches her hand. "You are our only hope. I have no place else to go."

She rolls her eyes. "I know I'm gonna regret this, but you can take the yacht. The side door to the yard is open, so go down to the dock, but make sure to stay hidden, so that Christos doesn't see you. I'll be down there with the key in the next five minutes."

Bastian nods and spins around. I let Vitaly go first to ensure he isn't taking off to alert the whole neighborhood, then follow behind. The garden is veiled in shade from a few large trees that hide us from view, but the private dock sits under the bright sunshine in the direct line of sight from the terrace of the house.

Bastian holds us back. "Let's wait for Solara."

Vitaly hops from one foot to the other. "I really need to piss."

"Can't that wait for another ten minutes?"

He groans.

Bastian juts his chin at a large bush. "Go behind there."

The boy disappears.

I fold my arms. "Who are these people?" Despite the dire situation we are in, the idea that we are getting help from a woman he slept with is like a knife twisted in my gut. I don't trust her as far as I can throw her.

"Christos Doukas is Cyprus's main representative to the UN. As the alternate, I usually stand in when he has other engagements or is unavailable."

"So you and Solara, you never . . ?" I let the words trail off in case Vitaly is eavesdropping.

"Oh, we had, and Christos caught us." He grimaces. "As you can imagine, it didn't go over well and he has had it out for me ever since."

I silently shake my head.

What the hell, Bastian.

An affair with a married woman is already bad enough, but with the wife of someone he closely works with.

Not a clever move.

Vitaly reappears at the same time Solara reaches the end of the garden path. She hands Bastian a key. "Tank is full and should get you to Turkey. Good luck."

"Thanks, Solara. I can't tell you what that means. I owe you big time."

"Just don't get caught or there'll be hell to pay."

With one look at the house, Bastian closes the gap between our hiding place and the sleek yacht in a few long strides. Vitaly is right on his heels. I'm about to follow when Solara grabs my arm.

Her brown eyes are full of concern. "Take good care of him. He deserves someone's love."

I smile. Maybe I judged her too harshly. "I'll do my best."

To have her approval makes the whole matter more bearable. Whatever was between them appears to be over, so I should not read too much into it.

The second I step onboard, the engine hums to life. Bastian motions me to get below deck as he navigates the boat away from the pier. He handles the wheel like a pro. I take off the wig, a tremendous relief, and toss it on the bed. Standing on the steps with just my head out, I let the airflow cool my face. The houses and yachts of Limassol blur to a line of different colors. We pass by our cruise ship and Bastian sets course toward the open sea. I sigh with relief. It proves premature.

A small boat from the harbor heads toward us, growing in size as it comes closer. Blue and orange stripes mark the sides, and the words *Marine Police* leave no doubt that it's an official Cypriot vessel.

Bastian mumbles "fuck" under his breath. "It's the coast guard. Vitaly and I will go under deck. Keep your cool and pretend to be Solara. Her last name is Doukas."

I take the wheel, slowing down to give the guards a chance to catch up. They pull along beside me and an officer signals me to cut the engine. He boards the yacht as soon as the sides of the boats touch.

A spate of Greek words assault my ears.

Shit, what should I do? "I'm sorry, but I don't speak Greek."

"I asked for your name."

"Solara Doukas."

"And your reason for driving in Cypriot's coastal waters?"

"Just going for a spin." I point at Limassol in the distance. "I live right over there."

"And are you alone?"

I look around. "Do you see anyone else?"

"Then I'm sure you don't mind if I check below?"

I raise my chin. "As a matter of fact, I do." One thing Marcel taught me is that a low-level cop is easily intimidated. "My husband is Christos Doukas. He is Cyprus's representative to the UN and a very important man, and I'm sure he wouldn't appreciate it if I'd called him to say that the coast guard is harassing me."

The officer swallows hard. Once. Twice. A third time. My bullying tactic is working.

Tipping his hat, he offers a contrite smile. "Of course, I'm sorry, ma'am. You are free—"

"Is there a problem, officer?"

The deep voice has me spin around and my breath catches. There, in the middle of the police vessel stands a man I'd recognize anywhere. Arms folded, he glares at me with the same level of recognition. It's the brute from the warehouse in Hong Kong, the one who held the gun to Sean's head.

Nico Dessler.

38

✦ ✦ ✦

CHELSEA

Limassol, Cyprus
~~~~~

His strong body odor precedes Nico climbing onboard Solara's yacht. His hard eyes take me in and manage to chill me to the bone. Deadly silence stands between us as he looks around.

He turns to the officer. "Did you check below?"

"No, sir. Mrs. Doukas asked me not to. She's the wife of a government official."

"Huh, Mrs. Doukas." Nico sneers at me. "Christos is a lucky man indeed."

My best line of defense is to stay quiet.

"Would you like me to check the rest of the yacht, sir?" The officer's voice is barely above a whisper. I might have intimidated him, but he's scared shitless of Nico.

"No, I'll do it." Nico pulls his gun. With one more glance at me, he takes the steps to the quarters below. The area where Bastian and Vitaly are hiding. Now we'll find out how deep Nico's loyalty runs.

I focus on my breathing to keep from screaming. Seconds trickle down in slow motion; they are almost at a standstill. My heart races in my chest and moisture forms on my cupid's bow.

Fuck, what is taking so long?

I lick my lips to fight the dryness in my mouth.

No shots ring out.

No shouts.

No battle of words.

The only sounds are the waves sloshing against the sides of the swaying yacht.

Nico's stench whiffs through the opening to announce his return. I've never been so happy to smell a man's sweat. He holsters the gun and juts his chin at the police vessel. "No one's down there, so let's go."

The coast guard tips his hat again. "Have a good evening, ma'am."

He and Nico cross over to the other ship. As the police boat speeds away, Nico remains standing in the middle of the deck. He locks my gaze; his eyes burn with the knowledge of the inevitable.

As long as Icarus is alive, neither Bastian nor I could ever be free.

39

✴ ✴ ✴

CHELSEA

Gweedore, Ireland
July 2024
~~~~~

The old farmhouse rests on a small hill in one of the most remote areas of County Donegal. The front overlooks the long-ass driveway, and so does Conor's study. Despite the top-notch equipment that secures the property, he likes to keep an eye on things. It's paranoia at its best that has guaranteed that he and the fam have remained safe throughout the years.

When we pull up in the rental, he's out in the yard, pushing a soccer ball around with his feet. I get out of the car just as he takes aim at the goal. The ball rolls forward, but the goalie makes no effort to stop it. Instead, the young boy is frozen in place with his mouth hanging open.

"Mam!"

He flies toward me; by the time I wrap him into a hug, a few tears have escaped and roll down my cheeks. Not even a day has gone by during these past six years when I didn't miss him with every breath.

"Let me take a look at you. You've grown so much."

His arms tighten around me. "Will you be able to stay this time?"

"No, not yet, but it won't be much longer. I promise." I kiss his hair, soaking up his scent. He still smells like the little boy I cradled close to my chest the night I dropped him off with Conor. I want to hold on to him forever.

When I finally release him, I find Bastian's eyes. His face is absolutely flabbergasted.

I tousle my son's hair. "Sean, this is my friend Bastian and his son Vitaly, and well, this is Sean."

Bastian's mouth opens and closes but no sound escapes. He doesn't need to mutter the question for me to understand.

How come your son is still alive?

Conor walks up. In his overalls, the heavy work boots, and the carpet of hair he calls a beard, he looks like any other Irish farmer.

"Conor Doherty." He stretches out his humongous paw and Bastian's hand gets swallowed up in the shake. To my amazement, Bastian keeps a straight face, even if his bones must be screaming in pain.

"Bastian Artino."

Conor juts his chin at my son. "Sean, you were going to check on the horses."

Vitaly's ears perk up. "You got horses?"

"Yeah, we have a whole bunch. Do you wanna see them?"

"I'd love to."

One look at Conor and a nod, and the boys are off into the fields. Conor works his bottom lip with his teeth, his gaze on Bastian. Uncertainty of whether he's a friend or a foe are all too evident in his features.

I got this, I mouth.

He clears his throat. "I'd better check on dinner. Stew should be done soon, so don't be too long."

He disappears inside the house and I lead Bastian to the little bench out back. We sit down and Bastian's question is out before I can even take my next breath.

"How is Sean alive?"

"When it came down to it, Nico couldn't pull the trigger. He and the other Disciple he was with let us go, but he was very clear: if Icarus ever found out that he had gone against direct orders, all of us would be dead. No exception. Your uncle would come after each and every one of us."

Bastian narrows his eyes. "What do you mean he went against direct orders?"

"Sean was never going to walk out of that warehouse alive, even if I had been able to give up Marcel. Icarus wanted to use Sean as a warning that he would stop at nothing, including killing a child, if anyone ever dared to double cross him again."

"I can't believe this." Bastian's hands are balled to fists and his knuckles are white. "I swear I didn't know."

"I believe you, but now you must also realize that the endgame was never revenge. Icarus has to die for us to survive. As long as he's alive, Sean and I can never be together. If he were with me, the risk that Icarus could find out that Nico didn't kill him is too high, so I've been hiding him here. I also owe this to Nico. He spared Sean's life and I couldn't live with myself if Icarus shot him because of it."

Bastian rubs the space above his eyes. "So it's us against the Disciples. We have to kill Icarus for both of our sons to live."

In that moment, Sean and Vitaly come running back toward the house. Their faces are full of life and their chuckles promise a budding friendship.

"I'm already on level thirty and got this really cool gun." Sean's eyes spark with excitement. "You have to see it."

Vitaly's stance is relaxed for the first time since I met him. "My grandpa never let me play video games."

The backdoor to the farmhouse opens and I just hear Conor's grumbled, "Get those muddy boots off" before the door slams closed again.

Bastian bites his lip, his eyes filled with awe.

I want to give him some time to decompress and stand up. "I'm gonna go inside and help Conor with dinner."

The stew smells divine and I soon chat away with Conor about Sean's school and the two new ponies he got for the farm. At some point, Bastian joins us but stays as quiet as a mouse. His gaze drifts back and forth from the sitting room where the boys are playing one of Sean's video games and me in the apron with a little bit of flour stuck to my fingers as I cut the oven-warm bread.

Setting the table, I lean closer. "You okay?"

He nods. "I want this."

"You want what?"

"This." He rotates his arms, which could mean anything from the loaf of bread to the entire house. He still has this *half-in-a-daze* expression and I let him be. He'll snap out of it eventually.

"Boys, dinner is ready."

They don't listen until Conor calls them to order; when they try to sit down, his stern face sends them into the bathroom to wash their hands. I fill everyone's bowl with stew, one eye on the boys and one on Bastian. He seems frozen in place and mostly smiles. Scraping chair legs and chatter signals the start of the meal. Sean leans over the table to finagle a slice of bread.

I swat his hand away. "Ask for it."

"May I please have the bread?"

Better.

I pass him the basket and he snatches a piece to put straight into his mouth. A second one is placed on the table next to his bowl. He holds the basket under Vitaly's nose, dipping the bread into his bowl with his other hand. "Do you want bread, too, Vitaly? You need to dunk it into the stew, then it's sooo good. Conor baked it himself."

Vitaly eagerly takes a slice. "You guys prepare your own food?"

Sean gives him a side-glance. "Of course. Don't you?"

"My grandpa has hired help."

"Well, we aren't that fancy around here." Conor chews in the same slow rhythm as he always does. When he eats, nothing can distract him.

Sean is the exact opposite; he wolfs down the stew as if he hasn't been fed in a week. "Conor, can we play a board game after dinner?"

"Sure."

Vitaly gapes at him. "You guys play board games?"

I want to roll my eyes. What did Icarus ever do to entertain him?

"Since Mam and Bastian are here, we could even play Cluedo."

"What's Cluedo?"

"It's this really cool murder mystery game. You have to find . . ."

I tune out, distracted by Bastian's odd behavior. I nudge him in the side. "Can I talk to you outside for a minute?"

He gets up without a fuss and follows me through the back door into the yard. Standing by the kitchen window, he stares back at the dinner table.

"Bastain, what's wrong?"

He doesn't turn his head. "It's just . . . I don't even know. I never had this."

"Had what?"

He puffs his cheeks. "All this. I never even knew what an ordinary family looks like."

I squeeze his hand. "A family like this is precious, and it's something worth protecting at any price."

40

✳ ✳ ✳

BASTIAN

Gweedore, Ireland
~~~~~

Chuckling under my breath, I pull Chelsea into the bedroom and quietly close the door. She giggles so hard behind her raised hand that her eyes sparkle with tears. The laughter is contagious and spurts of snorting cackles bubble out of me until my sides hurt from a stitch. Since our arrival at the farm a week ago, being silly and just letting go have become cherished moments.

"Man, I'm drenched." I run my fingers through my wet curls.

"I'll get some towels."

Chelsea heads for the ensuite bathroom and returns a few moments later. She's armed with a pile of towels that could dry off an army. Still smiling, I attack my wet hair. Chelsea shivers as she peels off her clothes, although I don't mind at all what the cold does to her tits. Her nipples are hard and alert, just screaming to be sucked. Add my throbbing cock that has been stuck in an aroused state since we started our walk through the fields, and it takes some effort not to bend her over the bed and fuck her.

Pulling the wet shirt over my head, I ogle her chest. Hard rain whips against the window and the wind howls like a siren. "I can't believe it just started raining like this. It's crazy. We were just watching the stars and then . . . boom."

"That's Irish weather for you." Chelsea tosses the towel on the bed and pulls down her panties.

Motherfucker!

I close my eyes, though I'm not entirely sure she isn't full-on teasing me.

Keep your cool, Artino.

We can't keep fucking like rabbits caught in our own pink bubble. Life will catch up with us sooner rather than later and we need to be prepared.

In the next breath, all my good intentions go out the window. Chelsea's warm lips capture my erection and she sucks the arousal off the tip with a wet *pop*.

Fuck, this is good.

I open my eyes and gaze down; the sight of her on her knees, totally submissive, gets my cock to jump. She licks the length of my shaft, gently squeezing my balls, and I have to suck the air through gritted teeth to suppress a groan.

She grins. "Remember, we have to be absolutely quiet or we'll wake up the whole house."

"Oh, I remember."

Though that's easier said than done when a woman gets down on you and swallows your full length.

Not only that.

She takes me so deeply that I shudder. Her eyes shimmer with a mischievous glow. She's challenging me to give her a good mouth fuck.

Still allowing her enough control to stop at any time, I thrust into her mouth as if it were her dripping wet pussy. She guides my hips to force me even deeper. Her lips are sealed around my shaft, providing an amazing friction that raises the heat in my core. I'm about ready to combust. The downpour hammers onto the roof in a steady rhythm, mimicking my movements.

As I push faster and harder into her mouth, hot flashes run through me. Lust takes over my existence.

Fuck, those lips.

I claw my fingers into her short hair to prolong the inevitable. Driving me against the wall, ignoring a *clink* as my phone drops to the ground, she takes full control of the action. A few more deep thrusts and fireworks go off behind my eyelids. As waves of pleasure set my nerve ends on fire, the height of my orgasm is prolonged by her swallowing my cum. My knees turn weak; as soon as she releases me, I stumble to the bed. Wiping my hand across my face, I catch my breath.

Fuck, the woman will be the end of me.

"Did you enjoy it?" Chelsea is still on her knees, my arousal glistening on her lips.

I beckon her closer with my finger. "You ambushed me. That was a bad girl."

"Aw." She pouts. "Do I get a spanking?"

"Oh, you want me to smack your ass?"

It's a rhetorical question. The gleam of desire in her eyes leaves no doubt that a good spanking is exactly what she wants.

I lick my lips. "Get on the bed."

As she crawls onto the covers and wiggles her ass, my cock is already hard again. Exhaling a shaky breath, I raise my arm.

My flat hand comes down on her butt cheek with a *smack*. She groans.

Crap. "Was that too hard?"

"No, but you almost made me come."

I massage the redness on her skin. As the tension leaves her body, I take another strike. She quivers with a soft moan. I rub the sore spot, my fingers exploring her folds. Her arousal seeps out of her. She is so ready that I feel compelled to take pity on her.

I flip her over and spread her legs. Blowing onto her swollen clit, I grin. "Remember, you need to be as quiet as a mouse or you'll wake up the boys."

She gives me this *fuck off* look but pulls a pillow closer. Pushing two fingers inside her, I explore her wet canal; the friction is by far not enough and I add a third finger. Her muscles clench around me.

Now we're talking.

I move slowly, relishing how her pupils dilate as the heat builds. She bites into the pillow, throwing back her head. Muffled moans still escape, but the wind rattles the shutters on the window hard enough to drown out the sounds of pleasure.

Yeah, come for me, baby.

I bury my nose into her heat and lick her hard clit. Her arousal zings salty on my tongue. Sucking her sweet spot, I give her the finger fuck of a lifetime. Her lust sings on my skin, sending throbs of pleasure to my shaft. When she becomes undone, her muscles tighten around me, the pillow barely able to hide her screams. She shakes so hard that her body almost convulses. I devour her overwhelming euphoria with greed, pushing myself over the edge with a couple of strokes of my cock. Cocooned in my own bliss, I keep my lips on her clit and my fingers in her wet pussy until both our aftershocks have died down.

She pulls me onto the bed and wraps my arms around her. "Sleep?"

"That is probably a good idea."

"Nah, I was just kidding." She pushes me onto my back and mounts me. "Once it stops raining, we can go outside again and you can show me the rest of the milky way."

I do like the sound of that. "And if it rains all night?"

"Then we'll just have to fuck all night."

41

✳ ✳ ✳

BASTIAN

Gweedore, Ireland
~~~~~

Waking up with the biggest sex hangover is worse than consuming a bottle of whiskey. I'm sore and drained of all energy, and the overstimulating euphoria I experienced after a dozen orgasms has left my soul raw and exposed. For the first time in my life, it hurts to release a woman from my embrace and see her walk into the bathroom. The coldness left behind on my skin sends dread to the pit of my stomach.

I don't want to lose her.

And the worst part is, I have not the slightest idea if she feels the same way about me.

What if she's just playing with me?

Tears well in my eyes and I cringe at my own vulnerability. Frantically wiping through my face, I try to hide my distress, but Chelsea catches me red handed.

She squints at me. "Bastian, what's wrong?"

"Nothing."

"Are you crying?"

"Of course not." I'm a man, taught to never shed a tear. At least not in public.

She drops on the bed. "Come here."

I allow her to wrap her arms around my midsection, though I avoid her gaze by turning my back to her. She's seen enough display of weakness.

Her embrace tightens. "You're shaking."

Don't lose it.

I control my breathing, inhaling especially deep and exhaling through relaxed lips. The tension doesn't ease.

She strokes my chest. "Do you want to talk about it?"

There's nothing to talk about.

I close my eyes. Sooner or later, she'll have to know the truth if I want any chance at a relationship. A secret like this would poison us otherwise. "You asked me once about Olivia, whether I was upset when she started to date Konstantin."

"Yes, I remember."

"The thing is that she never *didn't* date Konstantin."

"Oh." She stiffens. "So you and her had an affair?"

"Not exactly. She, Konstantin, and I, we were sort of in a relationship."

"All three of you?"

"Yes. We were living together and everything."

Awkward silence settles between us. "Well, it's different from what I'm used to, but I don't generally judge."

I free myself from her arms and turn around. "You don't understand. It wasn't by choice."

Her brows knit together. "What do you mean?"

Okay, where do I start?

"When I was fourteen, I ran away from home."

"Why?"

So maybe I should go back even further.

"I guess it all began when my dad refused to marry the woman my grandpa had picked out for him. Back then, arranged marriages were common and always furthered the best interest of the Disciples. Because my dad wasn't first in line to take over as head of the organization, my grandpa let it slide, so my father moved to the States and then met my mom. They had me and that's when Dad panicked. He knew that as a male Pappas' heir, I would get sucked into a world of crime eventually, so he legally changed our last name and tried to break off all contact. He almost succeeded, but my grandma convinced him to send me to Cyprus during the summers to get to know my roots. My father was big on traditions and agreed as long as I wasn't exposed to the dealings of the Disciples."

Chelsea clicks her tongue, her face expressing the obvious. My father was a fool for ever thinking that this could work out in his favor.

I pinch the bridge of my nose. "In all fairness, my grandparents did keep their end of the bargain and never directly exposed me to the Disciples. However, there was also Konstantin. He was twelve years older than me and the cool cousin. Fuck, growing up, I worshiped him."

"I guess he was like a big brother."

"I suppose. Anyhow, when I was about six, Konstantin moved to New York to start college. That's when he began seeing me behind my father's back. I had to lie to my parents, pretending I was meeting up with friends or had after-school sports practice, so I could spend time with him. Konstantin and I did the coolest things, we went to the zoo and rode the roller coasters on Long Island. As I grew older, he encouraged me to stand up for myself, teaching me stuff like boxing and karate. I was always small for my age and was picked on by bullies, so he made me feel empowered. He showed me how to shoot a gun. All in all, he was probably the biggest influence during my formative years and all through middle school."

"And I assume that impacted your relationship with your dad?"

I snort. That's an understatement. "I was angry all the time and the only weeks of the year I felt truly free were the months I spent in Cyprus. It all came to a head when I was fourteen and my father found out what I had been doing behind his back. He prohibited me from hanging out with Konstantin and we had an ugly fight. It was the first time my dad ever hit me—slapped me right across the face—and I saw red. Packed up whatever fit in my backpack and left."

"And let me guess. You went straight to Konstantin."

"Exactly. He and Liv took me in, and Konstantin got a lawyer involved the next day. With a little bit of prompting, I signed an affidavit that stated that my dad had been abusing me for years and I had a bruise to prove it. Konstantin was awarded guardianship, and when my parents tried to fight him, my grandpa got involved. He sent a few Disciples after my dad, warning him to let me make my own decisions. My parents tried to reach out a few times, but I was too stubborn to listen. Konstantin was treating me like an adult, and I wasn't going to go back to being a child." My chuckle is bitter; I was such an idiot and the final joke was on me.

"And your parents backed off?"

"They had to. My dad knew what the Disciples were capable of and he didn't want to risk my mom's life. I didn't care, I got what I wanted and felt on top of the world. All was good for about a year, but then, shortly after I turned fifteen, I was initiated as a Disciple. That's when Konstantin and Liv also decided they needed a new sex toy. It's when the abuse started."

Chelsea gulps. "They forced you to have sex with them?"

Ugly tears rise again and I turn my head. My throat closes; I choke on the words. The worst images of my nightmares find their way into my head; the memories of me being strapped in the sex swing with Konstantin fucking me while ramming my dick into Liv's pussy are so vivid that they send splinters of pain straight through my chest. I weep in silence; the tears flowing heavy. I can't form one single coherent thought that doesn't involve torment. Only Chelsea's rotating strokes on my back keep me grounded enough not to shut down. After what seems like an eternity, her tender touch even calms me.

"It went on for eleven years. Eleven years, three months, and twenty-one days, to be exact, until Anton saved me. I had just graduated law school and was given my own crew, and Anton was assigned to be my bodyguard. It only took him a couple of weeks to figure out what was going on, so one night, he showed up on Konstantin's doorsteps and told him I was moving out. Of course, Konstantin wasn't having it, but you've seen Anton. He is a big dude and his glare even gave Konstantin a pause, though Anton's threat that he'd tell Icarus the truth was likely the deciding factor. I packed my bags that same day, but it came at a steep price. I had to leave Vitaly behind and barely saw him after that."

"That must have been hard."

I swallow down fresh tears. "He was barely seven and considered Konstantin his dad. I was only Babá, a word that might mean father but was part of a language he didn't understand and had therefore little meaning to him. I doubt he truly missed me." I stand up and walk to the window. Outside in the yard, Vitaly and Sean are kicking a ball around, though they appear to be chit-chatting more than playing.

Stepping behind me, Chelsea leans into me, her hand resettling on my chest. Her cheek is wet against my skin. "I'm so sorry that you had to go through this."

"It's strange, even after I left, I never felt free until the day they died in the car bombing."

"Maybe you were scared that they would get control of you again, and that fear only dissolved with their death."

I stroke her hand. She so gets it.

Her soft lips on my spine send warm tingles through my body. "And I'm also sorry if I ever made you feel uncomfortable when we were having sex."

"You didn't." Anton saved me in that respect, too. He showed me that sex can actually feel good, especially once I allowed myself to be in control. "And . . ." For a beat, the words stall on my tongue. "You are the first person who ever let me be me. Enjoy the moment without strings or baggage." I laugh through more tears. "I'm probably not making any sense."

"No, you're making perfect sense and I'm glad I can share this experience with you."

Footsteps ring on the stairs and a "Mam" has Chelsea dive for cover behind the bed. "Don't come in, Sean."

I grimace. Encountering two naked people smelling like sex, one of them his mother, could be a life-altering experience.

"Mam, Conor wants to show Vitaly how to ride a horse. Can he?"

Fuck, if my son is getting riding lessons, I won't be far behind. "Not without me, Sean. I want to learn, too."

"Great, then maybe we can all take a ride together down to the lake?" Hope colors Sean's words.

I exchange a glance with Chelsea. She smirks, the spark in her eyes hinting that she'd relish some more family time with the potential of me making a fool out of myself by falling off a horse. "Just give us fifteen minutes and we'll be right down."

42

✳ ✳ ✳

BASTIAN

Gweedore, Ireland
~~~~~

Galloping along the path, I wobble on the horse but manage to hold on. If it weren't for my sore ass that sends painful waves up my spine with every stomp of the mare's hoof, this riding experience would be actual fun. I long to return to the farm, put my feet up, play one of the board games, and later, in bed, get a massage to reward my efforts. Chelsea leads the front of the line and I'd gladly follow her as long as I get to spend some time as a family.

Looking over his shoulder, Vitaly beams at me. "Isn't this great, Babá?"

The sparkle of joy in his eyes is breathtaking. I nod. "Does your butt hurt?"

"No, does yours?"

I want to roll my eyes.

Man, I'm getting old.

"No, I was just wondering."

The walls of the farmhouse appear in the distance; at least, this torture will be over soon. When I finally dismount the mare, my legs are in this odd limbo between tingling and numbness. My back is killing me, but I smile like a champ. No way I'm going to reveal the true state of my body. Conor, Sean, and Vitaly disappear inside the stables to clean and feed the horses. I stretch until my joints pop.

Chelsea grins. "Your ass hurts, doesn't it?"

"Is it that obvious?"

"Oh, yeah."

"I feel like a total loser." Or at least like the uncoolest dad in history.

"Don't worry, it's normal." She gets on her tiptoes and pecks my lips. "And it's nothing a hot bubble bath and some tender loving care can't fix."

"Oh, I like the sound of that."

"But first things first. The boys will be starving soon and I could use a cup of tea."

"If you insist."

We walk back to the house with our fingers entwined and rid ourselves of our boots and jackets. I stretch out on the sofa; Chelsea gets busy with the kettle and the cups for the tea.

"Green tea again?"

I nod. "With a little bit of honey."

Five minutes later, a steaming cup stands in front of me and I sip the hot liquid. The spreading warmth in my stomach radiates all the way into my lower back. The pain eases and just like so many times over these past four days, I'm totally relaxed.

This is the life.

It can't get any better.

The back door opens and the boys trudge in, chatter soon fills the air as they discuss what we should have for dinner.

With a grunt, I get to my feet. Time to pull my weight around here. "How about I cook some Greek food tonight?"

Chelsea lifts a brow. "You cook?"

"Of course."

Conor scratches his beard. "Not sure if we have the ingredients."

I smirk; he is as Irish as they come. Even pizza is exotic for him. "As long as you have chicken, rice, yogurt, cucumber and garlic, I'm all set." I can whip us up some chicken souvlaki with tzatziki.

Conor opens up the fridge. "Yep, that's all here."

"Then let me get to work."

I head to the sink to wash my hands, just as the boys drag Chelsea into the second living room for a round of video games. Conor rummages through his coat pockets and pulls out a little paper bag, placing it on the counter as he sits down on a barstool. Most people would have to pull themselves up, but Conor is so tall that the stool appears short.

He juts his chin at the paper bag. "Chelsea asked me to get your pain medication and I got the prescription filled this morning."

"Oh, thank you." In the last few days, the migraines have been manageable, although they will probably flare up again once I stress out. That has been the usual pattern. Filling up a pot with water for the rice, I set it on the stove and flick the switch to turn on the gas.

What's next?

I should probably mince the garlic. Getting a cutting board and a knife, I stop in my tracks. "Sorry, Conor, I hope it's okay if I take over your kitchen."

"It's more than okay." He slurps from the cup of tea Chelsea made for him.

As I peel the cloves of garlic, I glance up from time to time; he keeps scratching his beard and appears to be deep in thought. I slice the garlic, uneasy about the silence.

"So, Conor, other than running the farm, what do you do?"

"Cyber operations."

"Is that the same as cyber security?"

When his dark eyes cut into me, I detect a certain wariness.

"It's the opposite. Companies pay me to break into their systems to flush out weaknesses."

So he's a hacker. Now it makes sense how he could collect the information on the Disciples and evaded detection. "Are you any good at it?" A rhetorical question. Anyone who's called an IT god by Falk Herrera knows their shit.

"I've been told that I am."

"And is there money in it?"

Conor takes a sip from the tea, his gaze fixed on my knife annihilating the garlic into the smallest pieces. "Let's cut to the chase. We both don't trust each other, a fact I'm willing to set aside for Chelsea's sake, but make no mistake. If you betray her or hurt her in any way, I *will* find you and destroy you. I might not be able to shoot a gun or handle a knife the way you do, but I can locate anyone in the world, rob them blind without them even knowing or destroy their identities. If push comes to shove, I could even erase your name out of every database, making it appear as if you never existed, so you better think twice before doing anything shady."

I chuckle under my breath. "I've gotten my share of threats, but I have to admit, yours is probably one of the scarier examples." I find his eyes. "And I have no intentions to betray or hurt Chelsea." To the contrary; if someone will end up getting hurt, it's likely to be me.

"I'm glad to hear that."

"And you're mistaken. I *do* trust you, or I would never consider leaving my son with you."

He slowly nods. "Then what are the next steps?"

"I'm expecting a full-blown turf war any day now. Once that happens, Chelsea and I can move in for the kill." It'll be the best time to strike since the Disciples will be too distracted to see us coming.

"I haven't picked up much chatter. Are you sure this turf war is still happening?"

"Positive." It's the quiet before the storm. By now, the Albanian clans are striking allegiances to attack as one, a move that will wipe the Disciples out for good.

"Then let's hope your plan will work." Conor sips his tea with a blank expression. I don't know him well enough to determine if I convinced him or whether he simply closed down.

"But there's something I need you to do. It's to get Jackson Pierce off Chelsea's back."

That gets his attention. "What is it?"

"Just a sec." The water on the stove is boiling; I'm about to grab the bag of rice out of the cabinet when my phone chimes. One glance confirms it's from Nico. I dry my hands on a towel and open the message.

They know where you are. Get out.

43

✷ ✷ ✷

BASTIAN

Gweedore, Ireland
~~~~~

Conor cups his hands around Sean's shoulders. "You know the drill we have been practicing? This is the real deal. You've got ten minutes to get ready."

Sean gulps. His gaze flicks to Chelsea. "What about Mam?"

"For now, she can't come." Conor shakes him gently to regain his attention. "You need to be strong now, for all of us. No tears or crap to make your mother feel bad. Understood?"

He nods and Conor lets go of his shoulders. When Sean turns to leave the room, moisture sparkles in his eyes. Vitaly's forehead is one big crease; he looks utterly confused.

I nudge him toward the door. "Go with Sean."

My son shakes his head. "I want to know what's going on."

Chelsea and I exchange a glance. Even though there's little time, Vitaly will turn stubborn if I don't provide some answers. At twelve, I used to think that I knew everything and adults were total morons who didn't have a clue.

I pull him through the kitchen into the backyard. We sit down on the bench. He chews his lip, his gaze expectant. If

Konstantin taught me anything, respecting my son now enough to trust him with the truth will be crucial to ensure his cooperation.

"Vitaly, did Icarus ever talk to you about the Disciples and what they do?"

"He said they are my future. That I'd be helping him soon to run things."

I close my eyes. I got that exact same spiel a few months before my initiation. "Do you know that most of what we do is illegal?"

Avoiding my gaze, he nods.

"Do you know specifics?"

"Sell weapons."

So he has no idea about the drugs and the human trafficking. "Did Icarus ever tell you what's involved in order to become a Disciple?"

He shakes his head.

Good.

I let out a shaky breath. "The bottom line is that they are after me because I took you. Now that they found us, the farm is no longer safe."

He raises his head. "Are they after Sean and Conor, too?"

"Yes."

"Why?"

My head is swimming. This conversation is turning into a train wreck and I have no clue how to avoid a collision. "It'll take too long to explain, but Icarus wants Sean dead."

Vitaly's forehead wrinkles.

I take his hand. "I've never lied to you, so you need to believe me when I tell you that Icarus is not a good person." My gaze is drilling. "I don't doubt that he loves you very much, but he'll turn you into a killer."

My son avoids eye contact and tucks his lip back between his teeth.

My neck prickles with dark suspicion. "But then, you already knew that, didn't you, Vitaly?"

A few tears drop on his hand.

"You lied earlier. Grandpa *did* tell you what you need to do in order to become a Disciple, didn't he?"

A sob shakes my son's body. "He said I'll get to kill Mom and Dad's murderer. That it will make me feel better afterward."

A surreal buzzing spreads in my ears. According to my intel, the Bajris are dead, so for Icarus, Konstantin and Liv's killers have been brought to justice. Unless . . .

I refuse to go down that rabbit hole. There's no way he knows the truth. His assertion was clearly a ploy to make Vitaly's first kill more manageable. It's always easier to pull the trigger when there's a purpose.

"Do you understand now why you have to leave with Conor and Sean?"

He raises his tear-stricken face. "I want to stay with you."

The hope in his eye tears at my heartstrings. If I don't allow it, he'll feel abandoned, but I simply can't risk taking him with us on the run. "It's too dangerous to go with me." There's a chance I won't make it. I squeeze his hand. "Besides, I need you to look after Sean. Like a big brother. Promise me you'll do that."

He nods, wiping away the tears.

I tousle his hair. "Then let's go inside and get ready."

He obliges without further fuss. As we stuff random items into a backpack, I eye him like a time bomb. His gaze is vacant and I sense he's not fully onboard with the plan, but he also doesn't complain or try to get his way by nagging. It's as if he has shut down and accepted his fate for now, just to rebel eventually. Conor might be in for more than he bargained for.

When we get to Conor's truck and place his bag in the back, he turns away and slides into the truck before I can hug him goodbye. Sean is clinging to Chelsea but holds the tears at bay. She talks softly to him and seems to have more success in convincing him to do what needs to be done. Conor juts his chin in our direction, causing Sean to join Vitaly in the backseat. He closes the door.

Conor comes over to where Chelsea and I are waiting; it's well out of earshot of the truck. "You got everything?"

She nods. "Key to the deposit box and the new bankcard for funds."

"Make sure you destroy your phone chip before you go. From here on out, the only contact will be by encrypted email."

"I know the drill, Conor." Chelsea's voice is close to cracking and she tosses him an impatient look.

"Seventy-two hours. Not a minute more." Conor switches his attention to me and extends his hand. "You take good care of her."

"And you take good care of Vitaly."

We shake hands with a mutual understanding. In that moment, we each entrust the person who is most important to us to the other.

I step to the car and Vitaly lowers the window.

"I'll see you soon."

He nods but neither responds nor looks at me.

Fuck, how to get through to him.

"I love you, Vitaly."

This time, he doesn't as much as acknowledge me. The truck rolls forward; when the back tires spin, they leave Chelsea and me in a cloud of dust. My gaze stays on the backlights of the car all the way down the long driveway. They briefly light up as Conor pulls onto the main road. The truck disappears from view.

Chelsea wipes her face dry on her sleeve. "We should hurry and get out of here."

Since Nico sent the text, fifteen minutes have passed and we won't have a lot of time.

"What did Conor mean by seventy-two hours?"

"That's our check-in window. If we miss that, he'll assume we are either dead or captured, and he'll send everything he has on the Disciples to the authorities."

"Does he keep the info on his laptop?"

She snorts. "Conor has everything triple backed up in the cloud and has his own check-in contacts. One way or the other, the Disciples are going to go down regardless whether we make it or not."

At least there'll be some form of justice, even if I'd end up on the losing side.

"Alright, then let's get going."

Our bags are quickly packed and I haul everything to the rental that's parked out back. Popping the trunk, I let my gaze travel across the barn and the fields. I'll miss this place dearly.

"What about the horses?"

Chelsea looks up from her phone. "The neighbors will take care of them."

At least they won't have to be uprooted.

"Ready?"

"Yep."

Lifting her foot, she smashes her phone under her boot. The screen shatters into a million pieces; Chelsea kneels down to pick up the chip that has been forced out the casing and breaks it in half. If it weren't for the occasional text message from Nico, I'd probably do the same. In the commotion and the hasty departure, we never determined how the Disciples found us.

About to open the door of the car, a loud *pop* goes off inside the house. A flashing light rotates over the back door.

Chelsea tenses beside me. "That was the intruder alarm. Someone is coming up the driveway."

44

✴ ✴ ✴

CHELSEA

Gweedore, Ireland
~~~~~

Grabbing the small backpack with my wallet and essentials from the car, I run into the house. Bastian is right on my heels.

Where to?

The basement.

During one of my rare visits to the farm, Conor had shown me the shelter.

It's the only hiding place where we have a remote chance of survival.

I tear the basement door open, just as a car brakes on the loose gravel out front. Bastian steps to one of the windows and peeks through a gap in the drawn curtains.

"Definitely Disciples."

"Let's go." With one foot on the first step down the steep staircase, I cringe at the creak screaming from the wood.

We'll need to hurry or the old house will give us away. I make good progress, but Bastian is still at the top, frozen with his gun in his hand.

"What are you doing?" I hiss. "We need to hide."

"Don't you think we should take our chances up here?"

"No. We will be outnumbered." And I don't even have a weapon.

Bastian finally begins his descent down the stairs, closing the basement door in the same second the front door is kicked in. Steps pound on the hardwood floor in the living room.

A loud crack springs from underneath Bastian's foot, but it's drowned out by Anton's shout. "Search every corner of the house. I want them found."

Bastian takes the brief commotion to tackle the basement stairs. Three more steps and the loudest whine of wood shatters a sudden moment of deadly silence from above.

"Did you hear something?" Nico's deep, throaty voice is unmistakable.

"It sounded as if it were coming from behind that door. I'll check it out." Anton's words are sharp. He has taken charge. "Go and check the outside. They might be hiding in the barn."

Bastian leaps down the last few steps and pulls me behind the dryer. The basement door squeaks on its hinges. I hold my breath. About halfway down, we will be in open sight. The chirping of the birds, a sound I usually love, drifting through the ajar window hacks away at my nerves.

Anton cocks the gun with lethal intent. He might spare Bastian to interrogate him, but I'm out of chances. As he slowly descends down the stairs, the wood groans under his weight. Bastian raises his Glock. I squeeze my eyes shut.

The sounds of an old-fashioned ringtone hit my eardrums. The groans pause and Anton's "talk to me" gives us a temporary respite.

"I think they might still be here. Pot on the stove was warm and the teacups were half empty. If they left, it was in a hurry. Falk is checking out the computer to see if he can find anything useful and we are searching the house." Silence. "Icarus?" More silence. "I'm in the basement and the connection is really bad. Let me go outside and I'll call you right back."

Anton's footsteps move in the opposite direction and fade into silence. The basement door closes with a *thump*. It's now or never.

I leave my hiding place and run my fingers along the panel of the wall.

Where is that damn switch? And is it even this wall?

Shit.

I gaze around.

Focus!

I close my eyes, replaying the memory in my head. Conor had taken me down here.

The shelter is the perfect hiding spot. All you have to do is flip this little switch and the wall will open right up.

My mind throws a blank about the location of the switch. Panic wells in my chest.

C'mon, Chelsea, think.

My fingers search panel after panel, but all I end up with is a splinter and a small cut.

Fuck.

Anton's voice is back by the door. "I'll call you as soon as I have an update."

Clack.

The wall swings back without the slightest sound. I push Bastian inside the small space and replace the panels. Since I'm not sure whether the room is one hundred percent sealed off, I don't turn on the lights. The darkness threatens to crush me. Bastian's breath against my ear is strained with tension.

The creaking wood announces Anton's return. He walks through the basement and even opens the dryer. A barked "fuck," followed by a loud *bang* of shaking metal vent his frustration.

"Anton, you down there?" Falk's voice gets closer with every word.

"Yeah. Did you find anything?"

"Hard drive was fried and there were connecting cables for a laptop. The dude probably backed everything up to the cloud as well."

"Fuck." Anton's curse is like a growl. The wall that separates us vibrates from a blow. "What about Michail?"

"He found nothing. Face it, they're gone."

"Fuck." A cigarette lighter clicks and a whiff of smoke blends with the stale air of our hiding space. "Get Nico and Michail down here. We need to realign."

The ticking seconds stretch into minutes. I'm scared to inhale too deeply or even lick my lips. My nose itches from the smoke. Anton moves around the basement, spitting out mumbled curses and punishing the appliances with a few kicks. The wall quivers as several people join him.

"Did you find anything outside, Nico?"

"Half a dozen horses in the barn and a second car in the driveway. Engine was cold, so they must've left with a second vehicle."

"The perimeters were secured by a top-notch protection system," Falk enlightens the group. "However, that doesn't explain how they knew we were coming."

"They were obviously tipped off," Anton rumbles.

"But who would tip them off?"

"Who indeed?" A bullet moves into a chamber.

"Hey, what are you doing, man?" Nico's voice carries a slight edge.

"Where's your phone, Nico?"

Bastian tenses behind me.

"Right here."

"Unlock it."

I force my eyes shut, though that doesn't kill the sounds outside.

"Michail, search him. He might have a second phone."

I squeeze Bastian's arm. He has to do something.

His lips are right on my ear. "Not a sound."

"Oh, look, I was right." I can practically see Anton's triumphant smirk. "Let's see what we got here. Last message was sent not even thirty minutes ago. *They know where you are. Get out.* I guess we found our traitor."

"You should be on Bastian's side. Vitaly is his kid. Besides, didn't you and him have a thing?"

Anton sighs. "Yeah, but then he decided he likes pussy better than dick. And this is not about Bastian but simple loyalty. You fucking betrayed us."

In the next breath, a shot rings out. It hurts my ears and slices through my frayed nerves. My gasp is silenced by Bastian's hand over my mouth. I try to breathe into the sudden pain in my heart, fighting the tears that prick under my eyelids.

Nico risked his life for me and Sean.

And I didn't do the same.

Now he is dead.

Bastian's grip is iron-clad and his hand on my lips prevents me from screaming. On the other side of the wall, deadly quiet has settled.

Finally, a voice I've never heard before speaks up. "What should we do now, Anton?"

"Light up the place. If they are still here, we'll smoke them out.

45

✳ ✳ ✳

CHELSEA

Gweedore, Ireland
~~~~~

Nico's glassy stare spawns a revolt in my stomach. I refuse to look away, a dull ache pounding in my chest. He didn't hesitate to save me and Sean, but when it came down to the wire, I couldn't help him.

Bastian blinks away the moisture in his eyes. Hunkering down, he forces Nico's eyelids closed. A few words I can't make out are mumbled under his breath. It must be so much harder for him; they worked together for so many years and put their lives in each other's hands. That it was Anton who shot him must be the ultimate betrayal.

I squeeze his shoulder. "I'm sorry."

"He knew the risks."

"That doesn't make it okay."

"No, it doesn't." He looks up, his face chiseled in stone. "And I'm gonna get Anton for this, but for now, we have bigger problems. How are we gonna get out of here?"

I check my watch. It has been ten minutes since I made the call to the fire station and five since the shattered Molotov cocktails set the kitchen and living room ablaze. Heat creeps through the ceiling. It won't take much longer for the beams to cave and the fire to spread to the basement.

Where are the damn fire trucks?

"We have to call Conor."

"He said no more phone calls. Besides, how exactly is he going to help us?"

"Our families were involved in the IRA movement and his grandpa used to hide fugitives at the farm. There might be a way to escape we don't know about." I stretch out my hand for his cell. Desperate time calls for desperate measures and it might be our only chance.

With a frustrated exhale, Bastian passes me his phone. I dial Conor's number; it takes forever for him to answer. Plaster breaks off the ceiling and falls on my head just as his gruff "hello" drifts through the line.

"We are trapped in the basement and need a way out."

"Trapped how?"

I grimace; there's no easy way to tell him that his childhood home is being reduced to rubble. "The Disciples set the house on fire. I called down to the station, but I'm not sure the fire trucks will get here in time."

"Fuck."

Flames lick through the bottom gap of the door. So far, we've been shielded from the smoke, but that will change as soon as the door surrenders to the blaze. After that, we'll be in real trouble.

"Do you remember the little shelter in the basement?"

"That's where we were hiding earlier."

"In the left-hand corner is a hatch. Behind it is a tunnel that takes you to the barn. Make sure to let the horses out. I'll call the neighbor and he'll keep them for now."

"Okay."

"And get rid of the damn phone. They're probably tracking you as we speak." He hangs up without another word.

A *bang* blows the door off its hinges. There goes the gas stove. Fire rolls down the steep steps, licking dangerously close to my feet. Bastian jumps back.

"We need to go." His voice trembles with panic.

My gaze flicks to Nico. I'm tempted to drag his body with us, but that could seriously impede our escape.

Bastian squeezes my arm. "There's nothing we can do for him anymore."

Except for a proper funeral.

The smoke stinging my lungs makes the decision for me. Lightheadedness rushes to my head and I cover my mouth and nose with the sleeve of my jumper. Signaling for Bastian to follow me, I return to the small shelter. The torch of his phone reflects off the little metal hatch in the wall. It'll be a tight squeeze. I push back the latch and the door swings open with a squeak.

Smoke and heat from behind blast into the room, triggering a wild coughing fit. The dizziness sends a surreal buzzing to my ears. Every breath is an effort and my legs are heavy, barely strong enough to keep me upright. Bastian shoves me toward the opening; in my haste, I scrape my forehead on the rough edges. Pain shoots into my skull and clears the cobwebs from my head. A boost of adrenaline does the rest. Climbing into the tunnel, I crawl forward on my hands and knees. The ground is dry and a sand cloud stings my eyes. I take shallow breaths to avoid slowing down.

Bastian is right on my heels—literally—and his hands on my butt force me to scramble faster. It's the most unerotic intimacy and almost makes me laugh. Stupid as it is, his touch keeps me focused. With everything that has happened in the past hour, I'd lose my shit otherwise.

The heat and smoke in the tunnel become unbearable; my arms and legs are so weak that I'm about to collapse. Sudden sparks of light illuminating the exit releases another boost of adrenaline. I crawl faster until the top of my head collides with a bale of hay. Pushing it to the side eats up the rest of my strength. I drop onto the floor of the stables, panting to catch my breath. The world is spinning and I'm nauseous, my shirt and pants so sweaty that they stick to me like a second skin. The blaring sirens of the fire trucks pulling up to the farm rip painfully into my eardrums.

Bastian's condition is significantly better than mine; he looks as if he just stepped off the treadmill after some light, rejuvenating exercise. Ducking behind the large mower at the entrance of the barn, he peeks outside.

"The firefighters arrived."

Thank you, I'm not deaf.

At least not yet.

"Any sign of Anton or the other Disciples?"

"Nope, but I'm sure they are hiding and watching the house."

"Will they shoot us in front of witnesses?"

Bastian snorts. "Anton doesn't give a fuck about witnesses. He has an exit strategy, even if the whole country is looking for him."

So we are trapped once again. My gaze falls on the stable boxes.

"If the horses got loose, do you think Anton would watch them?"

Bastian turns around. "Probably not. Falk doesn't handle guns, so it's just him and Michail. Their main attention will be on the front and the back of the house."

"So we could ride out of here?"

He grimaces. "What if I fall off?"

"Running out to the car and hoping that Anton or Michail will miss you is the other option. Take your pick." I grin as I take a saddle off the stand.

"If you put it that way . . ."

Five minutes later, the mares are saddled and ready to go. I open the backdoor of the stables. Slapping the behind of Conor's stallion who is their usual lead, I prompt him to gallop across the field. The other horses follow without hesitation; as my mare steps out in the open, I swing myself into the saddle. Bending closer to keep my body low, I kick the mare's flanks and pick up speed. The other horses serve as superb coverage as the distance grows between me and the farm.

Please, don't let Anton shoot all of us down.

When I glance over my shoulder, I can't suppress a snicker. Bastian is bouncing up and down in the saddle, his face contorted in pain, though he manages to hold on. We reach the neighboring field and disappear behind a hedge. This should put us out of shooting range, even if Anton or Michail have a rifle.

I follow the path down to the neighbor's farm and dismount the horse in the backyard. The stallion did a good job; he baited all the other horses to follow him and grazes as if the lawn belonged to him.

A man steps out on the porch, an Irish sheepdog and a shotgun by his side. He wears overalls, boots, and a wool cap, his gaze assessing in an otherwise indifferent face. "Are you Chelsea?"

I nod.

"Conor called. He said you had a gas explosion?"

"I think the whole house might've burned down."

The man clicks his tongue. "All that modern technology can't help you with that one."

Except for the cell phone that brought the fire brigade on scene before the flames could spread to his property.

I offer him a smile. "We're going to stay with relatives for a few days. Do you have a second car we could borrow?"

"You can take my wife's car. She went with her friends to Mallorca for a hen party, so she won't be back for a week." He spits on the ground. "Not sure why a lass needs to waste that type of money when they are on their third marriage, but I'm no expert. Just minding my own business, as usual."

He's lucky that he isn't on his third marriage with that type of attitude.

Still smiling, I accept the offered keys. "Thank you."

"No worries." He turns toward the horses. "I'll keep them in the enclosure until Conor can get them sorted."

"Much appreciated." Walking toward the cars, I halt in my tracks.

Shit, it's a freaking Fiat Punto.

In lime green.

Now I'd love to meet his wife.

"I hope I won't bump my head," Bastian grumbles as he passes me. He's limping and when he fastens his seatbelt, he doesn't put the full weight on his ass. Poor baby needs a butt massage.

With a smirk, I get behind the wheel and start the engine. Pulling onto the main road, I take the route toward Bunbeg that won't take us by Conor's farm. Four tight bends later, we are on a long stretch of road that goes on for at least a mile. I'm about to sigh in relief when a car speeds up behind us. The driver tailgates us with their lights flashing; my money is on a youngster who just got their license and thinks the roads belong to them. The windows of the car are tinted, barring me from confirming my suspicion.

Just before the next bend, the driver swings into the other lane. I slow a little to let them pass. As the car pulls side by side, the back window is lowered. The reflection of the sun ricocheting off metal draws a quick glance over my shoulder.

I freeze.

The barrel of a gun is pointed right at my head and the person holding it is a grinning Anton.

46

✷✳✦

BASTIAN

Gweedore, Ireland
~~~~~

Chelsea hits the brakes hard. I'm tossed forward, the seatbelt locking. Pain rips through me and stifles my breath; my forward motion stops abruptly but not before my forehead taps the windshield.

Ouch.

That will turn into a nasty bump.

And it's a miracle the airbags didn't blow.

I rub the sore spot. Chelsea's sudden maneuver was totally unexpected, not only for me but also the Disciples. They sped by us, the car's red taillights not illuminating until they are almost at the bend. As they disappear from view around the curve, Chelsea whips the Punto into a small sideroad.

I glance at her. "I hope you know where you're going."

"Nope, no idea. I only visited Conor and Sean a few times throughout the years and my stays were limited to the farm."

Fantastic. This might turn into a dead end.

I don't say the words out aloud. No need to throw her into a panic. My shirt is soaked to my skin, I'm sweating enough bullets for the both of us.

She speeds up and I turn around, craning my neck. A car, still a dot in the distance, is gaining on us.

"Fuck. How do they keep finding us?"

"The phone. I forgot to get rid of it."

I roll my eyes. "Where is it?"

"In my front pocket."

I eye those mega fitted jeans. With her hands wrapped tightly around the steering wheel and her gaze fixed on the road ahead, she won't be able to give me much assistance.

"Can you raise your hips a little?"

"I'll try my best."

Her best is a small tilt; I try to slip my fingers into the front pocket, but when she jerks forward, my circulation is cut off.

"Watch out!"

I'm tossed forward again; this time, my shoulder slamming into the dashboard takes the brunt of the impact. Staring through the windshield, my eyes go wide. A huge tractor the size of a small house is heading right for us.

"Hold on!" Digging her teeth into her bottom lip, Chelsea yanks the steering wheel to the left.

Bushes and branches slap against the side of the car and the mirror on my side flies off. The grinding of metal on stone sends a shudder down my spine. Chelsea speeds up even more; with a counter-steer, she pulls back onto the road. The Punto sways from left to right, just as the rear window shatters into a million pieces.

I duck into the seat and peek over my shoulder. Anton must have gotten a shot off, but the Disciples are not as lucky with the tractor. The Subaru they chose as a rental is too wide and ends up with two spinning wheels in a ditch. Grinning, I turn back around.

Chelsea is still speeding as if she were practicing for the Formula One. "Try the phone again." This time, she tilts her hips more.

I'm about to peel the cell from her pocket when the Punto leans to the side, shooting around a bend.

"Fuuuck." Chelsea jams on the brakes.

Another crash into the dashboard leaves my shoulder numb. I squint through the window.

Is this for real?

There are fucking cows in the road.

Dozens of them, crossing the narrow street from one side to another at snails' speed.

"You can't be fucking serious?"

"In rural areas, farm animals have the right of way." Chelsea glances over her shoulder. "C'mon. Hurry up."

A farmer steps out into the road and ushers a few more cows to the opposite field, lifting a chain across the open gate to prevent more of them to follow. He raises his hand in greeting as we pass. When he drops the chain again, the cows immediately rush forward, just as the Disciple's car shoots around the curve. The Subaru comes to a screeching halt inches from a swaying obstacle. I chuckle.

Deal with that, motherfuckers.

Anton jumps out of the car and waves his gun around, screaming at the top of his lungs. His face is flushed red and it won't take much for him to shoot everyone and everything in sight.

"Here." Chelsea tosses me the phone. "Just throw it out of the window."

I have a better idea. "What's the emergency line in Ireland?"

"Nine-nine-nine."

I dial the number and an automatic voice requests me to select whether this is a medical emergency or a police matter. I choose the latter. The deep baritone of a man drifts from the speaker, informing me that I'm connected to a Garda Síochána. I put him on speaker phone.

"Hi. My wife and I just got into a verbal altercation at a grocery store and the three men involved are following us in their car. They're carrying guns and shot at us, and now they are threatening a farmer who came to our aid. We are fearing for our lives." My voice hitches in the right moment to give the whole claim a panicky vibe.

"Where are you?"

I look at Chelsea.

"We just passed a sign that said Meenanillar."

"Okay, if you stay straight, you'll get to Derrybeg in about 2 miles. The guards will meet you there. What kind of car are you driving?"

I smirk. "A lime green Fiat Punto." Not even a blind dude could miss that. "The men who shot at us are driving a black Subaru Outback. Looked like a newer rental."

"Okay, and what's your name?"

I grimace. "Conor Doherty."

Chelsea snickers under her breath. "He's gonna kill you," she whispers.

"Sorry, I couldn't hear you." The cop's voice is a slight-bit irritated.

"My wife said that she's scared that they are going to kill us."

"Stay calm and keep your speed. You'll be safe in a few minutes."

And Anton's ass will be hauled off to jail; without diplomatic immunity, it'll take Icarus a few days and some serious favor-calling to get him out. I lower the window and toss the phone into the closest ditch.

Chelsea snorts. "That was brilliant. I just hope Anton won't get into a shootout."

"I doubt it." Not even he's determined enough to gun down a law enforcement officer on foreign soil. Ireland might not have the death penalty, but prison terms for cop killers will likely be extensive and Icarus's connections couldn't bail him out.

Houses multiply on the side of the road; we must be getting closer to Derrybeg. Chelsea stays straight until we encounter three cars with the Garda sign on the doors, blocking the road. A cop waves us into the parking lot of a school. I have to hand it to them; they had five minutes tops to react and the efficiency of these police officers is impressive.

Not even thirty seconds later, the Subaru comes speeding up the road. The driver hits the brakes, the steering wheel already turned for a quick reversal when a couple of shots take out the front tires.

"Get out of the car with your hands up!" booms a voice from a megaphone.

Silence.

The Subaru sits under the orange sky, bathed in the evening sun, as if deserted. Without a doubt, a frantic phone call to Cyprus is being made. Finally, three doors open at once. Anton tosses his gun out, yelling, "We are unarmed," before getting out of the car.

Falk and Michail follow suit, dropping to their knees and locking their hands behind their heads. I'm pretty sure that

Irish cops aren't as trigger happy as their American counterparts, but Anton's crew doesn't take any chances. Law enforcement is not one to fuck with if you ever want to go home. That's the job of lawyers and bribes.

"You need to come down to the station for a statement."

I spin around to face a young cop who has appeared behind us.

Not gonna happen, buddy.

Chelsea and I need to leverage as much of a head start as possible and the illegal weapons' charges will already be enough to keep Anton out of commission for a while.

I smile. "Sure."

He hands us a card. "Here is the address and ask for Sergeant Walsh when you get there."

"Not a problem. Is it okay for my wife and I to have a cup of tea first? We are pretty shook up."

"That's grand. We have to book them first anyhow, which will take at least an hour." The cop tips his hat and returns to his colleagues.

Officially off the hook, I open the car door for Chelsea. "Would you like me to drive?"

"Nope."

"Where to now?" I stretch and pop my joints. My body is sore and my migraine has returned full force. To make matters worse, the bottle with the pain meds is in one of the bags we left behind in the rental at the farm.

"Belfast. It's about a three-hour ride. We can stay overnight there."

"Not gonna lie, I'm kind of hungry." And with the adrenaline seeping out of me, exhaustion is slowly creeping in.

"Let's drive for an hour or so and eat when we cross into the North. That way, we are out of Irish jurisdiction."

Sounds like a plan. "What do you need to do in Belfast?"

"Conor keeps a deposit box for me at a bank in case I need to change identities. It has a new passport, credit cards, and cash."

I have to hand it to him; the man is scarily resourceful when he wants to hide someone's tracks. "We should leave Ireland as soon as possible."

"I agree."

From across the street, I meet Anton's gaze. Handcuffed, he's being shoved into the police car.

You and your whore are dead, he mouths before the door closes in his face.

I chuckle under my breath. He's pathetic.

As the police cruiser slowly drives off, I pull Chelsea closer for a deep kiss. Anton's glare drills into my temples. For now, I won, but Anton won't give up, even if Icarus were gone. For him, this has become personal.

Breaking the kiss, I stare at the back of the police car where a shock of dark-blond hair covers a proudly raised head. No, if I ever want to breathe without fear again, I'll have to kill him, too.

47

✵ ✾ ✵

CHELSEA

Vienna, Austria
July 2024
~~~~~

"Geez, I'm pooped." I drop the heavy shopping bags on the floor of the Airbnb's living room and fall onto the couch. Vienna is wickedly hot and the humidity is stifling.

Bastian purses his lips, scanning the bags. "I think those clothes should hold us over for a while."

I roll my eyes. His definition of temporary wardrobe includes more items than I've owned this past year. "I'm ready for a shower and a nap."

"Me, too." He twists the cap of the painkiller bottle and pours four into his hand. Not sure if this type of overmedication should alarm me or whether it's just the stress. He turns on the tap, filling a glass with water. The pills disappear in his mouth and he smiles. "I hope you won't be too tired to go to the opera tonight."

"And miss a performance at Vienna's State Opera House?" Not a chance. Since I was a little girl and saw pictures from one of Mam's trips, I've always dreamed of going.

"Well, if you want my input, I'd love you to wear the black dress we got in the little boutique by the coffee shop."

That's the plan. I grin. "And why is that?"

"It looks absolutely amazing on you."

"Oh, does it?" I get up and stroll over to him. "Does that mean I'll get to pick what you wear?"

"You can pick my outfit any day."

I seal his mouth with my lips, relishing his exploring tongue. The tiredness seeps from my bones and heat spreads to my lower region. I pull the shirt out of his pants to trace the grooves of his abs with my fingertips. He fumbles with the button of my shorts, his other hand cupping my butt.

"I think we should finally test the whirlpool tub." The mumbled words against my earlobe tingle on my skin. His breath is heavy and his erection presses against my crotch.

Sticky as I am, a bath sounds like a solid plan. "As long as I get to scrub your back."

"I hope that's not the only part of my body you intend to put your hands on."

It certainly isn't. Lips glued together, we edge toward the bathroom. I can't get his belt open fast enough and dispose of his pants and shirt. He is even less patient, tugging and yanking my clothes to get to my skin. Our tongues roll in a heated rhythm; I drink in the spicy scent of his aftershave mixed with the saltiness of his masculinity. By the time we reach the tub, my nipples are taut and my pussy is soaking wet.

The tub takes forever to fill; I brush my teeth to distract myself and to keep my focus off his aroused cock. One wrong stroke and I'll orgasm right on his hand. He turns on the whirlpool jets and slides into the water, the desire in his eyes begging me to join him. Bubbles pearl on his chest; as I climb in, I can't tear my gaze off his sculpted muscles. He pulls me onto his lap. His cock is as hard as a rock.

Dipping the sponge into the tub, he lets the warm water drip on my exposed shoulders. Two of his fingers push inside me, soliciting a moan. The rotating motion of the soft, soapy sponge over my breasts sends little bursts of electricity to every part of my body; I'm on the verge of surrendering to my lust when he spins me to face away from him.

"Have you ever had anal sex?"

Marcel and I tried it a few times and it was okay. "Just make sure you stretch me first."

He kisses my shoulder and his fingers move from my pussy to my butt. Entering me feels a little intrusive and I tense, but when he shifts me so that a jet stream hits my clit, the world turns fuzzy. Having his fingers in both of my holes, fucking me slowly, with the water massaging my sex robs me of my breath. The heat builds so fast that I can't hold back. I cry out, my orgasm ripping through me in sweet waves of pleasure.

"Yeah, baby, come for me."

His fingers pick up speed and prolong the fire smoldering in my core; when I finally stop shivering, the tip of his cock is pushing against my opening. My butt is ready to take him, as a matter of fact, the friction is absolutely amazing. His fingers stay inside my pussy, providing a fullness I've never experienced before. He takes it all—my tight ass, my drenched canal, my swollen clit—stimulating my senses until I'm ready to shatter.

Wet skin on wet skin.

This is too good.

My moans come in spurts and the heat seethes in every nerve end, ready to break me apart.

"Harder."

My demand is met with a feral growl. He pushes me on my knees and I press my palms against the side of the tub for maximum resistance. From the mirror, his reflection sends tremors through my body. His eyes are closed, his jaw clenched, and every single thrust is followed by a groan. The bubbling water against my clit counters the raw force of his hard shaft. He squeezes my butt cheek, sending a sweet bout of pain right to the center of my core. My lust explodes, tearing him with me. Ripple after ripple of ecstatic pleasure takes over my world. I shiver in his arms long after he hugs me to his chest.

I tilt my head back to look him in the eyes. "I want to finger-fuck your ass."

He chuckles. "What about the nap?"

"Fuck the nap." When you can have sex, who needs to rest?

"Food?"

"We can eat after the opera."

"Okey, dokey." He leans in for a kiss, sliding his fingers through my folds. At this rate, we might not even make it out of the tub tonight.

~~~~

Looping arms with Bastian, we approach the Renaissance-style opera house. I stop to admire the intricate design of the facade. Two riders on horsebacks are at the top corners, overlooking the street and an arched balcony that houses five bronze statues. According to the tourist guide, they represent heroism, tragedy, fantasy, comedy, and love. The carved details evidence the passion of the artist for architecture and design; modern constructions today can't measure up to that.

Bastian leads me around the building to a side entrance and my gaze gets stuck on a magnificent fountain. The whole opera house emits so many historic vibes that I get chills. How many people over the years have passed through these doors? The freaking emperor and his wife even inaugurated the place. Simply amazing.

I lean my head against Bastian's shoulder. "I'm glad we picked Vienna as our escape."

"Well, it was more luck of the draw. We booked the first flight out of Belfast within the EU, which happened to be Vienna."

We picked a city neither of us had been to before, a tactic to throw off the Disciples. It's also an opportunity to breathe and recharge while Conor organizes a fake passport for Bastian. After that, it'll be back to fighting on enemy turf.

We step into the lobby of the opera house and I gape around in awe. Just like the outside, the interior is astonishing and carries an aura of forgotten times. The walls and ceiling are covered in art, some images painted directly on the marble, others carved out of stone. We walk up a staircase that takes us inside the auditorium. Gilded panels and dividers covered in a red fabric section off the private box with our seats on the first level. The view onto the stage is unobstructed.

Bastian organizes a glass of champagne for me. As usual, he sticks to water; except for the one night when he showed up drunk at my house, he hasn't touched a drop of alcohol. Painkillers are the only unhealthy substance he ever exposes his body to and then only by necessity. It's something I admire. As a caffeine, chocolate, and junk food addict who hates excessive exercise, I suck at a balanced lifestyle.

Bastian hands me a program and I flip through the pages. Tonight's showing is Giulio Cesare in Egitto, a musical drama in three acts. One of the glossy pages promises a baroque jewel that hasn't been performed in the State Opera in sixty-five years. Bastian was lucky to get us two tickets from a scalper.

The lights dim and the sounds from a live orchestra fill the large hall. It's my first opera and the high-pitched singing takes some getting used to, but after the intermission, I get the hang of it. Bastian absorbs the music like a sponge, and simply watching him with his gaze fixed on the stage and his lips curled in this entranced smile gets my heart to beat faster. My mind strays to the afternoon in the tub; I'm hot in my skimpy dress and can't wait for him to take it off. As the last notes ring out, I get to my feet with the rest of the audience and clap my heart out.

Bastian drapes his arm around my shoulders. "Did you enjoy it?"

"Yeah." The building alone made the performance worth it, even if the opera itself wasn't my cup of tea. I let my gaze roam over the excited faces of the people standing on the balcony across from us. When I meet a man's eyes, the breath gets stuck in my throat.

What the fuck!

My body goes rigid and I struggle to swallow.

'What's wrong?" Bastian's question is colored with worry.

"That guy over there, he works for Jackson Pierce."

"Are you sure?"

"Positive." He is the asshole who told me to strip.

And the fucker actually waves at me as if we were lifelong friends.

48

✳ ✸ ✺

BASTIAN

Vienna, Austria
~~~~~

When Chelsea tries to steer toward an emergency exit, I grab her elbow. "Not that way."

She tears loose. "We can't exactly walk out the front door."

"Trust me, Jackson brought enough men to cover every single exit. He's not one to take chances."

"How did he even find us?"

I shrug. "He must've gotten his hands on the airline's passenger manifest."

"That's impossible in the EU. The data laws are too strict."

There's no other explanation. "Could Conor do it?"

"Yeah, well, probably."

There you have it.

And getting me a new identity has now become an absolute priority.

Chelsea looks around. "So what's the plan?"

"We need to disguise ourselves." I pull her toward the backstage. "We are in a theater, so there must be plenty of props to change our appearance."

Fighting against the stream of people leaving the opera house, I usher her toward the auditorium. We sneak through a side door into the main section and end up at the stairs leading into the orchestra pit. Some of the musicians are still around, packing up their instruments. As we advance into the pit, they toss us puzzled looks.

A woman steps in our way. "*Zutritt nur fuer Philharmoniker.*"

I grimace. Speaking German would be useful.

Chelsea beams at her with the biggest smile. "Philippe Jordan is my uncle. He invited us backstage."

The woman narrows her eyes but steps aside. As if she owned the place, Chelsea continues her walk.

"How come you understood what she said?"

"I had German in school for six years."

Kudos to her for still remembering a single thing from high school.

"And who is Philippe Jordan?"

"The current music director. His name was on the front page of the program. Didn't you read it?"

"Nope." I kiss her cheek. "You are amazing."

Once again, this allegiance has saved my ass.

Chelsea pushes open the door leading to the back of the opera house and we walk hand in hand down the corridor. People buzz around us; I keep my face even and pretend I know where I'm going so as not to arouse further suspicion. After a few steps, my shoulders relax. Everyone is so hyped that no one pays attention to us. Singers stomp around with half their makeup removed and tease each other, their laughter and chatter filling the air. We pass an open door to a changing room covered in darkness and I nudge Chelsea's shoulder.

That's the one.

She catches on and we slip inside unnoticed. Closing the door, I turn on the light. It's perfect. Make-up, a few wigs, some costumes. This should be enough to fool Jackson and keep the bullets out of our heads.

I pull a jacket off a hanger. It's a longer overcoat that looks like something from the Barber of Seville. Chelsea options for a pair of breeches and a white, airy shirt that is loose enough to hide her tits. She spins in front of the mirror, wrinkling her nose.

"I was thinking, even if Jackson got his hands on the passenger manifest, how did he find us tonight? We've been in Vienna for two days and have been mega careful."

"Jackson has a ton of freelance soldiers working for him. They live in every imaginable country in the world. If he knew we were on a plane to Vienna, it would've taken him one phone call to have one of his goons wait for us at the airport and then follow us wherever we went."

"Without us noticing?"

"These guys are professionals. The Disciples followed you for weeks without you suspecting a thing."

She flinches and I grin an apology. When she snooped through my bag at the hotel room, she saw the pictures, so this shouldn't be news to her.

"And you don't think it's something else?"

"What else could it be?"

She shrugs.

I hand her a wig. "Here, try that."

Her black hair disappears completely under a blond, pageboy-style mop; she looks like a cute peasant from the Victorian era. I choose a gray hairpiece with cascading curls that reaches my shoulders. Some white makeup to hide my tan and some rosy cheeks for Chelsea complete the disguise. If Jackson recognizes us, he's even better than I thought.

Mixing with a group of singers leaving the opera house, we are swept toward the subway station. The bodies around us give us excellent coverage; Jackson wouldn't stoop so low to butcher a bunch of civilians. When I reach the steps that lead underground, I breathe a sigh of relief. Almost home free.

Chelsea loops arms with me and we tackle the stairs. We blend with the foot traffic heading for the platform. I'm still amazed by the honesty system; if we had no ticket barrier in New York City, every single person would ride for free. Plus the whole place is clean without a single beggar holding a cup under my nose—and it doesn't smell like piss. Unthinkable in the States.

A speaker in the ceiling announces that the next train is delayed by three minutes. I tug Chelsea against a pillar to hide her from view. For now, I'm not sure if Jackson bought her bullshit about shooting Marcel, so either one of us could be his target, or even both. Smiling, I focus on her face. She is torturing a lip, a habit I noticed when she's nervous.

Where is the fucking train?

My gaze flicks around and brushes a woman standing on the opposite platform of the tracks.

Is that Penina Cohn?

In that exact moment, she turns her head. I look away, though I'm certain she recognized me. A loud whistle on two fingers that has half the people in the station freeze confirms my suspicion. Jackson's head appears above the crowd. He stands on a bench, the elevated position not only giving him an excellent viewpoint but also leverage in case he pulls his gun. I instinctively reach for my Glock, a futile effort since I had to leave it behind in Ireland. Without the weapon, I'm even more vulnerable and exposed.

Time comes to a standstill.

Through the aviator shades, I can't see his eyes, but I don't have not the slightest doubt that he's glaring at me. Inching closer to Chelsea, I fully cover her, even if the move is silly. A man like him shoots a high-power projectile that will travel through me and right into her body. It's literally killing two birds with one bullet.

When his hand moves toward his armpit, my breath stalls. A surreal buzzing spreads in my ears. I should run, but my legs are paralyzed. A blow of a police whistle and people jumping aside tear me from my daze. Two transit cops run down the platform.

"*Auf der Bank stehen ist verboten!*" one of them shouts.

With thunder, the subway enters the station. As I push toward the opening doors, the cops signal Jackson to follow their orders. He steps down from the bench and takes off his aviator shades. For a beat, our eyes meet. His smirk speaks volumes.

I'll catch you the next time.

And he is right. Chelsea and I can't keep running. Sooner rather than later, either he or the Disciples will catch up with us.

The doors of the train close and the subway moves forward with a jerk.

Chelsea cuddles against me. "We made it. What now?"

"We can't go back to the Airbnb." And if I want Jackson off our backs, I'll need to proactively seek him out on my own terms.

"Then where are we going?"

"The airport." I lock her gaze. "We are flying to the US to speak to Jackson Pierce."

49

✷ ✸ ✷

BASTIAN

Falls Church, Virginia
July 2024
~~~~~

Cute little townhouses line the cul-de-sac that screams typical middle class, the residences of hardworking couples trying to make ends meet on a government salary. The woman emerging from one of the homes gives out the same vibe. Holding the hand of a little boy, she doesn't even look once to her left or to her right as they stroll down the sidewalk in the direction of a playground sitting at the end of the street. She displays the ignorance of an asset convinced that her employer will protect her identity at all cost. It's an illusion. Her real name was dropped casually by a CIA show-off after a brush with too much Rum and Coke, and it took Conor less than an hour to pull up her address.

They reach the playground and the little boy takes off running toward the slide. The woman plops onto a bench in the shade, scrolling through her phone. It's showtime. Nodding at Chelsea, we get out of the car.

I drape my arm around her shoulders. "How old do you think the boy is?"

"Maybe five."

That's what I thought.

Approaching the woman, I give her the widest smile. "Excuse me, my wife and I are looking at houses in the neighborhood. We have a daughter about your son's age, so we were wondering if you could tell us a little bit about the schools in the area."

She frowns, her smile more than reserved. Her guards are up, but thanks to Chelsea's presence, she is too polite to fully blow us off. "My son won't start kindergarten until next year, but we are planning on sending him to Saint James. It's a private catholic school, though all the public schools in the Falls Church are also very good."

"Oh, he looks so big. I can't believe he isn't five yet."

"Not until October."

Which would still fall within the time bracket. The little boy runs up, cheeks flushed and eyes sparkling with mischief and joy. It's mega hot and sweat has soaked his thick black curls. His mom pulls out a juice box—grape, which was always Vitaly's favorite—and hands it to him. She reminds me a lot of Liv. A toned body with long legs and good-sized tits, hard brown eyes that soften when she looks at her son, a wide smile that makes her appear younger. Looks-wise, she isn't my type, but if she puts on the charms, I can see how she might appeal to men.

Chelsea pulls out a bag of gummy drops. "Is it okay if I give him one?"

"Yes, of course."

She holds the bag open and the little boy grabs a handful. "Thank you, ma'am."

Chelsea's lips twitch. As he runs off, she turns to the woman. "He is so polite."

"My husband is in the military. It tends to rub off."

Chelsea sighs. "Shauna, that's our daughter, has a mouth like a sailor." She nudges my side. "I blame my husband for that. When she was little, I traveled a lot for work and he let manners slide."

I grimace, amazed at Chelsea's improvisation skills.

"I've been lucky. When Jayden was born, I transferred to an office job and mostly work from home."

I almost snort. After she returned from her undercover gig, the CIA likely considered her a liability and reassigned her to a government branch where she wouldn't attract attention.

Eyeing the juice box the boy left sitting on the bench next to the woman, I squeeze Chelsea's knee. "Let's snap a few pictures and then grab some lunch. I'm starving."

"Sure, that sounds good."

With my arm around Chelsea and our backs to the playground, I pretend to shoot a selfie with a loud, "say cheese, honey," aiming the camera of my brand-new burner phone in a way to get a good profile picture of the woman. Walking toward the playground equipment, I snap a few more photos, one capturing the little boy. Now I just need to get my hands on the juice box.

Back in the car, I start the engine and drive off, only to whip into a parking space after rounding the next corner.

Chelsea cranes her neck. "Why are we stopping? We got the pictures."

"I want to get the empty juice box."

"For what?"

I smile. No more lies is not something that will work here, but I'm also not willing to blatantly deceive her. "I simply need it. Please let's leave it at that."

She nods. "What's going to happen now?"

"I'm hoping to catch a red-eye flight to Houston tonight."

"You mean *we* are."

"No, you're staying here." I lock her gaze. "Meeting with Jackson is something I have to do on my own."

"Bastian—"

"No discussion. After you told Jackson you shot Marcel, he might kill you on sight and ask questions later. I can't risk that. Besides, I promised Conor, so please don't make me go back on my word."

The Conor excuse works. She pouts a little, but when I pull out the bottle with pain meds and choke down two pills dry, the defiance in her eyes switches to concern.

"You've been taking a lot of painkillers."

I pinch the bridge of my nose. "I've had really bad migraines lately, but I promise I'll try to cut down." I omit that my doctor will likely refuse to fill my prescription again after I asked for three refills in a week. Of course I couldn't tell him that I had to leave two full bottles behind because I'm being chased around the globe.

Chelsea's smile is crooked. "Just be careful, okay? I can't take down the Disciples on my own."

"Don't worry"—I peck her cheek—"I'm intending to return to you in one piece."

50

✳ ✳ ✳

BASTIAN

Houston, Texas
July 2024
~~~~~

Twelve hours later, I touch down at George Bush Intercontinental Airport in Houston and grab a taxi to the Mission Bay area. According to Conor's long, encrypted email that answered everything I asked for, the youth center I gave the cabbie as my destination is the only potential connection to Jackson Pierce. His number two, Penina Cohn, grew up in this part of town and still volunteers at the center from time to time. I drop an envelope for her at the reception desk with a note requesting a meeting with her boss.

Now the waiting game starts once again. I've given myself three days; if Jackson hasn't contacted me by then, I'll have to come up with a plan B.

At eight pm sharp, I enter the bar of my hotel not too far from the main entrance. Finding a seat with my back to the wall proves difficult and I opt for a barstool in a corner that I can turn to overlook the rest of the space. I order peppermint tea to settle my queasy stomach; as I wait, my fingers drum on the bar. Watching other patrons and staring up at the glass and chrome of the atrium with its elevators and balconies is the only thing that kills time. I sip the tea until it's all gone and order another cup.

Minutes crawl and I yawn behind my raised hand. The flight was exhausting and the adrenaline that has kept me going is slowly dissolving with the steam of the tea. My legs tingle. All this feels wrong. What if Jackson found a way to locate Chelsea? At this very moment, she could be lying in a pool of blood, the life draining out of her, while I'm sitting here at this bar like a complete idiot. What if the flight manifests isn't the way he's tracking me? For all I know, he has figured out Chelsea's new identity and is slaughtering her to get even for his brother's death.

The unrest grows with every mouthful of tea. Two hours pass and I decide to call it a night. I sign the tab to add the charges to my hotel bill and head toward the elevator. The glass-bubble compartment takes me almost to the top; as I ascend, the hotel bar shrinks under my gaze. I squint. In the exact same spot where I sat only minutes ago is now a woman who looks very similar to Penina Cohn, although from this distance, I can't be sure.

Should I go back down?

The elevator pings and the doors open. This is my floor. My finger already hovers over the lobby button to return downstairs when my bladder demands that I take care of pressing business. If the woman at the bar is truly Penina Cohn, she'll have to wait five more minutes.

With quick steps, I walk down the hallway to my room. The keycard against the pad beeps and I push the door open, just to freeze on the threshold. The light by the window is on, illuminating the part of the room that is now occupied by an uninvited guest. Zero emotions are reflected on Jackson Pierce's face; if he weren't breathing, I wouldn't be sure he's alive. He holds a glass in his hand that's filled with an amber liquid, an empty bottle on the table in front of him suggesting it's whiskey from my mini bar. A gun sits next to the small bottle. Even though the Glock I bought earlier is tucked in a halter under my armpit, I have zero doubt that he'd get a bullet off faster than me.

Jackson cocks his head. "You wanted to talk, so let's talk."

51

✷ ✷ ✷

BASTIAN

Houston, Texas
~~~~~

I let out a shaky breath. "Thanks for stopping by." Even if it wasn't the way I envisioned. A public place, like a hotel bar, would've made it much harder to shoot me.

"Well, it's not every day that a man I'm trying to kill is requesting a meeting, so consider me intrigued."

I fold my arms. "To be honest, I'm surprised that you'd risk burning bridges for Marcel. I'm still a Disciple, and even though I'm a hunted man, they will come after you if you kill me. Why endanger your life and your business reputation for a brother like him?"

"As you know yourself, family can be complicated."

"C'mon, Jackson. His whole life, Marcel did nothing but betray you. I mean, I get it. When you both killed your father after you couldn't handle the abuse, you alone took the fall because it was the sensible thing to do. You were only thirteen and faced juvie detention while Marcel would've been tried as an adult for first degree murder. But how did it feel when you walked out of those gates after being locked up for five years and Marcel wasn't there? After all, he was your big brother who was meant to take care of you. But no, he had joined the Disciples and didn't give a damn."

"He only joined the Disciples in order to survive."

"Truth is, he had moved on without you, and when you refused to join the organization and went into the military instead, he did everything in his power to make you change your mind."

Jackson eyelid twitches. "What are you saying, Bastian?"

"Did you never wonder how the military found out that you lied about your past? Your criminal record was sealed and you were going by a different name, so the only way they knew about the murder conviction was from him. It took Marcel one phone call to have your life blow up in your face. Sixty days in the brig and a dishonorable discharge—that's what your good brother did for you."

"I don't believe you." The moisture that has formed above Jackson's lip contradicts his statement.

I snort. "You were a running joke among the Disciples. Whenever your name came up with Konstantin, he'd laugh until he had tears in his eyes. He called you a fucking moron. But that's not the worst."

The muscle in Jackson's jaw jumps. "Go on."

I'm ready for the big blow. "Maren Birch. In order for the CIA to plant her with you, they needed insider information. Intel only someone who knew you extremely well could provide. Things about what makes you tick, what makes you vulnerable, your hopes and dreams, dislikes and fears. For Maren, you were an open book, all thanks to Marcel."

"You are lying."

"Am I?" I smirk. "C'mon, Jackson, you are a guarded man. You must've asked yourself how someone like Maren could've broken through your defenses. After Marcel fled Hong Kong, giving you up was his ticket back into the US. The intel he stole from the Disciples was becoming worthless, so he had to give the authorities something to keep them off his back. What better way to do that than give them a man they wanted even more than him."

Jackson sips from the whiskey, his eyes in another world. For someone who is usually in control at all times, my words must have struck a nerve. "How can you be sure Marcel sold me out?"

"I'm an alternate representative to the UN. Compared to most of the others, I'm significantly younger, and so are the aids to many of the bigwigs who are on the security council. We often grab a drink after the assemblies to gossip about the old geezers. Most of the Americans are military and CIA and as the nights carry on, tongues get loose. On one of those occasions, a CIA dude bragged that they finally had a way to get to the notorious Jackson Pierce. Of course that caught my attention. We were still looking for Marcel, so the name Pierce could mean a potential lead. I got the guy alone a few times and he was a lousy drunk. Spilled the beans without much prompting after I swore I wouldn't tell a soul."

Jackson mumbles "fuck" under his breath.

It's my cue to go in for the kill strike. "I propose that you back off. Permanently. Both Chelsea and I get a free pass for shooting your brother." The way I see it, I did him a favor.

He snorts. "Do you seriously expect me to back off based on some vague allegations?"

I shake my head. "I have a trade to offer. Maren Birch's real name and address."

He sets the whiskey glass down so hard that some of the liquid swaps on the table. "You are bullshitting. There's no way you got the real identity of a CIA asset."

"Don't take my word for it." I raise my hands not to spook him. "I need to take my phone out of my pocket."

"Slowly. There's a bullet in the chamber and the safety is off."

I expected nothing less. With utmost care, I pull the cell out of my jeans. Scrolling through the pictures, I find the one I took of the woman. "That's her, isn't it?"

He leans closer, his tongue running over his lips. "How did you get this?"

"Same UN contact let her name slip and I have a hacker who got her address." And there is more. "A little boy was with her. She said he'll turn five in October."

Jackson picks up the whiskey glass and downs the drink in one go. His hand is shaking. Another "fuck" is mumbled under his breath.

I pull up the boy's picture. "That's him. Now, I'm no genetic expert, but he looks like a mixed-race child to me. Granted, Maren's husband could be black, but if not . . ."

Letting the words trail off, I study Jackson's face. His jaw is clenched and my bet is that he'd do anything to get his hands on Maren's whereabouts.

I set the phone in front of him on the table, the picture of the little boy still on the screen. "Like I said, I propose a trade. Maren's real name and address, plus a DNA sample of the boy. In return, you'll leave Chelsea and me alone."

He stares at the picture for a long time. "You got yourself a deal."

"I need to get some stuff from my bag."

He nods. "Like I said, slowly."

I walk over to my duffel and retrieve the data stick with the woman's information and the empty juice box I stuck into a freezer bag. Placing the items on the table, I almost feel sorry for Jackson. Within a matter of minutes, his whole life imploded. "His name is Jayden. He looked really happy and healthy, so I hope you'll consider that."

Jackson's chuckle is bitter. "Even after everything Maren did, I'd never hurt her." Getting to his feet, he picks up the items. When he locks my gaze, his eyes are once again void of emotion. He has fully regained control. "Your migraine medication, that's how we've been tracking you. One of your flight attendants divulged the specifics. Outside the US, it's a rare prescription, so it was easy to follow up on alerts whenever it was filled. CCTV cameras did the rest. Thought you might want to know."

With one more look at the photo of the boy who could be his son, Jackson walks to the door. Nothing in his stance suggests he took a fatal blow to the fabric of his existence. Deep down, I don't envy him. Nothing is worse than knowing that you have a child out there you never get to see, but it's something he'll have to come to terms with.

52

✷ ✸ ✶

CHELSEA

Nicosia, Cyprus
August 2024
~~~~~

My heart races from my orgasm and I cuddle against Bastian to take advantage of his warm body. One leg wrapped around his, I stroke his ribcage. The smooth skin tingles under my charged fingertips.

"Why don't you have the lion head tattoo of the Disciples? Isn't it part of the initiation ritual?"

"It is, but I had it removed." He shifts his body to face me. A smile plays on his lips and he pecks the tip of my nose.

"They did an excellent job. I can't even feel the scar."

"Laser technology is amazing."

I trace the leaves of his vine tattoo. Across his front are at least a dozen and then maybe a handful climbing up his back. One is fairly new, but he hasn't laid on his stomach long enough for me to read the initials. "When are you gonna tell me what the leaves mean?"

He tenses. "Like I said, it's not important." His eyes lose some of their sex-afterglow shine; he has his guards up, a wall I haven't been able to penetrate. Secrets of his past that might stay buried forever. Not that I would ever hold that against him. We all have skeletons in our closets.

He rolls out of bed. "We should hurry. Solara is meeting us at the coffee shop in thirty minutes."

He's about to pick up his boxers when I hold on to his fingertips. "I'd never judge you for anything you did in the past."

"I know." He looks away, but not before I detect pain in his eyes. "But it's something I judge myself for, so I don't like to talk about it."

Fair enough.

I get out of bed and slip into a light beach dress and a pair of sandals. Compared to Ireland, Cyprus has been hot, even though Bastian claims it's cool for the summer. He actually wears a sweater. Tying his shoes, he winks at me. "You look gorgeous."

"Thank you, you look pretty decent yourself." I squirt suntan lotion on my hand and spread it all over the exposed parts of my body. My shoulders are still red from a bad sunburn and are tender to the touch. Even with clouds, the UV rays here are lethal for my skin type, a lesson I learned the hard way.

Bastian secures his gun in the halter; it's not even visible under the bulky sweater. "Ready?"

"Yep."

Hand in hand, we walk to the elevator of the Airbnb apartment and step into the road not even five minutes later. The coffee shop he picked for the meeting is right next door. Solara is already seated at one of the tables all the way in the back next to a door with the sign *Kouzína*. In every establishment, Bastian always chooses the same type of table.

Sitting next to the kitchen means access to the backdoor, guaranteeing a quick getaway if needed.

When we sit down, Solara doesn't remove her sunglasses and avoids Bastian's gaze.

He sighs. "How bad is it?"

"It doesn't matter."

"It matters to me. Take off the shades."

"Bastian—"

He lifts a brow.

Huffing under her breath, she tears off the glasses. The black eye is in full bloom and an angry dark bruise is just below the other eye.

Bastian's hands ball to fists. "This can't go on."

"Okay, then tell me what other options I have." She folds her arms. "The police won't do anything because Christos has them in his pocket. I can't work because of my immigration status, so I rely on his money. You can no longer set him straight because you are on the run. The only thing I could do to remove myself from the situation is to go back to Mexico and marry Enrique Salazar, and you know firsthand that he is ten times worse than Christos."

Bastian rubs the bridge of his nose; he has been battling migraines almost non-stop but had to settle for over-the-counter painkillers that are less effective. Most of the time, he suffers in silence, although moments like these get him incredibly irritated.

"I swear, once the Disciples are out of the picture, I'll get you citizenship."

Solara squeezes his hand. "I know, so let's hope this plan will work." Rummaging through her purse, she sets an envelope on the table. "Here is the invitation."

"Thank you. I really appreciate it."

She gets to her feet. "I have to go or the driver will get suspicious and squeal on me. I told him I had to use the bathroom, but that was ten minutes ago."

"Okay, I'll see you around."

She offers us a small smile. A lot is riding on our success and the stakes are high. Turning around, she slides the shades back on her face, and with her suit and her head held up high, she looks like an affluent businesswoman. No one would suspect her sinister secret. It's one thing that has passed me by; I've never had a partner lay his hands on me.

I meet Bastian's gaze. "How long has she been with her husband?"

"Four years. He found her in a strip club in Mexico where her gang-member boyfriend had her hooking. When Christos offered her a way out, she gladly took it and only found out after they were married that the grass wasn't as green on the other side as she thought. Granted, if she had stayed in Mexico, her life would've likely been worse, though that doesn't make Christos's abuse any better. I really hope we'll get the citizenship sorted out soon, so that she can leave him and start a new life."

I nod. Another person on the list who could benefit from Icarus's death. Sudden tears fill my eyes. The past has a way of catching up with me at the most inopportune moments. "You know, sometimes I think Marcel only married me because of my money."

"Don't say that."

"But it's the truth. And then, when I didn't give him access to the account and refused to spend a dime, he got me pregnant and came up with the idea of us going to Hong Kong, damn well knowing that this was the only way he'd ever get his hands on the cash." The list of things we needed went on and on to justify why he all of a sudden had to become a signatory on the account. A few tears fall. "I was so stupid and gullible." Chances are I never meant anything to him.

Bastian squeezes my hand. "Marcel was a master manipulator, but I'm sure he loved you in his own way."

"Then why did he abandon us?" And not only that. He started a whole new family.

"Chelsea, you need to stop, okay? Even if it were true, there's nothing you can do to change it anymore. Same with me. There are no do-overs, so we have to look forward and remember that the darkest times in our lives also gave us our greatest gifts. Sean and Vitaly deserve parents who don't dwell in the past but give them a bright future."

Fuck, he is so right.

Swallowing down the lump in my throat, I dry my face on my sleeve. "What does the invitation say?"

Bastian opens the envelope he got from Solara and slides out a card. "The memorial service is this Saturday, so a day later than expected."

"And you are sure Icarus will be in attendance?"

"It's a special mass for his deceased son and not something he would ever miss." He scans the card again. "Shit, it's in another venue than in previous years. We'll need to scout out the location for possible entry and exit points."

"What do you think triggered the change?"

He shrugs. "Beats me."

My gut twists. "I have a bad feeling about this."

"It's just jitters. We are so close to the finish line that it's normal to be nervous."

"I don't know." Unrest has been building over these past days. Not being able to talk to Conor, only communicating by encrypted email, lacking any reassurance has been sitting like a block of cement in my stomach. Sean usually struggles to readjust after a visit, and not having the farm and the horses to distract him must be especially hard on him.

Forehead wrinkled, Bastian scrolls through his new burner phone. "Still no response from Conor to my last email."

"Do you think something is wrong?"

"Like I said, it's just jitters. We need to keep our cool and things will go as planned. If you panic, you get sloppy."

Another good point. "Then let's look at the new venue."

"I'll also check with a few of my contacts in the States. If the turf war has started, we are looking at added security." Rising to his feet, he shifts his body away from me, but not before I detect a gleam of worry in his eyes. He is just as much on edge as I am and his jitters-claim is bullshit.

"Bastian, you can tell me the truth. I won't back out."

His chuckle is bitter. "Even if I tell you I'm scared shitless."

"As long as we are in this together, things will work out."

53

✳ ✳ ✳

CHELSEA

Nicosia, Cyprus
~~~~~

The Greek Orthodox church is massive with tons of statues and other intricate details on the walls and windows that are similar to those found in a Catholic church in Ireland. A sea of candles illuminates darker niches; the sharp scent of incense clings to the air. Almost every seat is taken and the murmurs of the visitors are respectful enough to a man they fear without hiding that they don't give a damn about the service or the deceased. It's a circus of the who's who of Cyprus, and walking down the middle aisle in hunt of an empty seat constricts my chest with a bout of panic. The dark sunglasses and long, blond wig can't hide that I'm so obviously an outsider. What if someone questions me? The invitation from Solara passed the scrutiny test with the guard at the door, but these people know I'm not her. If anyone catches sight of the envelope with her name, they'll expose me as an imposter.

With trembling knees, I squeeze into an open space at the end of a bench about midway down to the altar and give the woman next to me a small smile. She does not return the gesture, only regarding me with a frown. I take a few deep breaths to calm down.

Pulling the burner phone from my jacket pocket, I turn away from her and shoot off a quick text.

I'm inside.

Bastian's response is almost instantaneous. *Is it busy?*

Very. Why?

Usually it's a small affair.

I look around. The crowd gives me party vibes.

Why so many people this year? Maybe it's a special anniversary.

I don't get a response; he must be positioning himself for the ambush. Mass is meant to start in five minutes and Icarus is due to arrive.

I thumb-text another message. *Any sign of him?*

No!

What is taking him so long?

The front doors open and everyone turns their head. I almost drop the phone. Three men walk down the aisle, one of them Anton. The man in the middle stops at a Jesus statue and kisses him on the feet. I quirk a brow.

What's up with that?

Shades hide his eyes, but I recognize Icarus from the few photos Bastian showed me of his uncle. He is a bit shorter than expected, and stockier, but the part of the face I can see is a match. The third man sends a shudder down my spine. He has unusual soft features and carries a wide, energetic smile, but his good looks are nullified by the coldness in his almost black eyes. About to meet Anton's gaze, I look away from the group. They pass me and take a seat in the front row.

New panic settles in and my thumbs hammer the screen. For once, I'm thankful for autocorrect. *They are here. They came through the front door.*

So much for Bastian's assurance that his uncle never uses the main entrance of any venue.

Fuck. Who is with him?

Anton and some younger dude with long hair and psychotic eyes.

That's Rostya, my uncle's personal bodyguard. Anyone else?

I crane my neck, but the church doors are closed.

No idea.

For all I know, an army could be waiting in the street.

I'll move to the elevated spot in the front from where I can take the shot.

Should we abort? My thumb hovers over the text. Should I send it? The plan hasn't worked so far, but we expected a few hiccups. Bastian is in a better position to judge the situation. With a sigh, I erase the message.

Music fills the church and everyone gets to their feet. Mass drags on, especially since I don't understand a single word, and the heavy scent of incense gives me a headache. Almost robotically, I mimic the other guests whenever they stand and kneel to avoid drawing attention to myself. The panic still has a firm hold on me; my dress is drenched and the wig itches beyond belief. I'm desperate to tear it off, an urge that won't become a reality anytime soon. We've come too far and the end goal is almost within reach.

Calm the fuck down.

I wipe my palms on my dress to keep the phone from slipping. When Rostya turns around and finds my eyes, I almost choke on my spit. He winks before refocusing on mass.

A vibration from my phone has me jump.

In position.

I take a deep breath. My whole body shakes.

They just finished with the bread, so mass should be over soon.

More music and singing drives me close to the edge. The priest speaks to Icarus in a hushed voice and does something with his hands that could be a blessing. I hold my breath.

Is this the end?

Flanked by Anton and Rostya, Icarus follows the priest to the back of the church.

Shit.

He's taking the back exit.

No response. Bastian is probably scrambling to change positions again.

The other guests file out of the church and I have to fight against the stream of bodies to get to the front. Bending my knee, I make the sign of the cross and step onto the altar. My gaze flicks around. The door to the back of the church is ajar; a quick peek will confirm if Icarus has left already. I step closer and lean my ear against the door. Absolute silence raises the hairs on my neck. Even with Icarus gone, there should be a sound.

The door is torn open and I stumble back. In the next breath, I'm captured by an arm wrapping around me. Cold metal presses against my cheek. "Hey, Anton, you were right. Come here and check this out."

Anton appears on the threshold. A smirk spreads on his lips. "Nice wig, sweetheart. Too bad you couldn't fool me." With one pull, the hairpiece comes off. "Where is Bastian?"

"I dunno."

A backhanded slap takes me off my feet. I crawl to the side, but Rostya catches up with me. His hand slides under my dress and he squeezes my butt. My insides cramp with disgust.

"We can do this the easy way or the hard way. It's up to you. How much do you want it to hurt?"

I flinch back, which gets him to chuckle. "A fighter. I'm going to enjoy this."

Anton sighs and rolls his eyes. "We don't have time for this. Bastian is our priority."

"I got her phone."

"Then why didn't you say that?" With another eyeroll, Anton snatches the burner phone out of Rostya's hand. "Get her off the ground."

Grabbing a fistful of my hair, Rostya pulls hard to force me back to my feet. My scalp is on fire. Anton holds the phone under my nose. "Unlock it."

I shake my head.

"Use her print. That usually works." Rostya grabs my wrist so tight that the pain drives tears to my eyes. He guides my hand to the phone. I curl my fingers, but Anton bends my thumb back. The familiar tension warns that he's about to snap a bone. With a cry, I relax my hand.

"There you go." Grinning, Anton unlocks the screen and scrolls through the messages. "Let's see if our boy stuck around." He dials a number, his lips puckered while it rings.

"Hello." Bastian's faint voice is calm.

"We got Chelsea. You have five minutes to surrender or she'll die ... after Rostya had his turn. You know how that goes."

Bastian's response is too low to decipher.

Anton switches to the speaker and holds the cell close to my mouth. "Tell Bastian that you are okay."

I grit my teeth. No need to sacrifice both of us. "Save yourself."

My demand is met by Rostya's fist. The force tosses me across the threshold into the back room of the church. Crawling to the nearest table, I pull myself up and shake my head to kill the black spots dancing in front of my eyes. The priest is gone, but a third man sits on a couch in a corner. He has removed his sunglasses, and even though he has features similar to Icarus, his dark brown eyes and pudgy cheeks are no match. He was a decoy all along.

I glare at Anton. "You knew we'd be here."

"Of course. Icarus figured you'd seize the opportunity since it's one of the few times a year he is guaranteed to leave the house. And you guys walked right into the trap." He shakes his head. "So pathetic that Bastian will now lose his life because of a woman."

"He won't surrender."

He'll leave, just like Marcel did.

"We'll know in a few minutes how much he truly likes you." Anton checks his watch. "Three minutes, to be exact."

I ball my hands to fists until my nails cut into my skin. It's stupid and selfish to wish to be rescued. We will both die.

"Two minutes." Dropping on the couch next to the decoy, Anton chuckles. "And if he doesn't show, at least I'll get to shoot you."

Something he has been itching to do for the longest. "It must hurt that he chose me over you."

His blue eyes darken. "You need to shut up."

Oh, I got to him.

At least that's something.

Anton holds the phone to his ear. "You got sixty . . . fifty . . . forty-five."

The door on the other side of the room flies off its hinges. "I'm here." Bastian raises his hands and steps into the room. He drops on his knees, interlocking his fingers behind his head. "Now let her go."

"Tsk, no one said anything about letting her go." Anton steps next to Bastian and pulls out a set of cable ties. "But I promise to make it quick, for old time's sake."

54

✹ ✹ ✹

BASTIAN

Nicosia, Cyprus
~~~~~

I *should've* known.

Icarus is a creature of habit, always has been and always will be. The different date, the change of venue, the horde of guests that exceeded by far the few close acquaintances he'd usually invite. All red flags that should've told me that something wasn't right. In my hastiness to get to the finish line, I ignored them all, stepping right into the trap that my uncle laid so carefully out for me.

And the worst part is, I dragged Chelsea right along with me.

She's probably dead already, although Anton hasn't left my side, and knowing his revengeful ass, he's eager to personally fire the bullet into her head. He is petty that way.

When they lead me outside onto the terrace of my uncle's house, Icarus is in his usual spot at the round glass table with a whiskey glass at his fingertips. Splashing from the pool draws a quick glance to the shiny water, but the sun sits at an angle that disallows me to catch a glimpse of the visitor. It's likely one of the many girls who keep Icarus company whenever he has a down-moment and who will be sent away as soon as things get tight.

Icarus's glare drills into me for a very long time. I refuse to look away. Nothing to prove a weakness. I won't break down and beg for my life. It's the end of the line for me and Icarus won this round. It'll be up to Conor to win the war and save my son from a life full of crime.

My uncle rolls the whiskey around in the glass but leaves the drink untouched. "I've always known you have a defiant streak, but I never took you as the reckless kind. What happened to you? What made you turn your back on the Disciples?"

My gaze flicks to Anton. His eyes are hooded and his face is an unemotional mask. Usually, he has such a big mouth, but he must've kept Konstantin and Olivia's abuse to himself.

I refocus on Icarus. "Honestly, there were so many things that I couldn't possibly pinpoint it to one." The splashing in the pool is irritating; I squint against the sun, but the light only hurts my eyes and adds to the pounding in my head. "Don't you want to send your company away?" It's not like him to expose a stranger to Disciple business.

Icarus snorts and raises his voice enough to carry across the garden. "Hey, come and join us."

The splashing stops and the person pulls themselves out of the pool. I gasp, my heart dropping to my kneecaps.

It's Vitaly!

How did he get here?

And where are Conor and Sean?

As he comes closer, his gaze is stuck to the ground. Knotting his fingers together, he awkwardly shuffles his feet.

"Look at the man in front of you, Vitaly." Icarus's snarl slivers like glass shards on my skin. "He is the one who killed your mom and dad."

My son raises his head and finds my eyes. "Is that true?" His question is barely above a whisper.

I could deny it, but what's the point? Icarus wouldn't make this type of allegation unless he had iron clad proof. "I leaked information that ultimately led to their deaths."

"Why?"

"Because they hurt me very badly and kept me away from you."

Seconds stretch into a solid minute. Vitaly stares at his toes, his shoulders shaking from silent sobs. I want to reach out, comfort him, but my restraints prevent it. Besides, he might not even want me to console him. Even if I survive, I lost him forever. He'll never forgive me.

I glare at Icarus. "What gave me away?"

His cold smile rubs the triumph in my face. "I have to admit, your plan was brilliant. Blame it on Marcel Pierce and let the Disciples take out the Bajris, then cause a turf war to take us down. Only one small detail slipped your mind. A few months before Konstantin's assassination, his mother moved. Had some issues with the neighbors and wanted to be closer to the beach. That fact wasn't known to Marcel Pierce, so if he had sold the address information, he would've sent the Bajris to the wrong location."

I close my eyes. In my eagerness to get rid of Liv and Konstantin, I didn't cross-check all the details. A costly oversight.

"How did you find Vitaly?"

"What do you think?" Icarus's lips twitch. "After you left him with a bunch of strangers, he called me and begged me to come and get him. And it's not that I didn't warn you. Vitaly has been ready to become a Disciple for months and you weren't gonna stop him."

My shoulders slump. The ugly fight I had with my own father in which he warned me about Konstantin and the Disciples burns like a scolding nail in my head. I dismissed everything he said and only years of hardship made me regret many of the words I spoke that day.

"What happened to Conor and Sean? Did you kill them?"

"They are no longer your concern."

I close my eyes. I truly dragged everyone down and this is the end of the line. My plan failed in all respects.

I clear my throat to steady my voice. "Vitaly, please look at me."

He shakes his head, a few tears splashing on the tiles.

"There's a lot you don't know about your mom and Konstantin." I sigh; how could he ever understand? I turned him into an orphan that day. He never considered me his father. "And I was scared that one day, they'd hurt you, too. I love you too much and wasn't willing to take that risk."

The silence spreads like a hollow echo in my head. With every breath, the rift between Vitaly and I widens. I can no longer reach him.

"Enough of that." Icarus racks the slide of his gun and sets it on the table. "You had your chance to make amends with your son, Bastian, and you failed. Now it's time for Vitaly to get his revenge."

My son turns his tear-stricken face toward Icarus. My uncle gives him an encouraging nod. "Take the gun, Vitaly. Bastian killed your mom and dad. He deserves to die."

My gaze flicks to the small garden gate, but before any flight plans can take hold in my mind, the hard metal of Rostya's Ruger presses against the back of my head. If Vitaly fails, he'll do the job.

My son edges toward the table and picks up the gun. Spinning around, he raises the weapon. Taking aim at my chest. Tears roll down his cheeks in a relentless stream, but his eyes hold a determination that makes my heart weep.

I have no doubt he'll pull the trigger.

55

✳ ✳ ✳

CHELSEA

Nicosia, Cyprus
~~~~~

One push catapults me into a small cellar of the mansion Anton took us to. I stumble, trying to keep my balance. With my hands tied behind my back, it's a futile endeavor. I slam onto my knees, the pain adding to my dire mood.

I'm so fucked.

Once they dispose of Bastian, I'll be next.

"Mam!" The low shout cuts through me like a knife.

"Sean?

Shuffling in my peripheral vision confirms that I'm not imagining things. Sean struggles to get closer. Bastards chained him to the wall.

"Oh, my god, are you okay? How did you get here?" Panic rolls in my chest. "And where are Conor and Vitaly?" I scoot over to him and he buries his face into my lap. Sobs shake his shoulders.

"Everything went so fast. Those three men came to the house where we were hiding. They had guns . . . and they were going to shoot us"—he trips over the words—"but Conor told them he had information that could destroy them. That his friend would call the police if something happened to us. That's when they brought us here." More sobs turn into a hysterical wail.

I nudge him with my chin. "Sean, look at me."

He raises his tear-stricken face.

"You need to calm down, okay? Take a deep breath."

"Aren't you scared?"

Terrified is more like it. "If we want to get out of here, we need to work together, and for that, I need you to focus. Can you do that?"

He nods and bites his lip.

"Then tell me where Conor and Vitaly are."

"I dunno." Fresh tears pool his eyes. "They take Conor somewhere in the mornings to question him." A few tears fall. "They've been really hurting him."

I close my eyes. This is bad. "And Vitaly?"

"I haven't seen him, but he knew the men who caught us. I think he might've called them. Conor said he took his phone without permission."

Fuck.

Everything has gone to shit.

I look around. The room appears to be a wine cellar with cases stacked against the wall and two fancy fridges to keep a few selected bottles at the perfect temperate level. I exhale through tight lips. That's something I can work with.

I scurry over to the fridges and try to open one with the tips of my fingers. The metal is cold and pointy, turning my skin numb. Gritting my teeth, I refuse to give up; after endless attempts, the door finally opens and I stop it with my knee from closing again. Working out one of the bottles, I let it drop to the ground. The *clash* of shattering glass resonates magnified in the room. I hold my breath.

No approaching footsteps and the door to the cellar stays closed.

I release my breath.

So far, so good.

Picking up a larger piece of the broken glass, I return to Sean. "Here, try to cut the cable ties with this."

He hacks and slices; once, he slips and slashes into my hand. I bite my lip to suppress a cry.

"It's not working." The words quiver with tears.

"Keep trying."

"But you are bleeding."

I turn around and find his eyes. "Keep. Trying. It's fine if you cut me. Okay?"

He nods, large tears clinging to his eyelashes. The dull scratching of glass on plastic grinds my nerves. About to admit defeat, the restraints fall off. I rub my wrists, fighting against the pain. Blood is dripping from one of the cuts, another one barely oozes. I wrap the silk scarf I used to cover my head and shoulders in the church around my busted hand. The raging adrenaline in my bloodstream reduces the pain to a hollow pounding.

Sean is first on my inspection list. The chain attached to the wall ends in a dog collar that's fastened around his neck and secured by a small lock. What a fucked up improvisation for a restraint.

I grin. Picking the lock with one of the pins I used to secure my wig shouldn't be too difficult.

Thank you, Marcel.

Never thought that the crook skills he taught me could get me out of a bind.

The lock proves mega easy; a few jabs with the hairpin and it opens right up. I free Sean of the dog collar.

What now?

The window has bars and the only exit is the cellar door. My gaze falls onto the refrigerators. That should work.

"Sean, I need you to shout for help as loud as you can. Claim that I'm having a seizure."

My son's brows crumble but smooth when I pull a bottle from the fridge. I duck behind the door and nod at him.

He sucks in a deep breath. "Help! Help!" The words are shrill and bounce off the walls. "My mam is sick. I think she's having a seizure."

Ears pricked, I detect nothing but deafening silence. "Try again."

He shouts at the top of his lungs, his voice gaining momentum. The echoing shrillness hurts my eardrums but proves successful. Shuffling steps approach the door and a key turns in the lock. I raise the bottle.

"What's all this wailing and gnashing—?" When the bottle breaks on the man's head, his question is cut short. He faceplants onto the ground. Blood gushes from a wound.

Crap.

I press two fingers against his neck to find a pulse. It's a little faint, but he should be able to make it if he gets help within the next hour. I roll him on his back and pull the gun from the holster under his armpit. Releasing the safety, I move a bullet into the chamber. Best to be prepared.

"Stay here, Sean. I'm going to find Conor."

And Bastian. He likely needs my help more than my brother.

Sean shakes his head. "I want to come with you."

Too risky with the amount of potential firepower involved. "It's safer for you to stay here."

"But—"

"No "but"s, Sean." I cup his shoulders and shake him gently. "It's almost over and it's important that you listen to me. Can you please do that?"

He nods, a few stray tears running down his cheeks. The terror in his eyes churns in my stomach. The trauma he has suffered these past few days is almost as bad as what he lived through in Hong Kong. It's time to end this.

He stares at the man on the ground. "What if he wakes up?"

"We'll lock him in the cellar." I lead Sean into the room next door and gaze around. This part of the house is stuffed with lawn equipment, including a big riding mower. It'll offer Sean plenty of coverage. "Hide behind there in the corner. Do you still have your whistle?"

He pulls the little emergency whistle fastened on a string around his neck from under his shirt.

"Good. Blow that if someone comes too close."

"Okay."

I close the door to the wine cellar and turn the key. Sean has climbed behind the mower and I cover him with a tarp that's rolled up in front of the tires.

"I'll be back as soon as I can."

"I love you, Mam. Please be careful."

The teary timidness in his voice pulls at my heartstrings. I hate that I have to leave him. "I love you, too, Sean."

My mother's warning that death always comes in threes rings loudly in my ears.

Mrs. McKenna was the first.

Nico the second.

Who will be the third?

Fighting my own tears, I tackle the steps to the upstairs. On the threshold to the basement, I duck and peek around the door. Sunshine floods a large kitchen that lies otherwise deserted. The inside of the house is shrouded in silence. Biting my lip, I edge forward, prepared to raise the gun to scare any potential help that might sneak up on me. Murmuring voices drift through a cracked door. I tiptoe forward, staying low. Every muscle in my body twitches with adrenaline and sweat has soaked the fabric of my dress under my armpits.

I get to the door and peek outside, barely able to stifle a gasp. Fear and despair crush down on me at once.

I'm too late.

In the middle of the terrace stands Bastian, without a fighting chance of survival. Rostya has the barrel of a gun pressed to the back of his head; Vitaly's weapon is trained right at the center of his chest. Anton clutches the grip of his Glock still in his holster.

At least one of them will pull the trigger . . . and at least one bullet will find its deadly mark.

56

✳ ✳ ✳

BASTIAN

Nicosia, Cyprus
~~~~~

For years I thought about dying. Having a lethal bullet enter my head. Bleeding out in some ditch. Crawling through a forest until my heart stops beating. Pain was a common factor. I even imagined my life running backward in front of my eyes. That I'd feel remorse for every soul I took.

Yet that my son would be the one pulling the trigger was never anything near my doomsday scenarios.

I lick my lips, my throat so dry that I'm having trouble swallowing. "Vitaly . . ."

Should I tell him that I'll love him no matter what?

Should I beg for my pathetic life?

The latter is unthinkable.

I don't want to give Icarus the satisfaction. I don't want him to win.

"Vitaly . . ."

There really isn't anything to say.

Silent tears run down my son's face and his hand shakes so hard that the gun could drop at any second. It won't take much to pull the trigger. The resistance of the release is minimal and the recoil will be barely noticeable. The guilt will be a struggle, although depending on the brainwashing, it might not last for more than a breath. It didn't for me. To the contrary. My first kill was associated with pride.

I became a man that day.

Or at least the illusion of one.

In reality, I lost a part of myself I could never regain. The only reminder of the lives I took is my tattoo with a leaf for every soul I extinguished.

Moisture forms above my lip. I want to shake Vitaly, remind him of those precious moments out at the farm. Then again, they might've been only precious to me. He could've hated every second of it.

"Do it." Icarus's voice grinds like gravel. "He killed your mom and dad. He deserves it."

A sob shakes my son's body.

"Go ahead." Icarus's words carry a sense of urgency. "Show me you have it in you to become a Disciple and take your place by my side."

Another sob mixes with the whisper of the afternoon breeze. Tears drip off Vitaly's chin. He closes his eyes.

This is it.

He'll pull the trigger and end the life of the man he considers his enemy.

He swings around. A bullet rings out.

Silence.

For a few beats, time comes to a standstill. Icarus's face is thunderstruck. Then his body slumps forward.

Fuck.

Vitaly shot him.

My uncle's eyes lost all sign of life—he is motherfucking dead.

Rostya diverts the barrel of the gun from my head to Vitaly. Even with his boss gone, he'll follow Icarus's last order and take out any potential threat to the Disciples. He will avenge his mentor's death.

As I try to tear loose from my restraints, the ties binding my wrists cut painfully into my skin. I will be too late. Once again, I can't help my son.

The powerlessness is crushing.

Even my voice fails me.

It's as if I'm captured in a surreal bubble with none of my body functions still under my command.

Two more shots crack the shimmering afternoon air. Rostya sways. Blood seeps from a hole in the middle of his forehead. As he slams forward, the patio table breaks his fall. Glass shatters and the fine mist of whisky hits my face.

Anton lowers the Glock. He stretches out his hand. "Pass me the gun, Vitaly. It's over."

As if awakening from a daze, Vitaly turns his head and stares at Anton. A beat of hesitation, two, three. Taking a deep breath, he hands over the weapon. Anton sets both guns on the little side table by the pool lounger. His knife springs free. Cutting the ties around my hands, he grumbles, "I'm gonna fucking regret this." The dull side of the blade scratches against my skin. I rotate my wrists to restart the blood flow.

Pulling Vitaly into my arms, I rub his back. He weeps against my shoulder until my shirt is damp.

"I'm sorry, Babá."

"Shh, shh. There's nothing to be sorry about."

"I killed grandpa."

"He left you no choice." I pull him tighter. "He absolutely left you no choice."

57

✷ ✷ ✷

BASTIAN

Nicosia, Cyprus
~~~~~

"Bastian!"

Chelsea rushes toward me from a side door; the sight of her sucks a humongous amount of dread from my chest. Then new panic settles in.

If something happened to Sean . . .

"Are you okay?"

She nods.

My gaze flicks to Anton to access his mood. He stands by the pool with his arms folded, face grim and lips twisted as if ready to chew me out. Yet, he makes no attempt to go for his gun. For now, Chelsea is safe.

I stretch out my arm to squeeze her hand, holding on to my son with the other arm. Vitaly still has his face buried into my chest, even though he has stopped crying. I sense his worry. After leading Icarus's men right to Conor's doorsteps, he struggles to look Chelsea in the eyes.

"I found Sean and he is alright." Chelsea rubs Vitaly's back. "Don't worry, no one is mad at you."

With the next exhale, more apprehension seeps out of me.

Thank you, I mouth.

The last thing my son needs is blame or a guilt-trip.

Vitaly raises his head. "What about Conor?"

I meet Anton's gaze across the terrace. He rolls his eyes, pulling out his phone. A few seconds later, he growls into the receiver. "Change of plans. Get Doherty back over here asap." His forehead wrinkles as he listens to the reply. "Icarus and Rostya are dead, so I'm in charge. If you value your life, do what I say."

In another lifetime, I would've put him in his place. As the only Pappas heir alive, the Disciples are mine, but I have zero interest in running the organization. To the contrary. Let Anton have it.

Chelsea looks from me to Anton and holds out her hand. "Let's go inside, Vitaly, and get Sean. I think we could also use something cold to drink."

She truly is the most amazing woman. So intuitive, and so understanding.

Vitaly hesitates. "Babá?"

I give him an encouraging nod. "I'm right behind you. Just give me a minute to talk to Anton."

Frozen in place, I wait until they've disappeared inside the house. Chelsea shuts the door and pulls the curtain close; it's my cue to walk over to the pool. I lower myself onto the edge of the lounger closest to the table with the guns. Anton remains standing with his arms folded. In this position, I'd reach the weapons faster than he would.

"What now?"

His blue eyes drill into me. They are void of emotion. "I'm taking over unless—"

"Don't worry, I want no more part of the Disciples."

"Then you'll spread the word that you are retiring?"

"I will, though I can't promise you there'll be much left once the turf war is finished."

"Let me worry about that."

Some of the tension is soaked up by the stale afternoon heat.

"Look Bastian, I know that things will never be right between us again."

Too much shit happened that can never be erased.

"You shot Nico for having my back."

Anton scoffs. "I also saved your son."

"And you think that makes it okay?"

"No." He exhales through tight lips. "But when we part here today, I don't want to have to look over my shoulder for the rest of my life. And I don't want that for you either."

Which would allow Vitaly and me a chance at a fresh start.

"Are you suggesting a truce?"

"Something like that." He rakes his hand through his short hair. "I think it's for the best. For both of us."

Let bygones be bygones. I can live with that.

"What about Chelsea?"

His shoulders slump. "What about her?"

"Do I have your word that the Disciples will leave her and her family alone?"

He turns his back on me, his gaze on the mountains in the distance. Seconds stretch into minutes. His fists are pumping and I can practically see the wheels in his head spinning. When he finally turns around again, I wince at the pain edged in every wrinkle on his face. "As long as the information Conor has on the Disciples stays in the cloud, I won't go after them. However, if he leaks the intel to the authorities, all bets are off."

Considering the stakes, it's a fair compromise.

"I never wanted to hurt you, Anton."

His chuckle is bitter. "I blame myself. From the start, it was apparent that you were never that invested in us. I mean, you always cheated and never wanted to take matters to the next level. I should've respected that and broken it off."

"For all it's worth, I did like you a lot." And I'll always be grateful that he saved me from Konstantin and Liv.

"Not the way you like her. When you came back for her in the church, I could see it in your eyes. You love this woman, and from what I can tell, she loves you, too."

I smile, gazing at the house. I can definitely see a future with Chelsea, hell, one day, I might even marry her.

Standing up, I take Icarus's gun and secure it. As long as I'm on Cypriot soil, I'm more at ease with some firepower as a backup.

"I guess that's it." I look at Anton. "Time to say farewell."

He walks over and pulls me into a hug, holding on just a breath too long for comfort. "Take good care of yourself."

58

✳ ✳ ✳

CHELSEA

Gweedore, Ireland
November 2024
~~~~~

"Hey, watch out!"

As Conor swings the beam around, Bastian ducks but still manages to get a hold of the other end. Together, they lift the joist and lock it into the frame. Sean and Vitaly hammer away; my son's tongue sticks out as he is focused on the task. When I look up, I catch sight of the chasing clouds across the sky. A chilly bite fills the air, but it has been dry for the most part, which has helped in our endeavor to create a home for our boys. Life is better than it has ever been and I pinch a quick tear out of the corner of my eye to prevent outright balling.

"Guys, time for a break. I got tea and cookies right here."

The hammering stops and I meet Vitaly's gaze. "Did you bake the peanut butter oatmeal ones again?"

"I sure did."

The prospect has him practically jump off the ladder and he and Bastian join me at the fold-out picnic table. Conor helps Sean down from the beam; I add extra honey to my son's green tea to ensure he'll finish it this time. Conor scoffs; he still hates anything that's not traditionally Irish, but his face relaxes when I hand him the cup with his favorite Barry's tea bag. The silence is only interrupted by chewing and slurping.

Bastian hugs me from behind and rests his chin on my head. "I'd say another week and you won't be able to see the sky anymore. We'll literally have a roof over our heads again."

"I still think you should get a proper contractor to put on the shingles."

"Nah, Conor and I will get it done. Other than the wiring and plumbing, there'll be nothing in this new farmhouse that wasn't created with our hard-earned sweat."

"And are you sure you'll get it done by Christmas?"

"Yep. You'll have your tree right down in the sitting room in the spot where you want it."

I nod. It will be my first Christmas with Sean since Hong Kong and Bastian's first Christmas with Vitaly without Olivia and Konstantin. Everything has to be perfect, especially since Conor also agreed to invite my mam. Nothing but laughter and cheers in a new house to celebrate a new future, a new hope at an ordinary life as an ordinary family.

I finish the rest of my tea. "Okay, boys, one more hour, but then you need to come in and do your homework."

Sean pulls a face. "Can't we work again until it's dark? I only have a little bit of Irish left."

"Vitaly?"

"I'm already done with mine."

Four faces stare at me with different emotions. Sean's and Vitaly's lips are twisted with hope that I once again budge, Bastian's eyes hold a twinkle that tempt me to put my foot down, and Conor gives me this *you-better-let-them-be-if-you-want-that-Christmas-tree* look.

Snickering under my breath, I admit defeat. "Okay, let me get another hammer, so I can help, too."

~~~~

Dinner, a board game battle, and two bed-night stories later, I finally turn off the lights in the boys' bedroom just after ten pm. I'm pooped and my back hurts; I'm looking forward to lying down and should convince Bastian to give me a massage. He's in the kitchen, finishing off the dishes. The heavy scent of garlic and herbs is trapped in the small space of the rented camper trailer that constitutes our temporary abode; on second thought, a quick stroll through the fields to soak up some fresh air might be preferable to a massage.

I look around. "Where's Conor?"

"He already tucked in for the night."

So it's just us. "You want to get out of here for a few minutes?"

"I'd love to."

Careful not to wake up the boys, we sneak out of the trailer into the night. The cool air pricks at my skin and clears the cobwebs from my head. I feel giddy with my hand buried deep inside Bastian's down jacket pocket, and the scent of his aftershave teases my nose with every breath. The small living quarters have severely impeded our sex life and I relish every single stolen moment when we are alone.

"We should check whether the neighbor left enough hay for the horses."

Bastian chuckles at my suggestion. "That's an excellent idea."

We trudge along the edge of the field until we reach the barn. Bastian slides the heavy gate back. The inside is veiled in darkness; only the soft neighing of one of the horses and scraping hooves disturb my evil plan. I pull him between the harnesses and the carriage and lean so heavily on him that he topples over. A bed of blankets that smell like horses and leather polish buffers our fall. Giggling, I allow him to conquer my hips and sit up. He looks down on me with twitching lips.

"You did that on purpose."

I shake my head. "You can't prove I didn't trip."

"Don't force me to tickle you . . ."

Oh, he is going straight to torture. "Okay, okay, I admit it. I pulled you down on purpose."

"Did you now?" He wiggles his brows. "Well, that calls for punishment."

With one pull, he seizes one of the harness straps and loops it around my wrists. Another pull has my arms immobilized.

"Too tight?"

I shake my head.

With the slowest intent, he unbuttons my blouse. Stud by stud, with such excruciating breaks that my body weeps with need. Arousal gushes into my panties. When he finally gets to the end, I'm panting. He bunches up the fabric to use as a cushion for my head.

"The perfect bra." With a smirk, he opens the middle hook to expose my boobs, teasing my nipples with his fingertips gets them to harden like rocks. My clit aches with desire and I have to bite my lip to suppress a moan.

He frees me of my jeans and panties and takes a riding crop off the nail on the wall. Gaze locked with mine, he slowly pulls the soft leather through my folds. I shudder, heat pulsing in my core. As he circles my clit with the rougher edges of the riding crop, I have to press my fingernails into my palms to avoid spiraling. The restraints together with the friction of the leather send me into a sensation overload.

"Bastian, I'm about to come."

"Tsk, that's too bad." Abandoning my folds, he runs the keeper of the riding crop over the inside of my thighs. I buck my hips, so done with his games. I want his cock lodged deep inside me and drive me over the edge.

"Lie still."

A soft smack of the riding crop against the side of my ass stirs the heat. I'm so close to my orgasm that I'm dizzy with lust. He caresses my waxed pubic area with the leather of the whip before spanking me again. The radiating sting is a sweet symphony of pain and pleasure, a mix of our past and future. He relishes the control just as much as I enjoy his total dominance. He will always protect me.

When he drops his pants, his hard erection springs free. Lowering himself onto the blankets next to me, he strokes the hard peeks of my breasts. His fingers test my opening and I arch into his hand. He finally takes me out of my misery and covers me with his body. Sliding inside me, he takes me deep and hard; I only last a few thrusts before the heat ignites. Waves of pure ecstasy wash over me and I cry his name. Our bodies and hearts melt as one, quiver after quiver bearing witness to the ultimate pleasure.

He releases my wrists from the straps and pulls me into his arms. "Wow, that was something."

I grin. "We should check on the horses more often."

"I agree." His soft lips find mine for a brief peck. "How did I get so lucky?"

"You mean how did we get so lucky?"

"I guess we both hit the jackpot."

"In every possible way."

With a sigh, I snuggle against him. Six years ago, my life blew up in my face because of a man. Now it's fully mended again and I love every second of it. A joint future, a joint family, a joint soul . . . that's really all anyone can ask for.

THANK YOU FOR READING!

★ ★ ★ ★ ★

Please consider leaving a review! Reviews help indie authors like myself find new readers and get advertising. If you enjoyed this book, please tell your friends!

Arriving November 15, 2024

WRONG SIDE OF THE TRACKS

Ever since Brianna Hayes has shown an interest in the opposite sex, she has been attracted to guys from the wrong side of the tracks.

Those with all the tats.

Those who get into trouble with the law.

Those who regard women as nothing but play toys.

Yet, nothing could have prepared Brianna for Jay Ellis. As right-hand man of mob boss Gabriel Manzoni, Jay is a force to be reckoned with. Unfortunately, he has had a hold over her ever since she laid eyes on him for the very first time. And when he moves in with her under the pretence that he needs to keep an eye on Brianna's soon to be ex-husband, a battle of wills unfolds.

Because Brianna might be attracted to men from the wrong side of the tracks, but she is no baby doll.

Take a sneak peek at the first chapter . . .

Wrong Side of the Tracks

Chapter 1

Not sure what I was expecting when I barge into Jay Ellis's office, but it certainly wasn't his cock in the mouth of a pretty Asian girl kneeling in front of him while he sits at his sleek satin-black glass desk with his thighs spread apart.

"For fuck's sake, I said no inter—" The second half of the word gets stuck in Jay's throat as he pushes away the girl. He squints at me. "Do I know you?"

What a jerk. Okay, we only met once a little over three years ago, but our first meeting couldn't have left as memorable of an impression as it had on me.

"I'm Brianna, Ethan's wife."

"Oh, yeah, right."

"And I can come back if this is a bad time for you."

He looks down at his dick hanging flaccid between his legs. "Don't bother. I'm no longer in the mood."

While he zips himself up, I soak in his appearance. The bad boy crown still fits him perfectly. A chiseled jaw covered by just the right amount of stubble, wavy chestnut-brown hair that invites my hands to make it messy, and dark eyes the color of espresso beans. Arms sleeved with intricate tattoos to die for. And let me not get started on the abs that rope under his tight shirt.

It takes all my effort to tear my gaze off him.

The girl has gotten to her feet and wipes her mouth. Before she can turn away, Jay seizes her wrist and holds up a little plastic baggie containing a bunch of pills. "Why don't you come back a little later?"

"Of course." With a lick of her lips, she snatches the baggie from his hand and leaves without giving me the benefit of a glance.

I struggle to keep my jaw in place. "Did you just pay her with drugs?"

He chuckles. "Oh, baby doll, I don't need to pay women to have sex with me."

"Don't call me that."

"Or what?" With one smooth move, he's out of his chair. One pouncing step forces my back against the wall; luckily, my pinned-up hair works as a buffer for my head. He leans closer, resting first one fist against the wall, then the other, to lock me in with his body. Our lips are only inches apart. With my stilettos, he is not much taller than me, but his frame is imposing. Crushing.

"You think because you're Ethan's girl, you got some kind of special status? That's the problem with rich whores like you. You feel you can make demands because everyone who has less money than you is beneath you." His voice carries a dangerous edge that sends fear to the hair on the back of my neck but excites me at the same time. And why does his breath have to smell like damn peppermint? "But let me tell you, *baby doll*, there are people in this world who don't give a damn about your dad's money or his power. He isn't bullet proof, and neither are you, so don't think for a second you can come to my club and order me around." His thumb traces my bottom lip. "Your mouth looks like it enjoys cock. Maybe you should give me a blow job for interrupting a good fuck."

"Over my dead body." Despite my claim, my breathy voice is tinged with a sudden desire to taste his saltiness. I squeeze my legs together to curb the need between my thighs.

"Oh, baby doll, don't tempt me, because that can easily be arranged." As he steps back, his gaze is mocking. He shakes a cigarette from a pack and leans against his desk. "Now sit down and tell me what you want from me, or did you just come here to annoy me?"

What the actual fuck. He summoned me to this stupid club and now he acts as if I blew his perfect afternoon. I drop into the chair in front of his desk, regretting it instantly. The black leather looking comfortable on the surface is stiff as a brick. Not an incentive for any visitor to stay long. "One of your goons called me and said to come by the club straight away. That it was an emergency that couldn't wait."

"Oh, right. I actually thought he filled you in."

"Filled me in about what?"

"Ethan was shot." Jay lights the cigarette and takes a long drag, his gaze fixed on my face. "He's in the hospital, but I don't think it's too serious. From what I was told, it was a clean through-and-through, though it was in his chest, so his lungs could've collapsed."

I blink at him with irritation. So Ethan is back to his old ways and considering that he still hangs with Jay, he is likely dealing drugs again. "To be honest, I have no idea why you called me. I haven't seen Ethan in three years and would've already divorced him if I had known his whereabouts."

"Well, legally, you guys are still married and you are his next of kin. Ethan has no other family."

My forehead wrinkles. "What about his brother?"

"Dead."

That's news to me, but then again, a lot can happen in three years. "Look, I'm not sure what you want me to say. Under the law, I'm responsible for his medical bills, but that's about it." Who knows if Ethan even wants to see me.

"I'm afraid that's not how that works in our organization." Jay takes another drag, twirling the smoke around in his mouth. "Family is important, so I expect you to take care of him. I mean, it's for better, for worse, in sickness and in health, until death do you apart. As far as I can tell, you are both still alive, and this is a time Ethan needs you."

"He walked out on me. After only three months of marriage. And then he dropped out of school to return to a life on the streets that he preferred over our joint future. As far as I'm concerned, I don't owe him anything."

With a sigh, Jay crushes the rest of the burning cigarette into the ashtray. It only takes a few steps to close the distance between us; by the time he lowers himself to my level, his eyes have turned such a dark shade of brown that his pupils are no longer distinguishable from the rest.

Without skipping a beat, he cups his hand around my head and pulls me closer, making it impossible for me to breathe without taking in his woodsy aftershave. "Look, you seem like a smart girl, and I didn't think I needed to spell this out for you. As his wife, I'm holding you accountable for him. He will be staying with you until he has fully recovered, and that's starting as soon as he can sign himself out of the hospital."

"What if that's not acceptable to me?"

"Trust me, you don't want to go there." He strokes his fingers down my cheek and along my jawbone. The touch is gentle, but the darkness in his eyes leaves no doubt that it's intended as a threat. "You have such a pretty face. It would be a shame if something horrible happened to it."

I want to look away, but his gaze holds me hostage. He traces the curve of my neck, his nails edging along the opening of my blouse. All I can do is soak up his masculine scent. I should swat his daring fingers away now circling the outlines of my nipples that poke at him provokingly from under my shirt, but the parts of my brain that are usually in control of my muscle functions are paralyzed.

Being so close to him makes me feel alive.

Geez, Brianna, get a grip on your hormones.

He is a predator, a criminal of the worst kind, with an entourage of thugs who will dispose of me in the Hudson River without a second thought. Next to him, Ethan is a choirboy.

Shit, then why do I want to taste his tongue in my mouth?

I clear my throat to oust the friskiness from my voice. "What about the cops? Hospitals are required to report all gunshot wounds."

"Don't worry, Ethan knows how to handle the police."

"Then I should probably go and check on him."

"That might be wise before we will both do something we might not be able to explain to your husband."

My thoughts exactly.

With a curt smile, I get out of my chair. Shit, my panties are soaking wet.

Jay snaps his fingers in front of my face. "You listening?"
"What?"

"I said that before you go, I need your driver's license."

My forehead wrinkles. "For what?"

"Have to make sure you are twenty-one before I can invite you back to the club."

For real? That Asian girl didn't look like she was out of her teens. Since fighting him over this isn't worth the battle, I take my license out of my wallet and drop it on his desk.

He picks it up and turns it around to read the address. "Not gonna lie, I took you more for a woman who lives close to 5th Avenue to maximize all the shopping opportunities."

"Nope, I like the Westside more."

"Cool." My license disappears in the back pocket of his tight jeans that can't hide the bulge between his legs.

Not that I should notice these things.

I hold out my hand. "You saw my age, now give it back."

He snorts. "But that's my insurance policy, baby doll. You know, in case you disappear on me or abandon your poor husband at the hospital, I need to know where you live."

Did you like what you read?
You can pre-order *Wrong Side of the Tracks* now on Amazon to have the book delivered to you as soon as it is released on November 15, 2024!

Fire Rose

It's the Season to be Jolly . . .

EIGHT ONE-NIGHT STANDS FOR X-MAS

A SPICY WHY-CHOOSE HOLIDAY NOVELLA

Every year on Black Friday, BFFs Ava and Kari make a dare contest, from cookie baking to demolishing trays of Tequila shooters until they puke. For their college freshmen year, they take it up a notch:

Who can clock the most one-night stands before the last day of the semester?

For virgin Ava, this is a big leap into uncharted territory, but after a four-year losing streak, she's determined to take the crown. Problem is that her dares from days one, five, and seven aren't content with just one night.

Take a sneak peek at the first chapter . . .

Eight One Night Stands for X-Mas

Chapter 1

Legs tired and heavy, I drop into the empty chair across from Kari at the table in the food court. Fourteen freaking presents, two more than last year, leaving a big hole in my wallet but also a sense of accomplishment. I mean, who can boast that they've finished their entire Christmas shopping on Black Friday with maximum savings (even if the trillion other shoppers who fought me over bargains were kind of annoying)?

"I'm beat."

Kari grins. "I expected that, so I was such a good friend and already got your hot chocolate."

I eye the cup. "Where are the marshmallows?"

"What marshmallows?"

"Those small ones they always add."

"Why, I don't know what could've happened to them." She flutters her lashes at me all innocently. "Maybe they skip those on Black Friday. You know, too many people ordering. . ."

"Shit, you took them."

"Moi? Your best friend?" She opens her mouth and closes it with indignation. "I would never commit such an atrocity."

"Mm-hmm. Just like you didn't eat all the frosting off my birthday cake—"

"That was ten years ago, so you can't bring that up."

"The Statute of Limitations doesn't apply to BFF crimes."

She snorts—my latest lawyer jargon isn't something she appreciates. "Well, look on the bright side. At least I never stole your boyfriend."

"That's because I never had a boyfriend." Keeping a straight A average while enrolled in twelve AP classes during my high school years took a few sacrifices.

"Besides the point. Boyfriends are totally off limits. That's basic girl code."

"Then I vote to extend the girl code to anything sweet. Keep your paws off my marshmallows, my candy, and my birthday cake frosting."

"Duly noted." She slurps the milkshake through her straw. "So what are we gonna do for our Christmas dare this year?"

"Seriously? Are we still doing that?"

"Of course."

"Didn't you promise last year that it would be the last time?" I distinctly remember her claiming that we'd both become respectable adults as soon as we hit college. We were demolishing full trays of tequila shooters for three days until I finally threw in the towel due to the fear of permanent brain damage from alcohol poisoning.

"Nope, that wasn't me." She shakes her head, her lashes doing the fluttering thing again. "As you know, I don't make promises."

She is right about that.

"Besides, I have the best idea ever." She leans closer and bites her lip. That usually means she cooked up one of her crazier concoctions that gets us into trouble (and by us, I mean *me*). "Since this year was the year we both lost our virginity, and we are both non-committed, I say we go a little wild."

I arch a brow.

She squints. "I mean, you did lose your virginity at Ella's pool party this summer, right?"

It takes all my effort not to squirm under her drilling stare. I shouldn't have lied about that night, but I didn't want to start college as a pathetic dud. Who needs her BFF to get involved in her love life so you can finally score? Pretending that I kept up with our milestone plan we made at the start of high school was easier, though in hindsight, it might now come back to bite me.

But hindsight is a dreadful thing and I'm not about to fess up that I'm as untouched as the Virgin Mary. "Sure, Nathan and I hooked up that night."

"Cool, then this dare should work." Glancing at a family with a small toddler at the next table, she leans even closer and drops her voice to a mere whisper. "What do you say if we have a few one-night stands between the first of December and the time your dad picks us up for Christmas?"

Worst idea ever. "I don't know . . ."

"Are you scared?"

"No, but I'm a little concerned about my reputation. Aren't you worried that dudes might think you are easy?" And losing my virginity to a one-night stand is exactly the reason why I didn't end up with Nathan at the pool party.

"Nah, one-night stands for girls have become socially acceptable. Equality rules."

Kari has always been Queen Adventure. First kiss behind the swing set in our garden when we were in the sixth grade (with my older brother, so cliché), then titty play three years later under the bleachers after track and field practice. It's still a miracle to me how she got every single member of the baseball team to grope her without a teacher catching on. Of course, the big finale happened this year on Valentine's Day when she lost her virginity to Ryan Keller, our high school's bad boy, who convinced her to get a "Fuck the World" tattoo on her ass for graduation. When she proudly showed her parents a picture, they freaked out and almost disowned her.

And now she wants me to buy into her crazy one-night stand idea.

I scrunch my nose. "What about STDs?" Or pregnancy?

"Duh, of course we'll use condoms."

"Don't think it'll work. Come Monday, we still have two more weeks of classes, and then finals—"

"So you are scared."

Terrified is more like it, but I wouldn't admit that if hell froze over. "It's not that—"

"Then I dare you to have more one-night stands than me during Christmas dare weeks."

Fuck, she's going through with it. "What's the prize?"

"That's the best part. Winner gets first dibs on the car, and the loser has to keep the room clean and do all of the laundry for the entire spring semester."

That's big. With my internship next semester at the law firm, I could really use first dibs on the car. Taking the bus on a cold winter night is dreadful. "Okay, I'm in. How do we prove that we went through with it?"

"Dunno. Maybe take a pic of the dude's dick?"

"Bad idea. People today are sensitive about nudes."

"Okay, then what about the boxers? We claim them as trophies and whoever has the most wins. Of course, they have to be used and smell like a dude, or they won't count."

Having a drawer of used and potentially dirty underwear goes against my hygiene principles, but it's the fairest solution under the circumstances. "That should work."

And crossing the threshold to becoming a sexually active member of society had to happen someday and what better opportunity than dare weeks with a big prize on the line.

I crack my knuckles. My BFF is going down!

After my four-year losing streak, this is my time to shine. Men beware; there's a tigress on the loose . . . and I'm ready to pounce on you.

Did you like what you read?
You can pre-order *Eight One-Night Stands for X-Mas* now on Amazon to have the book delivered to you as soon as it is released on November 1, 2024!

A Special Thanks

Publishing is a team effort. Many people have supported me throughout the years and I'm grateful for all the guidance and motivation they have provided. Thank you, guys—I couldn't have done it without you.

A very special thanks goes out to my alpha reader Sophia—her comments and insights shaped this story in so many ways. She helped me when I was stuck, she motivated me when I wanted to give up, and she gave me the spark for many scenes and plot twists. You rock, girl!